A Mikayla Tale:

Coming Into Power (Book 1)

By

Tamara Smith

Table of Contents

Acknowledgment

Thank you to my wonderful Spouse, who supported and enabled me throughout this process. The existence of this book is due to his diligence and encouragement. I am blessed to have family and friends who embraced my new adventure and indulged my creativity. Thank you all for your input and validation to help me continue to pursue this dream.

Prologue

"This is not the life we wanted for our daughter."

"It is who she is, she needs to learn and be protected."

"We cannot protect her. She is so innocent, what if she falls into the wrong hands and gets corrupted? We need to hide her."

"She is more advanced than anyone in her training. At the age of 10, she is up against those who are 18. She can protect herself. The prophecy will come to fruition no matter what we do, so we should stay by her side and guide her."

"You and I both know the prophecy can be blocked and is not set in stone. She can live a peaceful life. Screw the prophecy. Why should she have to bear it all? Please, if you love me or her, we need to let her go."

Chapter 1: Introductions

Ten years later…

Mikayla's POV

I searched my closet for the perfect outfit. I wanted to be able to move freely on the dance floor, without attracting attention. This evening was a long-awaited girl's night at the Firestarter Club. It opened a few months ago and its reputation had grown to make it the most popular spot in town. The lineup was rumored to be so long, many patrons never made it inside. Jacqui, my best friend, managed to get VIP entrance passes for us. We were ready to party. It is going to be a time to let loose, have a few drinks, and dance the night away with my girls: Jacqui, Kate, and Tricia. I could hardly contain my excitement while working at the diner today with anticipation.

Since I got engaged to Elliott two months ago, I hadn't been out with my girls and was starting to feel a bit isolated. I needed to make a better effort to hang with my crew. Elliott and I were completely smitten with each other and only spent work hours apart. He had a lucrative job as a businessman being heir to a family business. I was a waitress working at the Pop Pop Diner, a quaint mom-and-pop establishment with some of the tastiest food. The owner was a sweet, old man who was like a father to me. I referred to him as Pop, even though his real name was Larry. While attending post-secondary nearby, I needed a place to stay and a job. He provided me with both.

One day I was walking by the diner and was famished. The smell emanating from the restaurant had my stomach growling and my mouth salivating. There was no way I could keep going on my way. I went inside to have a bite to eat and within 30 minutes the entire place was ridiculously busy. The staff was having trouble keeping up one waitress had called in sick. I needed some money so asked if he wanted me to help where I could. He graciously accepted my offer. I filled drinks, carried food to the tables, pitched in clearing tables, and helped to reset them for the next guests. I had no experience but did my best. When things finally calmed down, he paid me in cash and asked if I wanted to permanently work at the diner. I was ecstatic since I felt I was clumsy the entire day, but he said I didn't complain and was always smiling which made his customers happy. He told me, even though the customers had to wait, they still complimented the atmosphere and my attentiveness once it was their turn. I immediately accepted the position.

Shortly after, the renter living in the apartment above the diner moved out. I grabbed it right away to be close to work and school. It was now summer, so I was working full-time and had no classes to attend. One afternoon, two years ago, Elliott had come into the diner with a few of his friends. Yours truly was their waitress. It took him no time at all to ask me out on a date. He was handsome and polite, so I took a chance, and the rest is history. This little hole-in-the-wall diner brought me my job, a place to live, and the man of my dreams.

My phone rang while I was reminiscing about my life and how content it made me. I glanced at the caller ID, smiling happily said, "hello handsome". Elliott replied "hi beautiful. I know you are headed out soon, wanted to tell you I will miss you tonight and to enjoy your time out with the girls. You are mine again tomorrow." He was so sweet to be thinking of me and call. I asked him "are you going out tonight?". He told me he was too tired and going to watch a movie, stuff his face with some delivery and go to bed early. He would call tomorrow. Then, he told me not to have too much fun without him and wished me goodnight. I hung up the phone and felt flutters at how much love I felt from this man.

I glanced at the clock and realized I needed to hurry. I quickly grabbed a black pair of slacks, a black sports bra, and a white see-through blouse. As I put a modest amount of makeup on my face, I decided to wear my hair up with some strands dangling all around. I added a silver bangle bracelet, my platinum engagement ring, and hoop earrings. I put my driver's license, bank card, cash, and phone into a small black purse with a long strap that I could easily hold close while on the dance floor. Jacqui volunteered to be the designated driver (DD). However, I preferred to dance than to drink, and typically when she was the DD, I ended up driving us all home anyways. She always had men buying her drinks throughout the night. She was gorgeous, to say the least, and men flocked to her side wherever she went. She had long blond wavy hair, these almost transparent blue eyes, and a permanent light tan skin color. She did spend a fair amount of time in spas and gyms getting pampered and exercising to ensure she maintained her physique and appearance. With her beauty on the outside, she was equally beautiful on the inside. People often took advantage of her graciousness. She had very few female friends until we met in post-secondary, and we were instantly best friends. We met through a school assignment in which we had to do a business management report and presentation. Without that assignment pushing us together, we probably never would have met, but as fate had it, we were destined to be best friends. I am so grateful for that class, even though I have yet to use anything I learned in it to date. Jacqui was more than I could have ever asked for in a best friend.

I heard a honk and looked out the window above the diner to see Jacqui waving her hand out of the car motioning me to come on. I grabbed some open shoes that had a slight heel and straps that went up my legs just past my ankles under the black pants I was wearing. I grabbed my purse and a jacket to leave in the car for later, locked the door, and rushed down the stairs. I hopped in the front seat and eyeballed Jacqui from head to toe. She wore a tight-fitting red dress that stopped just above her knees. It had a V-shape in the back and front, exposing her back, cleavage, and red stiletto pumps. "Can you even drive with those shoes on?" I asked worriedly. She laughed at me saying "I've made it this far, haven't I?" I gave her a smirk and she stepped on the gas to our next destination.

Conveniently, Kate and Tricia were roommates in an apartment complex not far from the diner. Kate was the waitress at the diner who had called in sick the day I jumped in to help. Once she returned for her next shift, things were awkward for a bit seeing as I took some of her shifts, but eventually, we grew to be good friends. One day, she wanted to go out with her friends, but Pop refused to give her the time off. I heard her begging him to let her go and since I had nothing to do, I volunteered to work her shift making mine a double and told Pop it didn't have to cost him any extra overtime. I would do it at straight time. I made plenty in tips anyways and the evening shift always had more than the day shift since typically dinner meals cost more than breakfast. He agreed. The next day Kate brought me a key chain with an olive branch on it and said she was extending an olive branch as she could tell I was a good person and someone she should be friends with. After that, we hung out regularly and covered shifts for each other when needed. Kate's other friends eventually moved on and she was the third musketeer we didn't know we were missing until she came along. She was outgoing and knew so many places to have fun in the city.

Tricia was the newest to join the group about six months ago. She had come into the diner one night crying uncontrollably and asking for a table in the back. It took a while, but she eventually disclosed to me, she had just broken up with her boyfriend whom she dated since high school. She thought they were sweethearts for life, and she caught him texting another girl. When she confronted him, he said he loved her as a close friend but not as a lover anymore. He had hoped they could remain close friends since he enjoyed her company and talking with her, and no one knew him as she did, but he desired someone else to be his girlfriend. We had several girls' nights after that conversation doing all sorts of things like going to nightclubs dining out, hanging out watching chick flicks and of course, we had to have a few spa days to wash all those troubles away. Tricia took about a month to realize she was better off and now had several close friends to ease any troubles she may encounter in life. We all felt that way. We had each other's backs, and nothing was going to interfere with that. Tricia moved into Kate's apartment after her previous roommate ditched her for the rent money. Tricia needed a place and Kate needed help paying the rent. It all worked out in the end. Fate was bringing everything and everyone together.

My dream of a simple life has come to fruition. I can be myself, enjoy time with friends, embrace the adoration and love of a partner, and live happily with the basics of life. I have seen my fair share of high-maintenance women and it is shocking to me how many of them have partners scurrying behind them to do everything their hearts desire. I am missing something and by no means am attracted to those types of men. Of course, chivalry isn't dead to me, but I can hold a door now and then too. I wasn't rich, but I had enough to get by and was able to save so I could eventually move into a home I owned instead of the apartment above the diner. It's a quaint little apartment. It isn't large so I typically won't invite more than one person over at a time. Most of the walls are a mild yellow/beige color making every day feel like sunshine to me. The living room and kitchen meld together with a small built-in nook in the corner for a dining room. The bedroom is large with a walk-in closet; what girl couldn't use that? There is one bathroom which I won't lie; it could be bigger, but everything can't be perfect. It did have a soaker tub which at the end of a long shift was so easy to melt into with a candle, some bubbles, and light music.

As we pulled up to the front of the apartment building, I texted Kate. About five minutes later, the two of them came trotting out looking like models about to go to a photo shoot. I started to feel a bit underdressed given they all had on short-tight dresses, but I guess I missed the memo to dress provocatively. Granted I was more conservative than the rest of them and the only one who wasn't single at the time, but maybe I should have let loose a little more. Too late now, I thought to myself. I didn't want attention anyways. Looking at these three, I am thinking my plan succeeded. They all were on a level greater than me. I truly hoped they could find someone to make them feel how Elliott made me feel. They were all great women. They entered the car and immediately we pumped up the volume and listened to what we called our Girls Ramped Up CD. The first song burned on it was Girls Just Want to Have Fun, followed by several more female empowerment songs to get us in the mood to have a great time.

Chapter 2: The Firestarter Club

Jacqui pulled up in front of the Firestarter Club and proceeded to exit the vehicle. The rest of us looked in shock as she asked "are you coming? The valet will park the car for us. It is included with the VIP tickets." We all promptly hopped out of the car. She handed the keys to the valet, who greeted her by name. Stunned, we waltzed up the front path following closely behind her. The line-up to get in circled the building. The rumors were true. I couldn't even see the end of it. Then I heard Kate ask, "Jacqui how in the hell did you get these VIP tickets for such a prestigious venue." Jacqui smiled brightly and replied, "I have someone I want you all to meet" while waving us forward. We went into the club and directly to the VIP lounge. A security guard smiled and said "welcome back Miss Williams. We have been expecting you and your guests." He removed the rope blocking the entrance and stepped aside ushering us all to enter. We collectively looked at Jacqui in shock realizing not only did she get us into the club but also into the VIP lounge and the security guard recognized her so she must have frequented her before. What on earth is going on? We followed her to a booth along the side of the huge dance floor. In the booth was a handsome man who immediately stood to greet Jacqui with a kiss on her cheek and slid his arm around her waist turning towards us. We all stood their mouths dropped stupefied until he motioned for us all to have a seat at the semi-circle booth facing the dance floor. Jacqui introduced him as her beau, Matt, then pushed us to sit. As we each slid into the booth, Jacqui told him our names and we shook his hand with a quick smile and a greeting still a bit shell-shocked. After we all had been introduced, he said "I am so glad to finally get the chance to meet you all. I have heard so much about Jacqui's posse. I had to put faces to the names. Please sit and I will fetch us all some drinks and appies." He walked away before we could say anything, as we all turned to Jacqui. Her cheeks were blushing red, almost matching the brightness of her dress. "Isn't he the greatest? I met him a month ago and we have fallen deeply in love. It's crazy how you can instantly feel a connection with someone and know that it is right. I thought I would be single forever, but this man has changed me in such a short amount of time. He treats me like I am his entire world. I am the happiest I have ever been."

After about five minutes of silence, Kate finally spoke "that's excellent news Jacqui, we are so happy for you. This is a night to celebrate our friend and her newfound happiness." I hugged my friend immediately. "We are going to talk about how it has been a month and I am just hearing about this now missy, but you deserve every bit of happiness with your new love, and he is quite the looker." Just as I finished saying that he placed a tray on the table with loads of drinks. Matt indicated he didn't know what drinks we liked so he brought a variety for us to try. The appies were ordered and would be delivered to the booth. Then, he thanked me for the compliment with a wink. I was mortified and instantly looked away from him and to the tray of drinks to pick one up.

Matt sat with us enjoying some beverages and snacks he ordered. Getting to know all of us a little bit. He soon excused himself saying he had work to do. The nightclub was owned by his best friend, and he was responsible for helping run it. He had several checks to do and then he would return. As soon as he left, we all decided to hit the dance floor. We danced for a long time, just us girls having the time of our lives. I can't remember the last time

I was sweating this bad – maybe when Jacqui dragged me to the gym. I felt disgusting and having had a few liquids courtesy of Matt, it was time to head to the ladies' room. Jacqui and I went off the dance floor together and she showed me the way. She said she needed to freshen up too since Matt would probably be returning soon. The bathroom was extravagant, and I felt out of place. It was almost completely white marble: the floor, stalls, sinks, everything but the mirrors. Each stall had a small television in it and several women were at a very well-lit mirror reapplying makeup and checking themselves. A man walked by in front of me. I looked puzzled at Jacqui, who immediately saw my confused face and informed me the bathroom was unisex. In clubs, there are typically lots of hookups in the restrooms, so this club catered to that instead of pretending it didn't happen. There were condoms, wipes, sanitary napkins, perfume, and makeup all for purchase in the bathroom in this glorified vending machine. I went into a stall and heard noises coming from the stall next to me. I couldn't believe that people would be so bold. I hurried to finish and get out of there. It was making me uncomfortable to hear people having intercourse that closely. I flushed the toilet and exited the stall, then went to the sink to wash my hands and freshen up.

Jacqui soon came over to the sink next to me asking if I heard the couple in the other stall. She wiggled her eyebrows and asked if I would ever do something like that with Elliott. I asked her if she was crazy and said hell no. Pointing in the direction of the stall I told her, I had much more respect for myself than that. As soon as I finished saying it, the stall door opened and a woman walked out pulling her dress down straightening it up, then reached her hand into the stall beckoning a man to come out and join her. It happened so fast; Jacqui and I were both looking as he exited the stall. My mouth dropped to the floor as I muttered, "Elliott?!" They turned in the direction of the sinks and walked towards us when he caught my eyes and froze in place.

Chapter 3: The Reckoning

I never felt so betrayed in my life. This night has taken an ugly turn for the worst. My perfect life was shredded in a matter of seconds and my heart felt like it was ripped out of my chest, thrown on the floor, and stomped on repeatedly with heels. I immediately spun around and headed for the door with tears beginning to form in my eyes. I was holding them back with all I could muster. No way was I going to let him see he hurt me like this. I stormed towards the VIP section with Jacqui following right behind me. She kept trying to say something, but I honestly felt like my ears were deaf and I couldn't hear a thing. My mind was racing. I felt so hot and angry. I wanted to punch something. I wanted to punch him. How dare he ruin such a great thing and how long has this been going on? Is it just this once, multiple times, multiple women? How could I be so blind and stupid? His sweet call to tell me to have a great time was a ploy to get me to not call him since he was going out. I got back to the table and downed three drinks that were sitting there. I heard a commotion and looked over to see Elliott trying to get into the VIP lounge, but the security guard was not letting him pass. He looked my way as I raised my middle finger to him. Jacqui turned me so I could not see him and kept repeating he isn't worth it. I didn't know if I was more hurt or angry and felt completely out of control with my emotions. The others were still on the dance floor but headed over when they saw us come back and could visibly see I was shaken. Jacqui explained to them what occurred and instantly Kate wrapped her arms around me saying "he's an idiot and it is his loss. We are here for you." Tricia having been wronged similarly quietly stared at us while the others consoled me. They realized she wasn't saying much to make me feel any better and I noticed Kate raise her eyebrows at her and motion for her to say something. Tricia looked at me and said the most surprising thing I could have imagined. "Mikayla, I know it hurts now and nothing we say will make it feel better. When I was hurt, you all tried to cheer me up, encouraging me to go to all sorts of places and I had a great time, but it wasn't what helped me move on in the end. What you need to do is find someone to go home with tonight, rock his world and have the night of your life, then go home without a care in the world. I promise, you will feel better and will be able to leave this chapter of your life. If he has done it once, he will do it again, even if he hasn't already. He will try to keep you, having his cake and icing and everything else unless you stand up for yourself." All of us were silent looking at Tricia. She had such conviction and assurance that this is what I needed to do to move on quickly and unscathed. I was always a good girl. Completing my homework, never being late, working hard, and respecting others. I had never treated anyone wrongly or done drugs or slept around. Never lied nor stole. I was such a plain Jane; how could she propose for me to have a one-night stand? After a couple of minutes, Jacqui agreed with Tricia and Kate jumping on the bandwagon too. Kate spoke up "Elliott is a jerk. He tried to hit on me once, but I rejected him and told him I was going to tell you. He apologized and told me that he had a little too much to drink and it made him flirtatious, but he would never do anything to hurt you and to please keep it between us. I am so sorry I didn't tell you sooner. I am a horrible friend. Please forgive me and I agree with the others, you should do this to move on from him. It will keep you from forgiving him and making a huge mistake by staying with him."

I thought about all they had to say and looked up. Matt was talking to someone at the bar who was surrounded by females all attempting to get his attention. There were lots of men who had been dancing with us on the dance floor. It may have been the alcohol, but I felt a rush of self-awareness come over me. I was beautiful and sexy, and it would be Elliott's loss cheating on me – his fiancé, no ex-fiancé, the woman he was supposed to promise to love forever. How dare he? I told the girls I was going to have a one-night stand for the first time in my life. Matt had returned at some point during our conversation. I honestly didn't even notice.

We all got up and went to the dance floor. I was dancing seductively and with every man that came near us. My eyes were determined and just as the men started to swoon over me, I moved on to dance with the next. I giggled to myself, thinking it was like musical chairs except with men. When the music stopped, I would have a man in my sight and would go home with him. The song was almost over, and I moved on to the last man. I ground up against him as he came up behind me. I went down his body and then turned around and went back up again. Then I whispered in his ear, "your place or mine". He looked at me in amazement. His smirk on his face, I could only imagine what he was thinking as he gave me the elevator look up and down and then reached out to touch me with his hands. He wasn't the hottest guy in the club, but he was holding his own. He leaned in close to my ear, grabbing my butt cheek with one hand and moving the hair behind my ear with the other saying, "mine". Then, he guided me to the exit. As I walked past my friends still dancing, I told them not to wait up.

We walked past the bar where the man, who was talking with Matt earlier, was still surrounded by several women completely unphased by the attention. He must be used to it. As I walked by him with my soon-to-be one-night stand, unbeknownst to me, my scent wafted in his direction, and he knew right away that I was meant to be his. He jumped off the bar stool pushing his way through the sea of women and chased after them. From the girls' booth, Matt watched him heading out and said he needed to take care of some business to Jacqui and then ran after him. They made it through the VIP lounge and into the main section when Mikayla felt someone grab her hand from behind. She stopped and the man she was walking with also stopped. "She's coming home with me" the man stated in a domineering and possessive voice. "Like hell she is" the other man retorted. Just then Matt came up with three beautiful women and told the man she was originally leaving with that he would be compensated and would have a good time if he stayed including free access to the VIP lounge for a month. The man grinned slyly looking at Mikayla "that's an offer I cannot refuse. I would have rocked your world though baby" and walked away with Matt. Mikayla stood there feeling slightly dejected but also disgusted at his words. She looked up to the man that remained and said, "lead the way then". As she was once again being pulled towards the door, she shrugged to herself seeing this guy was cuter than the last, all the ladies were throwing themselves at him all night and he chose her. She should count her lucky stars that someone as handsome as him was taking her home and she would be able to use him to move on from her cheating fiancé.

They walked past the valet to a car that was in the first spot in the parking lot of the club. It was a black Ashton Martin Victor. He opened the door for me and held my hand as I slid into the passenger seat. While he walked around the car to his door, I saw a sign in front of the

16

parking stall that indicated owner on it. It had the name Jason Bloodright on it. I made a mental note of the name and figured when I had the chance, I would google him quickly. I stared out the window watching the scenery of the nightlife while he drove in silence. I was glad he didn't want to waste time with small talk. This encounter wasn't about me finding someone and getting to know him but getting over someone, so I didn't want to make any type of connection with him. I needed time to heal and maybe be single for a bit, focus on myself and of course, I was going to over-analyze how I missed Elliott's behavior and wonder how frequently his cheating occurred. It was going to drive me mental. I was lost in thought thinking of all the times he said he was going to bed early or he had to work late. How many, if any, of them were true? The nerve of that guy. I gave him all of myself and this is how he treated me. I was kind and generous and loving and adored him, but he would openly bump uglies with that tramp of a woman in a bathroom stall. I looked down at my hand and noticed I was still wearing the engagement ring. I glanced at the man driving and when I thought he wasn't paying attention, I slid the engagement ring off my finger and into my purse. Then I leaned back on the seat and thought more of how I detested Elliott and how I wasn't going to hold back tonight. It was going to be a night to remember.

Chapter 4: A Turn of Events

Jason's POV

I was at my nightclub sitting at the bar talking with my beta, Matt. He had found his mate and was an excited puppy dog whose owner returned home. Tonight, he met her friends and they seemed to be having a great time as Matt and I glanced at them laughing and smiling together. They all went onto the dance floor, and we watched them act as if they were the only ones there and being carefree. Most of the people in the VIP lounge were regulars. Other than Jacqui's friends, I didn't see any new faces. The air was stuffy with all the sweat and body heat in the lounge, so I indicated for the fans to be turned up. The second the air blasted out onto the dance floor; the sweetest smell reached me. It was of chocolate-dipped strawberries and funnel cake: two of my favorite desserts. I looked at the dance floor unable to ascertain which of Jacqui's friends was emanating this sweet, delicious scent. My wolf, Titus, was yelling "mate" in my head. Women were always swarming around me. Today was no different. However, I was even more put off than normal once I knew my mate was in the club.

I turned to Matt and told him to tell me what he knew about Jacqui's friends. One of them is my mate, but I am unsure which one. I can't see them well enough on the dance floor, but they are the only new faces in the lounge tonight and I can smell her from here. I try to get a better look, but these vultures are surrounding me hoping I will choose one of them for the night and take them home. Indeed, I normally will choose someone sometimes to take home and have a great time with, but I never fell for any of them. They all only wanted the money and power that came with my name. I doubt they knew anything about me other than the size of my bank account. I would enjoy my night of pleasure with them and then make myself scarce before they would wake up. One of my household servants would politely usher them out of the house and send them on their way in a taxi. It had happened enough times that I was known for it, which was unacceptable I know, but I was not finding my mate and I am a man with needs. Women kept coming hoping they would be the different one. Most ended up being angry and ranting in the news for their fifteen minutes of fame. It wasn't every night just when the need became overbearing, and I couldn't concentrate on my pack or my businesses. Every man has their limits.

I watched as Jacqui – whom I had met a few times now – stalked off toward the restroom with one of the others. Matt informed me her name was Mikayla and of the bunch, she was the only one who wasn't single and has a fiancé. As he started to tell me about the others, I immediately put up my hand to stop him. The smell was faint now and almost completely gone which means my mate must be Mikayla. Of all the luck, I had to have a human mate who already has a fiancé. How was I going to separate them and make her mine? Wolves can find their mates as soon as their 18th birthday. I kept waiting for her to appear but when she didn't, I started seeing other women, never getting attached so I could accept my mate whenever she finally crossed my path. I opened the nightclub to meet more women a few months ago. I can't believe it worked and she has finally come to me. I am 26 now, so, it has felt like forever waiting for her. Now that she is here, I have this overwhelming desire to grab her and fling her over my shoulder like a cave person and drag her home with me and keep her there like our own beauty and the beast story until she falls for me. "It's

Mikayla" I informed Matt. He smiled at me. "I cannot believe that we are best friends and have found mates that are best friends. What are the odds? The moon goddess has favored us." "How do you figure that? She is engaged to someone else. That isn't something so easy to work around. She's in love with someone else. It's horrible news." Matt waived over the bartender to refill our empty drinks. "Have faith Jason, it will work out in the end. The moon goddess would have a plan."

Fifteen minutes later which felt like hours to me, I saw Mikayla looking distraught and racing back to the booth Matt had arranged for them all. Jacqui was right behind her and so was a man I recognized as a frequent customer in the regular club but never in the VIP area. My security guard stopped him from following the girls into the VIP lounge and I immediately had the urge to give him a raise. The man was yelling for Mikayla, and she just ignored him continuing to walk away. She looked furious. I had such a better view of the booth than the dance floor. She was beautiful. Her angry face was adorable. I just wanted to walk over there and wrap my arms around her and ask her what I could do to make her smile. If her mad face looked like that, I could only imagine what a smile would do to me.

Her other friends joined her blocking my view completely. Matt had been sitting with them on and off most of the evening, so I asked him to go over and find out what was happening. He nonchalantly walked over. It appeared they barely noticed his presence as the other girls tried to comfort their friend. I mind-linked him "what happened". He messaged me back "wait a minute". It felt like forever. I watched their faces go between shocked and angry and empathetic. It looked like they all went silent and then one spoke. I could tell she had determination behind her words but no idea what she was saying. The others all stared blankly at her, then one by one, they all started to nod in unison. Then looked to Mikayla for what appeared an approval. She nodded her head and they all headed to the dance floor. "WTF Matt. What is happening?"

Matt walked back over to me at the bar and had a huge smile on his face. "The moon goddess doesn't play around. When Mikayla and Jacqui went to the restroom, they heard someone having sex in one of the bathroom stalls. They were just about to leave when the couple exited the stall, and it was none other than her fiancé." Jason looked appalled. He looked over at Mikayla. He was happy for himself but sad for her. What an ass, he thought to himself. Matt continued "Apparently, Tricia had something similar but not as bad happen to her and it took her a while to get over it listening to everyone's advice. The only thing that got her past it was to have a one-night stand. She suggested it to Mikayla saying it will ensure she will not go back to such a vile man. Kate then confessed he had hit on her once but chalked it up to alcohol. The other girls encouraged her to have a one-night stand saying she has never done anything scandalous in her life and lived by some high and mighty moral code, but it was time for her to get in the game and forget about him. Having a one-night stand would not only make him angry but would ensure she would never go back to him having moved on herself."

"What are these girls thinking? That is a terrible idea. Whom is she going to have a one-night stand with? It must be me and then I will have to make it more than a one-night stand and win her over."

Matt and I looked over at the girls all dancing on the dance floor. Mikayla was dancing quite seductively now, and men were all gathering around to dance with her. Titus was going insane repeating "mine" repeatedly in my head. It was all I could do to keep him calm while we watched her on the dance floor. She flitted from one man to another arousing all of them, then moving on to the next. She was a sight and even from this far away, I felt the need to have her. It was driving me crazy seeing her with these other men, touching her and rubbing up against her. I wanted to break all their hands to teach them to keep them off her. She belonged to me; how could she be so forthcoming with them all? If she was a wolf, she would know right away, I was her mate, but being human, they do not have the same pull to the bond. Figures! How am I going to be the one she goes home with?

Matt decided to head over to dance with Jacqui. He said his wolf was getting too antsy having all these men around the women, so he had to claim her as his. I unfortunately knew the feeling. Shortly after he got there, the song stopped, and Mikayla whispered in the ear of the man she was dancing with. A smirk appeared on his face as he pulled her towards the VIP lounge exit. I jumped off the bar stool and ran to stop them. Matt ran after me as well. I didn't know what to say or do, I just couldn't let her go with another man. I grabbed her hand and pulled her towards me, halting both her and the man in their tracks. He was a regular in the VIP lounge so we knew he would be happy and leave if we gave him some perks. Matt instantly by my side told him to let me take the girl home and he would compensate him generously with a guaranteed good time and free VIP access. The man could not turn down the opportunity after implying to Mikayla she missed out on a good thing. Repulsive. With that Matt led him away and I looked at Mikayla. She looked at me and said, "lead the way then". My wolf was doing somersaults in my head, and I couldn't help but smile as I walked her toward the exit.

We got into my car, and I was driving her to my villa. I typically would take females to my downtown home, which was closer to the club, but Mikayla was different. I wanted to treat her better and show her a time she would never forget and hopefully make her fall in love with me and forget about that scumbag. I wanted her to remember this as the night her life changed for the better, not a terrible scar she had to get over. Forget the idea of a one-night stand. This is not the type of woman she is, that was clear. I was mind-linking with my staff at the villa that I was bringing home a guest and that they all had the night off and to make themselves scarce in the next 20 minutes. It would take about 30 to get there. I also mind-linked Miss Flint, the woman who raised and has taken care of me that I was taking someone to the villa instead of the downtown home and to be there in the morning. I caught Mikayla's hand moving in my peripheral as she slipped her engagement ring off her finger and put it in her purse quickly. She started to look up in my direction to make sure I wasn't seeing anything, so I turned my eyes away quickly. After a minute, I looked back in her direction, and she was staring out the window. If only I could read her mind and know what she was thinking about.

Chapter 5: Night at the Villa

Mikayla's POV (sexual content)

The car pulled up to a secured gate that slowly opened as we approached. As we moved down the driveway, it was a gorgeous villa surrounded by the most beautiful gardens I have ever seen. There was a fountain in the middle that we circled. The moonlight sparkled off every drop splashing into the air. It was a clear night all the stars were visible in the sky. The driveway was lit up with lights all perfectly spaced and leading up to the front of the villa. He parked the car in front and proceeded to get out. I waited for him to come around and open my door. He took my hand and helped me out of the car before closing the door and leading me up the stairs to the door. He hit a button to the right and leaned towards a light. The system indicated "retinal scan complete and accepted – welcome home Mr. Bloodright," and the door unlocked. He opened it and we walked in. The foyer was huge and had a spiral staircase leading upstairs. There were double doors to the right and left and straight was an open-concept forum that I could see all the way through with floor-to-ceiling windows in the far back. The air was fresh, and I smelled a hint of vanilla.

Jason looked at me and asked if I wanted something to drink or eat. I nodded no. I couldn't delay this any longer or I would get cold feet. I leaned into him planting my lips on his and giving him a passionate kiss. I must have taken him by surprise as it took a few seconds for him to reciprocate, but when he did, it felt like butterflies fluttering in my stomach. His tongue entered my mouth and started to dance with mine. I could taste the liquor on his breath. We continued kissing for I don't even know how long before he easily lifted me. I straddled his waist with my legs and wrapped my arms around his neck as he carried me up the winding staircase to a room. I could feel his hard member pressing up against me already. He reached for the knob and then kicked it open with his foot. Walking in he kicked the door back closed and then set me down still kissing me. It was as if our lips were stuck together and could not come apart or we would come apart. He walked me backward and I hit the bed and fell on the edge with him standing there looking at me. His hand grabbed my cheek stroking it and then putting one of my loose strands of hair behind my ear. "You are mine," he said to me as he reached down and started to unbutton my blouse. I looked up at him from the bed as he did one button after another. I was kicking myself for wearing a sports bra and these ridiculously hard-to-remove shoes that were strapped up my leg under my pants. In my defense, I wasn't thinking when I dressed that I was going to be trying to have a hot and steamy sexual encounter with a man I just met.

He pulled my blouse down off my shoulders pushing me onto my back on the bed as he removed it. He straddled on top of me leaning down and kissing me again. This time slowly kissed my lips, then moved to my chin, then my neck leaving a trail of kisses and a warmth wherever his lips touched only to cool as he moved down further. I was starting to get in my head thinking, I cannot believe I am doing this. What was I thinking letting them talk me into this and here I am? I can't stop now. Do I want to stop? This feels so good now. I need to just enjoy this. I am enjoying this. I better take control and make things happen faster. I am here for an unforgettable one-night stand. Why is he taking his time like he wants to make love to me? I decided to move things along, so I reached down and grabbed the hem of his shirt and lifted it above his head stopping the kisses he was trailing down my body. I proceeded to kiss his chest. Oh my god, he had a chest to die for. It was chiseled with an eight-pack and a V-line down into his pants. He worked out and his skin was so soft. His cologne was turning me on even more with its tantalizing scent. It was sweet but masculine like a morning dew scent. I wrapped my legs around his torso and motioned for him to roll over so that I was on top instead of him. He was way stronger than me so the only way to make that happen is if he was willing. He let me roll over with him and I kissed down his chest, then sat up and undid his pants while he lay there on the bed staring at me. His eyes sparkled with the only light coming from the moonlight outside the window and his clock radio. I stood up sliding his pants off him. He was so hard. His cock was trying to stand at attention, but his boxers were preventing it. It is a pet peeve of mine to leave socks on, so I pulled those off first, then I proceeded to pull off his boxers. He let me have my way with him and I felt so out of sorts. This wasn't me. I usually was the one having things done to me or leading me to do things. Not me taking charge and making things happen, but I had to get this over with. It was now or never, and I had to move on. Something about it felt right. I thought it would be foreign to me, but things were moving naturally other than the thoughts in my mind. Overthinking things again. His member was straight up in the air as I hovered over it, I made eye contact with him, then I grabbed it with one hand. I leaned down to it, still watching his eyes with mine, and licked it from the shaft up to the head, then I used my hand to move it a bit so I could do the same all around it. He moaned slightly at the feeling of my tongue on his manhood. This was going to happen, and it felt exhilarating.

Jason's POV (sexual content)

26

Our eyes gazed into each other's as she used her tongue awakening all my sensitivities. Little tingles where her tongue and hand stroked me had me losing my mind as I tried to lay there calmly holding her gaze. I knew I was not going to be able to hold out long with this woman. I have never felt the urge to just grab a woman and pin her down and take her repeatedly. My wolf was howling in my head almost making it difficult to control myself. I let her take control so I could focus on controlling my wolf. Before I knew it, she was taking my entire manhood into her mouth and swirling her tongue around my head. Then she took it out and used her tongue to stroke my shaft, then back up again and engulfed it into her mouth. Oh, my goddess, it was amazing. This girl was going to send me over the edge before we even got started. I needed to stop her, but could I? I hadn't even gotten her fully undressed yet. Maybe she changed her mind and didn't want this, so she was giving me head to stop me from sleeping with her. It was so hot the way her eyes stared into mine and not letting go the entire time. I had to stop her. "Stop," I said and moved my hands to stop her from moving. I let out a moan and then pushed her off me. Sitting up I grabbed her and yanked off her sports bra, then threw her on the bed on her back. I undid her pants and panties pulling them down her legs, but they got stuck on her shoes. I looked at her shoes trying to figure out these things. Goddess! Why can't she just have glass slippers like Cinderella that come off easily? I gave up and lifted her legs up putting my head between her legs under her pants and panties. With her legs in the air above me, I placed my lips on her and kissed her. I used my tongue to lick her core and up her womanhood. She was already sopping wet and fully aroused. It made me almost painfully hard thinking about how much she wanted me right now.

I kept licking and sucking her as she reached her hands up to take off her shoes which were now in the air. I couldn't help but laugh in my head at the situation. How could this be so awkward? I wonder if she is thinking the same thing. I wanted to take my time with her, but her moans were making me into a wild animal. My wolf wanted to take her here and now. It was taking all my self-control to indulge her a little before I penetrated her. I heard one shoe hit the ground with a thud, but I kept going. She started moaning even louder and telling me yes and to keep going. She struggled to remove the second shoe as I started to move faster over her, then I put two fingers inside her pulling them in and out. She was so wet, and she was thrashing around a bit, almost like she wanted to tell me to stop but didn't at the same time, having an internal fight with herself. Once the second shoe hit the ground, I gave her my all and she came within seconds. I pulled my head out from under her pants and panties and pulled them off now that the shoes were gone, making a mental note to discard those shoes as soon as the opportunity presented itself.

I repositioned her laying fully on the bed instead of across it then pulled a condom from the bedside table. I put it on and pushed her legs open sliding myself into her wet core. I started slowly moving in and out of her knowing she had one release already. I pulled almost out and then slammed back into her making a slapping sound when I connected with her. She yelped and took a deep breath, looking up at me with her brown eyes. I did it again and then again. Each time I thrust inside her; she made a gasping noise. It was so arousing to me I wanted to hear it repeatedly, knowing it was me that was making her gasp. She had me so horny I couldn't stop myself and we came together letting out a moan of my own. I didn't want to be finished with her that quickly. I pulled off the condom and then motioned for her to join me in the bathroom. We got into the shower together and I kissed her under the waterfall spout. Feeling her body with my hands and her feeling mine. I reached my hand between her legs and started playing with her again as the water ran down my hand to her core. She stopped me by grabbing my hand. I could tell she wanted more so why she was stopping me I had no clue until she got down on her knees. She used her mouth to grab onto my member again and continued sucking it until it got hard again. Being a wolf, I have increased stamina, so it wasn't long until I was ready to take her again. I pulled her to her feet, then kissed her again. Then turned her around and lifted one of her legs slightly, inserting myself into her and penetrating her wet core that was calling out for me. My hands moved up to her soft breasts and squeezed them as I pounded her from behind. Then before I reached my edge, I pulled her head back by her hair and kissed her neck. She came first and within seconds I pulled out of her and came in the shower.

We cleaned up in the shower, then went to lie down in bed. I woke up two more times in the night completely hard and taking her. She was exhausted by the fourth time, but she was smiling, and I felt some pride thinking that I was able to take her mind off that jerk and provide her an escape from him permanently. I pulled her into my embrace. It was warm and comforting. I wanted to hold on to her forever. I slowly drifted off to sleep listening to her breathing.

Chapter 6: The Slip

Mikayla's POV

This must have been the best sexual night of my life. I feel so satisfied. I was tired after the emotional night and then had sex twice. The third and fourth times I was surprised I felt anything at all, but it all felt so good continually. I lost count of how many times he pushed me to the end. No wonder he had girls swarming around him at the club. He had his arm draped across me, but I figured I could look at my phone now and see what I could google about this man. I had heard his name before but was never into following gossip or the latest and greatest about famous people. To me, they were just people like everyone else. I slid out of his embrace. I looked around the floor for my purse before heading to the bathroom with my phone. I locked the door, then proceeded to google his name. There were a bunch of articles about how rich he was, how he was a bachelor and how he owned so many different ventures. I then searched his name with woman and a few news articles came up. I clicked the first one and it was an account of a woman whom he took home, they had a passionate night together. Then, in the morning when she woke up, he was gone, and the housemaid called her a taxi and sent her on her way. He didn't exchange numbers or talk to her again. She called him a player and a disgrace. I opened the next article, and it was a similar story from a woman who thought she found mister right and he was so charming. They had a romantic novel night together and the next morning, she was given the brushoff, not even by him but by an employee of his.

I shook my head and congratulated myself for ending up with the perfect one-night stand. He wouldn't want her to stay any more than she wanted to stay. It was a fun night and that was it. I was going to be the one to disappear from the bed and he would wake up alone, not me. After what Elliott did to me, I am not feeling all that great about males right now and I am going to have the upper hand from now on. I snuck out of the bathroom and picked up my clothes, getting dressed quietly. I grabbed my shoes and slipped downstairs running into a staff member. Instantly the staff member asked if she could help me. I asked for her to call me a taxi so I could return home and told her I would wait outside. I also asked her for a piece of paper and a pen so I could leave a note for the man of the house. The woman asked me to wait in the foyer, then made the call for the taxi. She returned with a pair of slip-on shoes, a sweatshirt with a zipper, and a bag for my dress shoes. "I think these will be your size. They are more comfortable to go home in." She then handed me the paper and pen. I wrote Jason a note and then handed it back to her. I thanked her and asked if she could let me out so I could wait outside for the taxi. She said she would be glad to and that she informed the taxi driver to come inside the gate to pick me up at the front. "No need" I mentioned to her as she opened the front door. "I will walk to the end of the driveway to meet the taxi and you can close the gate, so you don't have to wait. Thank you for the shoes and shirt." I waited for only a few minutes before a taxi arrived and asked me where to. I gave my address looking back at the beautiful villa and promising to remember this night forever.

Jason's POV

I woke up at 7:00 am what I thought was early, but I guess I was mistaken. The bed was empty. I felt the other side and it was cold, so Mikayla must've been up for a while. I got up and checked the bathroom and there was no one there. I threw on some sweatpants and headed downstairs. Miss Flint heard me coming as usual, meeting me in the foyer and indicating breakfast was ready. "Where is Mikayla?" I asked her.

"Was that the young lady that was here last night? She came down about two hours ago and asked me to call her a taxi. I gave her some alternate clothes and shoes as per normal and sent her on her way. I didn't realize you were still upstairs, usually; you are gone from the house and off to get work done," said Miss Flint.

"What? She left?" This is new territory I thought to myself. She took this as a one-night stand and left before I got up. I started laughing out loud. Miss Flint looked at me curiously and then pointed to the table "she left you a note". Interesting. I walked to the table picked up the note and read it.

Dear Jason,

Thank you for an amazing night and for helping me to move on with my life.

Sincerely,

Last night's one-night stand

I sighed then laughed again even louder this time. Miss Flint left me standing there informing again that breakfast was ready and maybe I should seek some professional help today. I wasn't acting normal. She always spoke her mind with me leaving nothing to the imagination. If only I could read Mikayla's mind. I can't believe she just up and left like that. Come to think of it, it is a terrible feeling even though I did my best to provide everything the girls would need the next day, food, clothing, a ride home and escape from the walk of shame, but it still felt wrong. Last night was amazing, didn't she think so too. I followed

Miss Flint to the kitchen informing her along the way Mikayla is my mate but is human so is unaware. It was rare for Miss Flint to lose her composure. She had been serving our family since I was a pup and was like a second mom to me. She smirked slightly and I could tell she was trying to hold back her laughter. "Just let it out. The irony has not escaped me, hence my laughter earlier when you said I needed to seek help." With that, she let out the loudest wail I had heard from her since I was a young boy. She finally started to calm down and wiped tears from her eyes. "It has been a while since I had a belly laugh like that. Good luck Jason." she said as she left the room continuing to snicker.

The breakfast was heavenly as usual. Miss Flint was a culinary master. I had worked up quite an appetite last night. While I gorged on the meal, I mind-linked Matt, "are you awake?" "Yep," he replied, "what can I do for you this fine early morning?" "Matt, can you believe this woman? She ditched me this morning leaving me lying in bed to wake up alone, then left me a note thanking me for helping her move on." There was silence. "Hello, earth to Matt. Did you hear what I said?" Matt responded "Jason, I cannot stop laughing, this is new territory for you. I only have one word for you man: Karma."

"It's not funny man. Well, it is a little bit funny, I laughed at the hypocrisy of it all as well, but I need you to focus. I must find her. She is my mate. Get Jacqui to tell you everything about her. She didn't even sign the note with her name, she signed it last night's one-night stand."

"I guess she figured out who you are then after you grabbed her in the night club. I told you, woman saying things about how you disappear on them in the morning was going to come back to bite you. If only you were a stand-up guy like me."

"Matt, you are asking for a beating in our next training session. Get me what information you can on her. She's my mate and I am going to win her over."

"Chill Jason, I am just teasing you. I have never seen you like this, but I can empathize with the pressure of the mate bond. Thank the goddess Jacqui is a wolf and understands our world even though she was a rogue and pretending to be human for the last few years. How are you going to explain all this to Mikayla and win her over?"

"Through any means possible."

"Jacqui and I will come over. Where are you?"

"At the villa"

"See you soon"

Chapter 7: The Morning After

Mikayla's POV

Once I arrived home, I was still exhausted from last night's escapades. I decided to run a bath and soak for a while, relaxing and maybe even snoozing. I ran the water, turned on some quiet soft music, added the bubbles, lit a vanilla-scented candle, and turned off the light. I stepped into the water and slumped down until just my head was sticking out of the water. It felt so good. The events of yesterday clouded my thoughts. How lucky I was to have such great, dependable friends. They would be there for me over the coming days, weeks, months whatever it was that I needed from them. They all sent me multiple messages already to check if I was okay in our group chat. I just replied that I made it home, mission accomplished, Elliott is over, and I need to sleep and relax now before work.

Elliott also tried to contact me several times. I ignored all his calls and text messages. They finally stopped a few hours after I caught him with his hands in the cookie jar. I guess he either figured I needed time to cool off or he was finishing his night off with the other woman; probably both - who knows. I don't even know why I am still so mad about it all. We only planned our entire future together. What a jerk he is. At least I found out about this before we got married. I can still cut all ties and send him packing much easier this way. I am way too trusting. I didn't even see it coming. I can't believe I am single again. I must've jinxed myself by thinking everything in my life was falling neatly into place. Thank goodness I didn't give up my apartment like he tried to make me last week. How dare he? Today I am taking the day for myself, then heading to work tonight. Tomorrow I am off. I will pack up his things and return everything along with his ring, then block his number. Why am I wasting my time thinking about him?

I can't believe I had a one-night stand last night. I so didn't think I had it in me. I feel a bit exhilarated and with Jason nonetheless. At least I never told him my name, that makes it seem final as well. If I took the time to talk to him, I am sure he would've sweet-talked me into anything. His dreamy eyes and strong handsome body. He has a lot of money; I would've thought him to be more snobbish and stuck up than he seemed to be. He was considerate of my desires and needs far from being selfish, at least in the bedroom. I wonder how many pairs of shoes and sweats are in his home to give to the girl of the evening. Do they have every size and multiple? How often does that happen? The process seemed established, provide clothes, call a taxi, and send female of the night out the door. What am I thinking? I instigated this, not him. He is who he is, and it was just one night. An incredibly exciting and euphoric night but it is in the past. He has tossed several women aside, why would I be an exception and even if he did treat me differently, our worlds are vastly different for us to be together. Goodness, what's wrong with me? I just got out of a relationship, why am I thinking about this guy?

Focus Mikayla on yourself and not men. Breathe in, breathe out. Time to relax and wash all my sorrows away. It's a new day and I am not going to dwell on the past and how it didn't go my way. I am meant for something else.

Jacqui's POV

"Are you serious? Mikayla is Jason's mate. This is so exciting. I thought I would have to leave her and join the pack. This is amazing. We will be together."

"Mikayla isn't a wolf, Jacqui. She doesn't feel the mate bond like we do. Jason stepped in and took her home after you and your girls planted the idea that she needed a one-night stand to get over Elliott. After a supposedly incredible night, she ditched him in the morning, and he woke up alone. He wants us to head over so you can tell him all about Mikayla so he can win her over."

"Wait, she ditched him? The powerful, rich beyond imagination, sexy, number one bachelor in the city, alpha of our pack, Jason. Wow, she took that one-night stand, use him, and lose him mantra to heart. That's my girl."

"Are you with us getting her on board or not? And what do you mean by number one bachelor? You realize you are my mate!"

"Sorry. I am with you of course. Mikayla is my girl. She may be putting on a cool, didn't impact her front about last night, but that isn't who she is. I would bet my life she is overanalyzing every aspect of last night right now.

"Let's head to Jason's then, he has already mind-linked me five times to find out if we have left yet."

Jason's POV

My pack and I have a scheduled training session today. It is important to stay on top of things. I am the Alpha of the Moon Eclipse Pack and have been for five years since my father passed on control to me so he and my mother could live their lives. The Full Moon Pack is adjacent to us and has been extending its borders in the other directions. We are a strong pack and equal to their strength, but it is only a matter of time before they claim war against us and try to forge forward. Their Alpha, Justin, is a pathetic excuse for a leader. He treats his people horrendously keeping the spoils for himself and letting them fend for themselves. He barely joins them on the battlefield to lead them as an Alpha should. I have been in search of my Luna for years. An Alpha is stronger once he has his Luna by his side and they are mated and marked. I need to win Mikayla over for my people and I need to get her to the safety of my pack before Justin figures out, she is my mate. She will be in danger once he discovers this truth. I can't get her out of my mind, where is Matt and Jacqui.

"How much longer?"

"We are here, open the gate."

Jacqui had never been to the villa before. She was awe struck looking around the place. Then she asked me if this is where I took Mikayla?

"Yes, I wasn't going to take her to a motel."

She responded, "oh boy, this is worse than I thought."

Matt and I looked at each other puzzled. I then motioned for them to join me in the living room and asked if they had eaten yet. Miss Flint had put together some snacks for us. We sat down and I asked Jacqui to explain what is worse.

"Mikayla dreams of a simple life. She doesn't like extravagant things. She admires them for their beauty, but she can't stand show-offs, snobs, pretentious people, and those who throw their wealth in others faces. She is a waitress by choice. Girl has got a brain on her, but she chooses to serve others. It makes her happy to make others happy. She is the most selfless person I have ever met. She is down-to-earth. She craves for a family and someone to adore her, so she is more heartbroken than she will let on by Elliott cheating on her. It will take time for that to heal even though she will for sure show a strong front. You are going to have to get her to know the real you. You portrayed in the news will be a complete turnoff for her. After spending some time with you, I know you are not that person, but you will need to convince her of that. Here is the address where she lives and works. She works at the diner tonight and is off tomorrow. I don't know her schedule after tomorrow. She lives in an apartment above the diner. We attend the University together in the Fall, Winter, and Spring but we are off for the summer. I drag her to the gym regularly, but she hates it even though she tags along. If it doesn't work out at the diner, you can come to the gym. We can say I brought Matt, and you are his best friend who wanted to join too. If she finds out I set her up, you are both going to be in hot water by me. She will for sure hate me doing this."

"Thank you, Jacqui. This is good information. Matt and I have training today. I will make an appearance at the diner today and try to convince her it is fate bringing us together. Technically, it is true."

Matt sent Jacqui home in a taxi. He and I went to train with the warriors in the pack. I owed him a good whooping for laughing at me earlier and I was going to keep him away from Jacqui tonight. He needed to accompany me to the diner, so it looked like a legitimate, we just heard about the place and stopped by type of situation. I will bring Kirk, my Gamma, and Luke, my brother so it looks like a real boy's night out.

Chapter 8: Stalking Much

Mikayla's POV

On days like this one, I am glad I live above my workplace. I can drag myself out of bed at the last minute, throw on a pair of jeans, my diner shirt, and my name tag, and scoot downstairs in under 5 minutes. At least Pop never let me down. He's getting older for sure and has trouble keeping up with tasks. I help where I can when I can, and he has hired more staff to get by lately. The diner has become infamous over the last two years since I started here with a word-of-mouth reputation. Like any restaurant, it has its busy times and slower times to recoup. It's Saturday today, so I am planning on a busy night. I threw on my clothes and headed downstairs to start my shift. Kate had worked the morning shift, so we would overlap a bit.

"Kate, how on earth did you get up this morning to work?" I asked her.

"I knew I couldn't call you to cover me," she said with a smile. "How are you doing?"

I replied, "Tricia may have been right. I feel great and am ready to persevere and close off ties with Elliott."

"What about Jason," she responded, "he is quite the catch. Every woman thinks so. Are you going to see him again?"

"Jason is a womanizer. I can't trust him. His reputation proceeds him. Don't get me wrong, last night was a night for the record books. However, I am moving on as a strong, single woman. I don't need a man to make me feel better. I only need my friends."

Kate updated me on the tables and where my help was needed. The diner was slow for a Saturday, but it usually picked up around 5:30 pm for dinner. I started helping to clear tables. Kate's shift ended at 3:00 pm so we said our goodbyes after she checked up on me for the umpteenth time. At 4:00 pm, I was soon to have my first break. First, I went to the restroom. When I came out to grab a quick bite to eat, none other than Elliott was waiting for me at the break table in the back. He stood up abruptly when he saw me walk out.

"We need to talk. I made a one-time mistake. Please forgive me. I love you; my family loves you and you are all that I want in this life." He pleaded continuously for me to take him back and wouldn't even let me get a word in.

I finally raised my finger to my mouth and said, "Stop! Can I say something?" He nodded in response. "Yesterday morning, you were my world and my everything, by this morning you were nothing to me. I cannot trust that you have not cheated other times and that you will not do it again. You have no issue lying to me. Kate told me you hit on her once as well. I will not be made more of a fool than you have already managed to do. Please leave. I am not working tomorrow. Please come by the apartment. I will have all your things boxed up for you to take and return the engagement ring. I want nothing to do with your future anymore, Elliott."

"Mikayla, be reasonable. We have invested two years into this relationship, and you know you are my shining star. I am sorry I hurt you, but I cannot let you go. You mean too much to me."

"Goodbye, Elliott, my break is over. I need to get back to work."

"I am not leaving," he said sternly.

"It is a free country and as a patron, I cannot kick you out of the restaurant, but you and I are over. I am not changing my mind. I could never trust you again."

I went back to work utterly frustrated that Elliott would not leave and would not leave me alone after what he had done. He had no right to pester me at work like this. I didn't want to cause a scene in my workplace, even though I know Pop would understand. His business didn't deserve to be punished for Elliott's infidelity and bad choices. I continued working and asked Brenda, the other waitress, to take the side of the diner Elliott had positioned himself.

It was now 8:00 pm and Elliott was still showing no signs of vacating the restaurant. He kept ordering things so we wouldn't make him leave and worked on his laptop. He was probably updating his dating profile. Wasn't I ignoring his calls and text messages enough to get him to leave me alone?

I ran into the back to make sundaes for a couple who was holding hands and doting on each other. I could practically see the hearts in their eyes. Good for them. Frankly, I normally liked that kind of thing, but it was making me ill today. Like really world, you must rub it in my face like this while the cause of my despair is watching me intently and refusing to leave me be.

When I came out, I carried the sundae with two spoons to the couple at the front booth and passed by another booth with four men. They must've just come in, so much for my next break. I sent down the sundae, then turned to take their order. "Welcome to Pop Pop's Diner…" I paused for a minute as he stared at me, and I stared at him. Almost memorized in his eyes, I couldn't think or talk. What was he doing here? Could this day get any worse?

I will just pretend I don't know him. I am just another notch on his belt, so I am sure he won't remember me or think I am the girl from last night. "How are you all doing this fine evening?" They all indicated they were doing well and excited to eat at the diner they had heard so much about. "Do you know what you would like to order, or do you need a few more minutes with the menu?"

"What do you recommend?" said Matt.

"Hey Matt, long time no see." What are these guys playing now? Can't I just have a normal uneventful shift? "It depends on your mood. I like everything on the menu. If you are looking for something hearty and filling, I would recommend the lasagna. If you want something on the lighter side, the BBQ chicken flatbread on the appetizer menu is good. The chocolate chip cookie is the best dessert, but it takes a bit to make, so if you want it, you should order it with your meal."

"We will have one of every appetizer on the menu. Please bring them as they are ready. We have been training all day and have worked up quite the appetite. We will each take one of those cookies you mentioned and water for us all. Need to replenish ourselves after last night and today's exercise." Jason smirked and winked his eye.

"Sounds good, I will be back with those waters shortly." I turned around to input their order and rolled my eyes. Clearly, he remembers.

After inputting their orders, I went back to the couple with the sundaes and provided them their bill. They asked questions about where they could go nearby for fun for couples. I politely gave them some suggestions. They thanked me and left. At least I got a good tip from them.

I grabbed water for the four men and a water jug so they could refill them, and I would have to go back to the booth as little as possible. As I was placing the water on my tray, Brenda came over. "Oh girl, those guys are so fine. All of them are watching every move you make when they can catch a glimpse. I heard Elliott mumbling some profanities under his breath while you were interacting with them. You are so lucky. I regret trading sections with you now."

"Brenda, it is a slow night tonight, so how about I help get them served and then see if Pop will let me go for the night, and then you can flirt with them all you want."

"You would do that for me. You have such a nice man in Elliott, I hope I can find a successful, handsome man to take care of me too."

"Elliott and I are no longer together. I will ask Pop if he is okay if I disappear tonight. If it gets busy, then he can call me back down to help you."

"You are such a sweet girl; Elliott is going to regret it for sure. Those boys are too young for me, but you should keep the table and see if you can replace Elliott with one of them. At least you can make him jealous by flirting with them."

"I have no desire to play such games Brenda but thank you for the advice. I would rather just leave the situation tonight."

Having wolf hearing, Jason and the others heard the entire conversation between Brenda and Mikayla. Jason instantly mind-linked someone and asked them to post that he has been spotted at the Pop Pop Diner, fully knowing his groupies would be there in no time taking up the seats and ordering food just to be in his presence like they always did. Then the restaurant would be busy, and Mikayla would be forced to stay.

I went in the back to ask Pop if I could go early given it was a slow night. It was now 8:35 pm. Pop agreed that I could punch out at 9:00 pm if things were still slow. The diner closed at 11:00 pm on a Saturday so it wasn't too late. One of us often went home early, although typically I would stay since I just lived right upstairs and didn't have to commute. Pop asked me if everything was okay. I let him know that Elliott and I broke up, but he still wants to be with me but it's over. Elliott was refusing to leave the diner but kept ordering so we could not ask him to leave without causing a commotion. He understood then.

Suddenly five minutes before I was ready to leave, the door was on a swivel. People just kept coming in and sitting at the tables. Brenda and I were swamped running from table to table to take orders. The kitchen was having difficulty keeping up.

Jason's POV

I watched Mikayla running around the diner meeting everyone's needs. The other waitress was older and seemed tired. She wasn't keeping up at all, so Mikayla was handling 75% of the restaurant. This wasn't what I intended. I didn't want her to leave before I got a chance to talk to her. Although in hindsight, bringing these guys with me and all sitting here, I didn't get an opportunity to talk to her, especially since she was acting as if she only knew Matt. I knew Mikayla had a late night and early morning, so I hoped she had rested during the day. I felt bad for making this all happen.

The booth I was sitting in was a round booth in the corner and I could see in full view the entire diner and everywhere Mikayla went. I also saw that Elliott jerk sitting in a booth on the opposite side of the diner. He was watching her almost as intently as I was. What was this guy getting at stalking her like this? He had his chance and blew it.

I watched Mikayla go over to Elliott's table and talk to him. I could feel the jealousy building up and Titus was fighting for control. He would start a brawl and not even care. "Calm down Titus. We cannot start a fight at her workplace and throw money at it to clean it up afterward. You heard what Jacqui said about Mikayla not being impressed by the flaunting of money and I am pretty sure she will not be too thrilled about a fight breaking out."

Mikayla and Elliott, both looked over in our direction and she pointed at me. I didn't take my eyes off her even though most men probably would have turned away. I couldn't. I wanted to know what they were talking about. The diner was too loud for me to make out their voices even with my wolf-hearing capabilities from across the way.

Mikayla promptly walked to the side of our booth where I was seated. She leaned over the edge and whispered in my ear. "I know you planned everything happening right now. I just don't know why and frankly I don't care. Since you decided to show up at my workplace uninvited; you can help me out. Kiss me right now." She leaned closer to me.

"What?" I looked up at her with curious eyes and she winked at me, then leaned further down letting her lips touch mine. I could feel the sparks igniting and instantly felt like the entire diner disappeared and it was only her and me in the room. I reached my hand up to her cheek and pulled her even closer, delving my tongue into her mouth. Her body was half over the side of the booth. I was going to pull her into my lap. She started to kiss me back passionately but after a few seconds quickly pushed herself away from me, saying rather loudly "I am at work sweetheart, save it for later." Then she smiled at me, winked again, and walked away.

"What just happened?" Luke asked.

"Oh, sweetheart! It seems our future Luna has managed to use you and ditch you again." Matt smirked.

"I like her." laughed Kirk.

"If it gets Elliott out of her life, then she can use me all she wants. Especially if I get a kiss like that." I retorted. "Don't be jealous."

They all laughed at me, each taking turns to taunt me and tell me that I had my hands full with this one. Meanwhile, she was starting to get very unfriendly looks from my groupies after our kiss. I usually am in such control over things. How on earth did they get so out of hand so quickly and how is it that every woman throws themselves at me except for my mate?

Unexpectedly, I felt some rogues crossing our pack territory boundary. As the alpha, anyone who wasn't a pack member or given permission to enter our territory would automatically alert me. Shortly after I felt their presence, I was mind-linked by one of my warriors on patrol. "Jason, we have four rogues on the attack on the Eastern border. We are chasing them, but they are not exiting the territory."

"We are on our way. Keep them away from the homes and pack members." I responded.

"Fun is over gentlemen. Time to go, we have an issue at home." I told the others. I glanced around to see Mikayla one last time, but she must've still been in the kitchen. I left a quick note on the table, and we all left.

The pack house was an hour's drive from our current location. We all hopped in the SUV with Kirk driving well above the speed limit to get us home and ensure the protection of everyone. I knew my warriors were excellent at combat and they wouldn't let the rogues harm anyone. Rogues typically were just looking for food or supplies on the outskirts. They would dip quickly into the territory if they noticed something but would immediately exit. The behavior described by my warrior was abnormal, so we needed to investigate. Rogues could be functioning, or they could be completely deranged. A lot of it was determined by how long they remained in their human or wolf form respectively. Look at Jacqui, you wouldn't even know she was a rogue until the mate bond kicked in with Matt. She was able to mask the fact that she was a wolf and live amongst the humans for years. It was very impressive.

On the other spectrum, I had seen rogues that had gone completely rabid and were unable to communicate. I don't even know if at that point, they can shift back into their human forms or if they would want to. Our pack has had to put a few of them down, but most times we tried to be reasonable. It wasn't our goal to kill and ask questions later. Unlike, Alpha Justin, he tormented and tortured rogues in experiments and gave packs a bad name. I had taken a few escaped rogues into our pack after finding out the cruelness they had endured in his territory once they were caught.

Mikayla's POV

It would be time to close the diner soon. Pop came out and announced the last call for the kitchen. It was still crazy busy. I had never seen it like this at closing time. Jason was very popular, especially with the ladies, but his friends sitting with him were all laughing and carrying on. It looked like it was at his expense as he kept shrugging and even let a little pout expression appear on his face. I admit it was adorable. Why is he here anyway? It couldn't be a coincidence that we had a one-night stand last night and now here he was visiting the diner no matter what he said his reasons for being here were. Given that Matt was with him, it dawned on me that my bestie must have something to do with them knowing where I work and how to find me. Next time I see her, I am calling her on it and will find out the truth of the matter. I can tell when she is lying to my face.

I had been in the back putting together dessert orders while Brenda served them. Luckily, she hated doing the dessert preparations so when I told her I need a break from the people and would do all her dessert orders; she jumped at the opportunity. After applying drizzle, whipped cream, and cherries to several different dessert types, I finally finished and went back to the front to help. Jason and his friends were gone, and the diner was already half empty. Brenda informed me everyone was finishing up the desserts and most tables had already requested their bills. Looks like we will get out of here at a reasonable time after all. Where did Jason go?

I went to clear the table when I saw a note. I picked it up.

My Dearest Mikayla,

Thank you for dinner and a kiss. Something has come up and we had to leave abruptly. I will be back tomorrow to pay the bill and provide you with a tip.

Yours Truly,

Jason

Are you kidding me? They ate almost every dish in the restaurant and just left without paying. How am I going to explain this to Pop? Calling me dearest. I am not his dear anything. Unbelievable the men I have in my life. What am I going to do if he doesn't come back tomorrow? I guess I do know who he is, but I don't want to have to go looking for him. Ugh!

Shaking my head, I clear the table, pocketing the I.O.U note that was left behind. Brenda and I delivered the remaining bills and started cleaning up the restaurant. I informed Pop about the payment showing him the note. He wasn't too happy but said Jason had talked to him earlier and he is confident he will come back tomorrow as indicated in the note. Pop was raving about what a great talk they had about potentially franchising his diner and he was a nice fellow with a good head on his shoulders. Jason managed to schmooze Pop also. Guess he was born with a silver spoon in his mouth, and it changed to gold as he matured.

After locking up the shop, we all left. I went upstairs to my apartment. I kicked off my shoes, then grabbed a pint of Ben and Jerry's chocolate fudge ice cream, sat on the couch, and scanned my PVR recordings to determine which tv show I had been neglecting. Any good breakup deserves a good tv binge. I was dreading seeing Elliott again tomorrow. His stuff was all over my place and a constant reminder, so I wanted it all gone, but I didn't want to see him right now. Hopefully, after tomorrow, things would start to feel normal as I closed that chapter of my life.

Chapter 9: Duty Calls

Jason's POV

"Bring them to the packhouse," I instructed.

My warriors walked four rogues into the common area. Matt had already cleared everyone out so we could talk to the rogues and find out why they were there.

"I am Alpha Jason. You have entered the Moon Eclipse Pack unannounced. Why are you here?"

"My name is Trevor Blackwell. This is my mate, Kathryn, and our children Tristan and Isabella. I was a warrior in the Full Moon Pack. My family denounced Alpha Justin right before leaving his territory. We are seeking asylum for information."

"Why would you denounce your Alpha? It leaves you and your family as rogues."

"He could track us if we remained a part of his pack. We have no intention of ever going back there. He is a ruthless ruler. He forces the men to train and work in his army, killing and taking over other territories – some embrace it and some like myself have nightmares over the atrocities he forces us to commit by choice or by command. The mated women are safe but those that are unmated and of age are taken and forced into servitude until they can find their mates. They are forced to cook, clean, and satisfy the needs of the men. Once they find their mates, depending on the male, they accept their mate and free them from the horrific life they lead, or they reject them in disgust at knowing how they have been defiled. My daughter is coming of age, so we had no choice but to leave. I had an opportunity, so we left immediately, leaving everything behind but the clothes on our backs. Please help us relocate to another pack. We have heard good things about you Alpha Jason and your pack but Alpha Justin plans to attack you soon and create a huge war. I can provide you with information on his methods from his attacks, defense, and spies to aid you. All I ask is that you get my family to safety and never send them back to him."

I mind-linked Matt "do you believe him? We already know one of the spy methods is to send his men out as rogues and have them infiltrate other packs to provide information."

Matt answered, "the spies we know he sent out usually are one rogue that claims to not have a family so his family is held hostage to ensure he keeps his word and provides helpful information. Although Alpha Justin is smart, he may know that we already know that and has changed his methods but then how would he force them to comply? He also seems nervous about the war. He isn't asking to join our pack due to the impending war but asking that we relocate him elsewhere."

"Tell me, Trevor, how is it that you escaped with your family? I know Alpha Justin has several methods to ensure escape is difficult for any in the pack."

"Alpha Justin arranged for me to be a spy and infiltrate your pack. When that occurs, they have the family members kidnapped so he can ensure compliance. A close associate of mine found out as he was one of five men ordered to grab my family. He mind-linked me secretly. I mind-linked my family to get out immediately and being a warrior, I knew a gap in his security that would allow us to escape near your pack lines. We denounced him, then climbed down the cliff and went through the water. It was risky but nothing would be worse than leaving my family unattended and knowing my daughter was coming of age. I don't agree with his methods, and he has only gotten worse with power with every pack he has overrun. I am a strong warrior, so received many accolades and plenty of the spoils of war, but there are others in our pack that are starving and barely surviving. Alpha Justin says we are thriving and those that are reaping the benefits agree and follow his lead. Most of those with daughters are worried as I am, although some have accepted it as a way of life now."

"Trevor, you must understand that we cannot fully trust what you are telling us given what we know of Alpha Justin and his infiltration tactics. Your family will be accommodated here in the packhouse under supervision tonight. You are to always stay in your suite. Warriors will be placed at your door to ensure compliance. We will arrange for your family to be moved and accepted into an alliance pack tomorrow. You will need to remain here to provide us with what information you can on Full Moon's war strategies and at the end of the week, you can join your family in the new pack. Whilst in the new pack, your family will be under 24-hour observation until they can be deemed not to be a threat to others. It will be the Alpha of the receiving pack who will determine when they are comfortable with dropping your security. Any wrong move by yourself or your family will result in you all returning to rogue status. Matt, make the necessary arrangements."

I mind-linked Kirk, Luke, and Matt to meet me in my office in an hour once Matt had time to sort out the arrangements for the Blackwells.

I went to the office and started working on the new paperwork that arrived. The mail brought daily issues that required attention and decisions to be made as well as information on all business and financials. Suddenly, I couldn't get Mikayla from my mind. She may have kissed me only for the sake of getting Elliott to back off, but the sparks were still there. I wish she was a wolf too so she could feel the mate bond. It would make life so much easier for me. She would probably already be here with me right now and my tensions would ease so I could concentrate on the impending war coming to our pack. I have always known it was only a matter of time and it seems the time is almost upon us. We have been training hard with my brother's guidance. Luke has traveled to many packs gaining knowledge on fighting techniques and bringing them back to our pack. We have multiple training sessions a week led by all sorts of people. Thinking during the war is just as important as physical capabilities. Luke has studied and trained with the best of them. He keeps locating new packs to travel to and learn from.

Luke and Kirk enter the office interrupting my thoughts. "Hey, Jason, any progress with Mikayla" Luke snickers.

"Bite me Luke" I respond in a huff.

Matt enters just as Luke and Kirk sit down on the sofa. My office was big as we had many meetings in here with internal pack members and external visitors. I had a large mahogany desk which I am sitting at with my feet up on it now leaning back in my chair. Kirk and Luke are sitting on the couch and Matt sits on the chair. I put my feet down and scoot my chair over to where they are all sitting. We start to discuss everything Trevor has told us and what our next steps are going to be to protect the pack, as well as put together a list of questions to discuss with Trevor in the morning. Kirk and Luke will take the lead in obtaining the intel from Trevor, then start forming a plan with security measures. Matt and I will be going back to the city to check on Mikayla and hopefully attempt to get her to come back to the packhouse. I have no idea how to explain all this to her or how she will take it. Her friend Jacqui is going to also be there to help us since Mikayla trusts her.

Chapter 10: A Shocking Revelation

Mikayla's POV

I woke up on the couch with the light from the tv flashing in my face. I sat up and stretched my neck feeling it was a bit sore. I drag myself to the bathroom to get ready for bed and shortly after fall into bed. Jason kept coming into my mind. The night we had together was amazing and despite me sneaking off in the morning, it felt kind of nice sleeping in his arms all night. Tricia was right. Jason helped me move on from Elliott. Don't get me wrong, Elliott was still in my heart. Love doesn't fade that quickly, but I knew it was over and I wanted nothing to do with him. I would never trust him again. Who knew how many times he has lied to me or cheated on me? I look at my clock it is 3:00 am. Why can't I sleep? Maybe I can get Elliott out of my mind once I give him all his things. With that, I get out of bed and find a garbage bag in the kitchen. I start going around my house putting all of Elliott's things in the bag. I wanted to remove all traces of him like he never existed. I'm unsure what time I gave up and went to bed exhausted. My alarm went off at 9:00 am waking me from my slumber and I had at least fallen asleep in my bed this time. I got up and went to the bathroom to do my morning routine. After showering and getting dressed, I made myself some breakfast. I had asked Elliott to stop by at 11:00 am to get his things including his engagement ring.

There was a knock at my door. I looked at the clock and it was only 10:30 am. I opened it with the chain on to see an annoyed Jacqui standing at the door with a smirk on her face, "you didn't think you were going to have to do this alone did you?" she questioned.

I raise an eyebrow at her and let her in. "What are you doing here Jacqui? I can handle this on my own and don't think I don't know it was you that informed Matt and Jason where I work so they could come and harass me yesterday. Traitor!"

"I confess it was me. Jason is a sweetheart, and it would be so cool if you ended up together as he and Matt are best friends, and we are besties. I know you wanted a one-night stand, but it isn't your style, and you never know, maybe it was meant to be. You should give him a chance. According to Matt, he is quite smitten with you. He has never stopped in his tracks for any female. Please forgive me. I am here to make amends by ensuring you have some support while dealing with Elliott."

"Jacqui, I appreciate you being here to give me strength, but this is something I need to do on my own."

"Okay, I get it. How about I hide out in your bedroom in case you need someone to help kick his ass out, and if not, then I will just chill? He was kind of stalky last night and I have a feeling he isn't going to let you go so easily. Besides, after you are done and he leaves, I am taking you out to lunch so we can discuss what happened with Jason. I want all the details."

"Fine, you can stay in the bedroom and wait him out. We can go for lunch afterward. I am quite hungry and don't want to cook or eat at Pop's until I can see Jason to get the money for the bill to give to Pop. However, you know I do not kiss and tell so you can forget about the details."

"We will see about that" she winks at me as she heads to my bedroom closing the door behind her.

I shake my head in frustration and do one last look around the apartment to ensure I have collected all of Elliott's things and then I grab the ring from my purse placing it back in the ring box it came with, giving it one last glance.

Jacqui's POV

I feel a bit bad going behind my best friend's back. I mean I have known her for two years and my mate for only a few weeks and I am doing things for him, not even for him, but for his friend. I planted a monitoring device in her living room. It was a simple monitor which would provide the video and sound for what was going on in the living room. I adjusted the sound so it was low so Mikayla would not be able to hear me from the bedroom listening in on her and Elliot. Then I texted Matt that I was about to call him and not to talk. Matt and Jason were downstairs in the restaurant and Jason had already settled the previous night's bill with Pop. I facetime called Matt who put his side on mute immediately so nothing could be heard from their side and then I positioned the phone, so it was facing the video monitor. We could see Mikayla lost in thoughts as she stood by the bookcase. Poor girl had her heart broken and now she had not one but two guys wanting her. I can't wait for her to accept Jason. I feel it will happen eventually. He is her mate even though she doesn't feel it like we would being werewolves. Human mates still can feel a connection, it just takes a bit for the bond to show. Once he marks her, she will feel it immediately.

A knock at the door interrupts Mikayla's distant gaze, as she strolls towards the door. I see her glance at the bedroom and then motion to open the door. Elliott walks in like he owns the place "Hi Beautiful". I unconsciously roll my eyes at his boldness.

"Hi Elliott, thanks for coming by to pick up your things. I have them all packed up here in a bag for you and here is your ring back." Mikayla points to the bag on the floor.

"That's it, after our time together, you just want to hand me my stuff at the door and shoo me away like a bug. Can't we have a chat first? I did drive all this way to see you yesterday and today."

"Today wasn't about seeing me, it was about picking up your things and as for yesterday, I didn't ask you to stop by I told you that I didn't want to see you. What you did hurt me. I cannot forgive you and I am certainly not going back to you after seeing you and hearing you with another woman. Please don't make this any harder than it needs to be."

Elliott took a step towards her, and she took a step back. "Mikayla, I don't want this to end. You are the one I want to end up with, otherwise, I would not have proposed to you. What we have is special, you can't just throw it away over one drunken mistake."

"Do you think I am an idiot? First, you called me to tell me you were staying in, so how did you suppose you ended up going out and getting drunk, resulting in sex in a bathroom stall? Second, if you think I believe this is the first time and it hasn't happened before, you are mistaken. You lied to me, and you cheated on me. Then you tried to get all possessive by showing up here yesterday. I don't owe you anything and we are over. I have moved on and so should you. It isn't even a conversation. As I told you yesterday, my mind is made up."

"You mean you've moved on with the player from the club. He loves them then leaves them. Everyone knows that. He's been with multiple women and casts them aside as quickly as he meets them. He isn't relationship material. At least I want to stay with you."

"While you are out sleeping with others. It doesn't matter. You and I are through."

"I am sorry to hear you say that Mikayla, but our journey is not over." Elliott took two strides and was at her side. "You are coming with me either willing or by force, but we have somewhere we need to go."

"I am not going anywhere with you." Mikayla tried to push him off. I dropped my phone on the bed and headed for the bedroom door, snarling under my breath. As I swung the door open, I heard from my phone "we are on our way, stall him."

I entered the living room to see an unconscious Mikayla in Elliott's arms. "What have you done?" I screamed at him. My wolf was coming to the surface. I could barely contain her.

Elliott looked into my eyes and laughed. "You are a wolf, clever girl hiding your scent all this time. I had no idea."

He laid Mikayla on the couch then turned to me and I saw his eyes going a black color when I realized that he also was a wolf hiding his scent. What the hell is going on here? He lunged at me, and I dove out of the way and transformed immediately. Our wolves had just started pacing back and forth in the living room waiting for each other to make the first move when Matt and Jason busted down the front door. Jason growled in fury. I could see his eyes glowing golden color and his claws were half out. His alpha aura emanated from his body. I felt the need to submit to him. Elliott must have felt it as well. He quickly jumped through her living room window shattering glass everywhere and landing on the fire escape. Matt and I ran to the window after him. I shifted back into my human form, having shredded my clothes, I was completely naked but could see Elliott running through the alley toward his car. He shifted before reaching his vehicle and then used the code on the window to unlock it and he must've had an extra set of keys inside as he instantly drove away. Matt looked at me and told me to go put some clothes on hiding me from Jason's view. Jason only had his eyes on Mikayla checking her pulse and feeling her head.

I ran to the bedroom, grabbed some of Mikayla's clothes threw them on, and rushed back to the living room.

"We are taking her to the pack doctor. She is unconscious and we are unsure what he gave her. It looks like he injected her with something through the video. Grab some things for her, she is staying at the packhouse. It isn't safe for her here until we figure out what Elliott was up to" Jason ordered as he carried her bridal style out of the apartment.

Matt said "hurry, grab some of her things and meet us downstairs. You must come too; she will need someone she trusts to be around when she wakes up to keep her calm and know she is safe after what occurred."

Chapter 11: The Whole Truth

Jason's POV

I thought I was already stressed and anxious but seeing Mikayla unconscious in that jerk's arms brought me to a whole other level. I was sitting in the backseat with her laying across the back and her head resting on my lap stroking her hair. I only kill when necessary, but that wolf was bad news. Did she know he was a wolf? Does she know about our life and existence? Where was he trying to take her? There are so many unanswered questions.

Matt is driving and Jacqui is in the passenger seat looking back every few seconds at her friend. I can see the anger written all over her face when she finally speaks "I cannot believe he is a wolf. Mikayla attracted all of us to her and doesn't even know it as far as I can tell. How would she have so many in her life?"

Matt chimes in "we need to find out if he belongs to a pack or is a rogue. If he belongs to a pack, there are only four in this area, and we know he isn't from ours but what if he is from Full Moon Pack? Whomever he is or whatever his motives, he was willing to force her to go against her will so it cannot be good."

I look down at Mikayla "why did he want you and where was he taking you? I won't let anything happen to you. You are mine."

We arrived at the packhouse within an hour. I carried her to the room next to mine. Sylvia, the pack doctor was already waiting upon our arrival and followed me upstairs. I placed her on the bed and Sylvia started to check her over. She lifted one of her eyelids to look and I swear I saw a bright blue spark in her pupil but then I blinked to clear my eyes and looked closer, and it wasn't there. After ten minutes, Sylvia made an initial assessment. "She appears to be in a deep slumber. She most likely was given a sedative and will wake up when it runs its course through her system. Without knowing how much she was given; I cannot guess when she will awaken. I will take some of her blood and test it. Once I see how much is currently in her bloodstream, I should be able to come up with a wake window give or take an hour if she hasn't already woken up by then."

I nod to Sylvia as she takes a blood sample and then leaves the room.

Matt and Jacqui are still there with me. We decide that Jacqui should be the first one Mikayla sees when she wakes up. Knowing Jacqui was in the apartment when Elliott was there would make sense for her to be there. Besides, Matt and I had to follow up with Luke and Kirk regarding the information from Trevor and the plan they have drawn up.

I kissed Mikayla on the forehead as Jacqui crawled onto the bed on the other side of her. I look at Jacqui and tell her to mind-link as soon as she is awake.

Mikayla's POV

I sat up abruptly on the bed drenched in sweat and breathing heavily. "You're safe Mikayla." I turned to see Jacqui lying next to me on the bed. I started to sob, and she instantly wrapped her arms around me and tried to comfort me telling me everything was going to be okay and that I was safe. After drenching her clothes, which I noticed were mine. I looked around the room and it was unrecognizable. "Where are we? Why are you wearing my clothes?"

She paused for a minute and then started with "don't be upset". Really? Anyone who needs to say those words knows that what they are about to say is going to be upsetting. I look up at her and already my face is showing signs of being upset. "I am not making any promises Jacqui. What happened?"

"Elliott gave you a sedative and tried to kidnap you. I didn't tell you when I got there that Matt and Jason were downstairs waiting in the diner. Jason paid Pop the outstanding bill. I planted a video monitor in the living room, and we all watched and listened to your interaction with Elliott. I can't explain it, but something felt off about him the night before to the three of us and we have pretty good instincts, so we wanted to be around just in case. Thank goodness we were, otherwise, who knows where he would have taken you or what he would have done to you. We are at one of Jason's homes now safe and secure. He had a doctor look you over to ensure you were okay and I have been waiting here for you to wake up. Matt and Jason are on their way and will be here shortly."

"How long have I been out? What happened to Elliott? Why did he try to take me? How do you know Matt and Jason are coming now? What is going on Jacqui?"

Matt and Jason enter the room as I finished my barrage of questions. Jason walks over to me on the bed, and I lean away slightly. He has a look of adoration on his face and while it is somewhat calming, I have no idea why he is giving it to me when we only just met. He sat on the edge of the bed and reached out to push a stray hair behind my ear. Then said, "we need to tell her everything."

Jacqui and Matt in unison like it had been coordinated say "what?"

"I know it is a lot to take in, but he tried to kidnap her. It could be related to me or the impending war. She needs to know what is happening and I must trust the mate bond and the Moon Goddess's decision to put us together. The pack doesn't have time to wait, and I need to put them first. Besides, how do we explain everything without telling her? She is already questioning things. Without the whole truth, things will not make sense. I want her to know everything."

Jacqui and Matt look at each other and shrug.

Now I am getting irritated. I was almost kidnapped by Elliott but seeing as I am here in Jason's house just makes me feel like I was kidnapped by them, and Jacqui is in on it too. She's my best friend. How could she do this to me? Am I this bad a judge of character? Someone needs to start talking. "Well, is someone going to enlighten me or am I going home?" I pushed Jason's hand away from me as I spoke.

Jason started "I am going to rip the band-aid off and then go into more details. Please try to remain calm while we explain everything – except why Elliott tried to kidnap you, which we are still trying to ascertain. We are werewolves. I am the Alpha of the Moon Eclipse Pack, and you are currently in our pack house. We are one of the larger, stronger packs in the area. Werewolves have destined mates that are established by the Moon Goddess. A werewolf can tell their mate anytime they meet them after their 18th birthday. The mate will have a pull and a certain scent that entices each other to form a permanent bond. You are my mate Mikayla, which is why I feel overly protective, and possessive and love for you already. Jacqui was a rogue werewolf, masking her scent for years and living amongst humans until she ran into Matt. They instantly knew who they were to each other

65

given both were werewolves and could sense and smell the bond they had. A rogue is when a werewolf doesn't belong to a pack but since Jacqui met Matt and they have mated and marked each other, she has joined my pack. We can mind-link each other, which means we can talk into each other's heads. Jacqui informed Matt and me the moment you woke up and here we are. I know this is a lot to take in, do you have any questions?"

I took in all of what they were saying and looked Jason in the eyes. "Just one, can you take me home please?"

He had a look of sadness flash upon his face and then it turned to determination. "No, it isn't safe for you there now. You need to remain here."

"So, what you are saying is you saved me from Elliott kidnapping me only to kidnap me yourself."

"That's not what we did, we saved you. You are my mate; I want nothing but the best for you and your safety. Didn't you hear all that I just told you? We are werewolves and…"

"Stop! I know of the existence of werewolves already and I need to stay away from you all."

Jason let out a growl in anger as he rose from the bed where he was sitting next to me. I followed to get up. "You are staying here for now. We must figure out why Elliott wanted to take you and where he was going to take you. You are my mate which makes you the future Luna of this pack and we are about to go to war with another powerful pack that will not hesitate to use you against me. I cannot risk having my judgment clouded and making irrational decisions to risk the safety of you, myself, and most importantly the pack. If you know anything about werewolves, then you know my hands are tied in this. We need answers before I can allow you to leave."

"You cannot keep me here against my will."

"I can and I am. Try to be reasonable Mikayla. Get some rest. Feel free to freshen up and relax. Jacqui brought some of your things for you. If you need anything, other than to leave, let Jacqui know and she can inform me through mind-link. Let's go, Matt, we have work to do. Jacqui, bring Mikayla down to dinner in two hours." Jason ordered as he walked out of the bedroom. I heard the door lock behind him.

"Jacqui, you have to help me get out of here."

"Mikayla, I cannot go against my Alpha's orders, even if I wanted to. He is right. It isn't safe out there for you. You are my best friend, and I couldn't live with myself if I helped you leave, and something happened to you. Please can you just give him a couple of days to at least figure out what Elliott was planning? He is also a werewolf. I came out of the bedroom to stop him from taking you while Matt and Jason were on their way. He turned into a wolf and attacked me. I was able to hold him off until they arrived, but he was much stronger than me. If they had not been there, he could have killed me and taken you to Goddess knows where to do Goddess knows what. I was so scared. He fled out the window when he felt Alpha Jason's aura and escaped. I am begging you to trust me just this once. He could attempt to kidnap you again. I have never led you astray."

"No, you haven't but you haven't been truthful with me either. You have chosen to plot against me with Matt and Jason. Telling them where they could find me and planting a monitor behind my back and now agreeing that they should have me locked up here to stay. I thought you were my friend. You have lied to me for years being a werewolf. I am wondering if I even knew you at all."

"It isn't like that Mikayla. I only wanted the best for you by trying to connect you with your mate. It is the most amazing feeling, and everyone speaks very highly of Jason here. The monitor, I know was crossing a line, but if I told you they were downstairs and wanted to eavesdrop because we felt something was off with Elliott, would you have let me place the monitor and stay? I was worried for my friend and did what I felt was right to protect you."

"I don't need you to protect me. I need you to be honest and stop trying to play matchmaker with me. This is my life, or it was my life. Now I am just a prisoner. I don't want to even look at you right now." With that said, I stalked off to the bathroom and slammed the door.

I was angry, to say the least. Who do these wolves think they are holding me prisoner and telling me I cannot go? I should have continued practicing. I am so weak now. My parents left me when I was young. They gave me a letter telling me to stay clear from werewolves and to hide my gifts from the world. It was crucial to my survival, but they didn't say why. Up until they sent me away, I was taught about all supernatural creatures, including werewolves. I know the mate bond would pull Jason to me and while I wouldn't feel the bond in the way that he did, I would feel at peace and happy with him, like he was my soulmate and fated to me. I was already thinking about him more than I would care to admit, but how could I ignore my parent's warning in the letter? Should I even listen to them given that they just left me so abruptly? I loved them and I knew they loved me, and all that love faded away so fast and is forgotten and then Elliott tricked me, and that love was all a fake. How can I trust that Jason is any different or that this love he feels for me is not going to fly out the window as quickly as it came? The only good thing about this is the incredible bath I see before me. It is huge and has jets. There are bath bombs, bubble bath, Epsom salts, potpourri, candles, and scented oils. I have never seen so many bathing options before. I started the water, then added the bubble bath. There was still sunlight beaming through the window, so I didn't need the candle yet. I stripped down and soaked into the bath turning on the jets once the water got high enough. I had to think of a way to get out of here.

Chapter 12: Mikayla's Secret

Jason's POV

Matt and I went back to my office where we left Luke and Kirk drawing out our plan of defense. We were not responsible for starting this war, but we were not going to lie down idly and wait for Alpha Justin to take us over either. He may have been successful in the past conquering other packs, but my pack was ready to put up the fight of a lifetime to ensure he was unsuccessful.

I stormed into the office with Matt hot on my heels. "How can she know about wolves already and then asks me to let her leave? Ungrateful for us having saved her life. She has only been in my life for three days and they have been a long three days. This is not the fairy-tale mate bonding I was described growing up."

Matt spoke up, "Jason, you need to calm down. We anticipated she would be grateful, but she is right, we saved her from her kidnapper only to kidnap her ourselves. She will come around, but we are going to have to give her some time. Let her see what it is like to be here, a part of the community, and continue to show her how much you care but getting angry and almost letting your wolf out isn't going to help the situation."

"Let's focus on the plan for now and start executing. Did you have any reason to doubt any of the intel Trevor supplied during your interrogation?" I changed the subject and addressed Kirk and Luke.

Kirk spoke first, "he gave us some crucial information if it is accurate, then we have some ideas on how to get ahead of the attack. We must make some adjustments in our border defenses and the patrols we are currently running.

Trevor was able to point out some gaps that Alpha Justin and his men have been discussing. Luke and I have drawn up the details and they are ready for your review and approval."

"Jason, if what Trevor said is true, we don't have a lot of time to waste. We need to inform the pack immediately and ensure all the women, children and elders are safe. The warriors need to be on guard and working rotations. We have already recalled those that are on missions and in the field. You need to inform our alliances, so they are ready as well." Luke warned.

"Leave me with the documents and the plan. Matt and I will review it. After dinner, we will all reconvene in the office to update any details and approve the plan assigning implementation tasks. If you have everything from Trevor, send him off to meet up with his family and then rest until dinner. Jacqui and Mikayla will be joining us for dinner, so I want you all there tonight."

"Yes Alpha" they all spoke. Kirk and Luke walked out closing the door behind them and Matt walked over to the desk.

"Let's get to it," I said.

Matt and I discussed the plan, making minor adjustments for about an hour. There was a knock on the office door interrupting our thought process. "Come in" I answered.

Sylvia entered with a file in hand. "I need to share my findings with you regarding Mikayla. Has she told you anything about herself?"

"Is something wrong with her?" I raised an eyebrow pleading in my mind she was going to say no.

Sylvia sat down and then continued, "I was reviewing her blood sample. Based on the amount of sedative she had in her system; she should still be unconscious until well into tomorrow. However, Matt mind-linked me that she was already awake, so I took a closer look at her blood. Are you aware that Mikayla is a witch?"

"A witch? You must be kidding. She hasn't shown any signs of.... Wait a minute. I did think I saw a blue spark flicker in her eye when you lifted her eyelid earlier today, but I blinked, and it was gone so I thought it was my imagination. Jacqui didn't mention anything about her being a witch. Her scent would have given it away immediately and she doesn't show any signs." I was speaking more rhetorically but I guess it was out loud, so Sylvia responded.

"If she hasn't been practicing magic, then her scent would be of a human, and the fact that she is a witch would be undetectable unless her blood was scrutinized. I am 100% sure of it after running some tests. Her magic kicked in and was fighting off the sedative without her even knowing it. You may even be able to detect it in her scent if you concentrate on it now."

"Sylvia, I will take that file. Thank you for bringing this to my attention right away. Matt, contact Dylan and have him conduct a full investigation into Mikayla and her history. I want a full report by end of day tomorrow."

Sylvia exits the office and I walk over to the bar to make myself a drink. I need something to take the edge off. This has been one heck of a weekend.

"Make me one too" Matt sighs.

"We need to finish reviewing the tactics report for later. It is almost time for dinner." I remark as I hand him his drink.

"We can take a minute to mull things over. This is a lot to take in."

Mikayla's POV

It was time for dinner. I was going to have to play nice for a bit until I could find a way out of here. I wasn't going to stay. I had money put away so I could find a hotel to stay in for the time being. I would need to grab some items from my apartment that my parents left for me.

I asked if I could use a phone to contact Pop to tell him I needed a few days off, but Jacqui already thought of that and had contacted Kate and told her that I was going to be away and for her to work out covering my shifts. Other than asking Jacqui for the phone, I hadn't said anything to her. I was still fuming mad. I got dressed after my bath in a pair of jeans, a pink cashmere sweater, and white keds. My hair was put up into a high ponytail. My lips were feeling a bit chapped, so I put on some lip-gloss, but I wasn't about to get all gussied up for Jason and his pack. I wasn't planning on staying.

Ten minutes to dinner time and we both looked towards the door as we heard the lock turn. A young lady walked in announcing it was dinnertime and we should head down. She would tidy the room while we were out. Admittedly, I was looking forward to dinner. I hadn't eaten all day and I had heard my stomach growl a few times since awakening from the sedative. As we made our way down the stairs, I could smell the most delicious-smelling food. My mouth was watering already even though I had no clue what we were about to have. Jacqui led me into the dining room and my jaw dropped to the ground. It was decorated like a fancy Christmas party dinner you would see in the movies. Beautiful white silk tablecloths with gold trim laced throughout. There were several round tables spaced around the huge room. There were black curtains drawn and draping down the floor-to-ceiling windows. I saw French doors leading out to a balcony. I could see a garden and in the middle of it was a fountain spraying water in different directions glistening in the moonlight. There was a chandelier in the center of the room and hanging lights throughout the rest of the room in the shape of lanterns. On the far wall was a line of people walking through a buffet-style line. As I followed Jacqui to the line, everyone was turning to look at me. I avoided their gaze looking at their plates of food and how high the food was piled. On every table were cutlery, a coffee cup, and saucer, a basket of buns, a dish with butter, water, and wine glasses with a bottle of wine in the center. We got to the back of the lineup. Everyone who was in line to stepped to the side so we could move to the front of the line and get our plates. I stopped at the end of the line and stepped aside also not realizing they were doing it for me. Jacqui whispered to me what was happening, and realization dawned on me. "Please do not step aside for me. There is so much food here for all of us. I can wait my turn like everyone else." I received a few shocked looks; others were confused like they didn't know what to do. "Please get back in line and load your plates as if I was any other wolf." No one was moving, it was a bit frustrating. I wasn't about to skip the line.

"You can all continue. Mikayla wishes to wait her turn to grab her food. We will wait with her." Jason's sexy, masculine voice rang out from behind me. I turned to see Jason and Matt standing there smiling with two others. I recognized them from Jason's initial visit to Pop Pop's, but I didn't know their names or who they were. They also sent a smile my way and one of them even winked at me. I immediately turned my head back to the line. He and Jason looked so much alike that it was uncanny. I was so hungry, and the line was moving slower than I would have liked but it would only be a few minutes until I was able to eat. I told everyone I would wait my turn. In my mind, I want to push everyone out of the way and grab handfuls of food and shove it in my mouth. The image of me doing that in this setting makes me giggle to myself. Jason must have picked up on it as he asks me "what's got you laughing?"

"Nothing, I am hungry. I was picturing myself going a little over the top with stuffing my face in front of all these strangers and imagining their reactions." I laughed. I am guessing he imagined something like me and started to laugh himself. His laugh made me feel warm fuzzies inside like I had been outside in the cold freezing and took those first couple of bites of soup that warm you up from the inside. He leaned closer to my ear and whispered "thank you for containing yourself this long, it is your turn. Grab a plate and don't be shy at filling it up."

I grabbed one of everything to try until my plate was full which was only about halfway through the buffet line. It was more than enough for me. I looked back at the four men behind me. They each had two plates in their hands and were directing the serving staff to continue to pile them up high. My eyes almost bulged out of my head thinking of how wasteful they were being. We got to our table which needed fewer things on it to fit all our plates. After some maneuvering, we all managed to fit. The table sat eight people and there were only six of us, so we had the extra space. If two others had been sitting there, we certainly would not have fit. I grabbed a bun and started buttering it, then passed the basket and butter to Jacqui.

We all started digging into our meals. As we started to slow down a bit, Jason spoke "Tell us about yourself, Mikayla, where did you grow up?"

I didn't want to share right now any personal details. It would make it that much harder to leave the more we know about each other. I kept it vague, "I don't like talking about myself very much. I was in a loving home with the best parents ever. When I was ten, they passed away. My life changed. I was raised in foster care until I turned 18. I received a scholarship to attend school and used the money my parents left me to supplement the rest. I got a job at Pop Pops and then decided to reside there to make life easy. I will be going back to school to complete my business degree come the fall. Oh, and I have recently been kidnapped and held against my will by a stalker and his pack." Jason's fork is midair frozen and the others all gape at me as well. The entire room goes silent as everyone looks in our direction. I hear mutterings around the room.

Jason informs me, "wolf hearing is better than human hearing, so your joke about being kidnapped was heard by everyone and they believe you are being serious that their future Luna doesn't want to be here when they are all excited, I finally found you."

I got his hints that I was about to be the cause of a huge uproar, so I decided to keep the peace and play along. I instantly thought of how to use it to my advantage. "Sorry, I forgot about the wolf hearing. Don't worry everyone. It was a joke as Jason has stated. You will see me out and about tomorrow of my own free will to prove my sarcasm. I will attempt to be more cautious of my words in the future given everyone is listening in on my conversations."

I smiled and raised an eyebrow at Jason, whom I could tell was torn between happy I shrugged off the whole kidnapping comment and angry I found a way to get out in the open tomorrow. We stared into each other's eyes like we were in a staring contest. Neither of us backed down.

Luke jumped in "maybe we should share and tell in a more private setting".

We finished dinner praising the food. Then we got up to get dessert. It looked so enticing but I honestly could not eat another bite. I asked if they had to go containers which got a few smirks but one of the servers motioned for me to wait and ran into the back room. She grabbed me a plate and put a few items on it. I thanked her and took the plate. "I am ready to go back to my cell, I mean, room."

Jason rolled his eyes and then said, "Follow me".

He led me back upstairs and to my room. I opened the door and walked inside. The bed was made, and fresh towels were laying on the end of it. I turned around to see Jason walking in as well when I put up my hand and said "this is the end of the line for you. Goodnight." And I closed the door with him stepping back slightly so it would not hit him. I heard him say "Goodnight Mikayla" through the door before hearing it lock and his footsteps walking away.

Chapter 13: The Escape

Jason's POV

My room was right next to Mikayla's. Even though she gave me the cold shoulder at her door, knowing she was on the other side of the wall had me and my wolf at ease. He was going stir-crazy that he couldn't mate and mark her.

"Titus, you need to be patient. She is very strong-willed and if we force it, it will ruin our relationship."

"What relationship? She isn't coming around. If anything, she is even further away, if we mate and mark her, then she will feel the bond more and will come around, probably faster than waiting for her."

"I do not want to force her with the mate bond. I want her to want to be with us. She needs time to absorb everything. She was in love with another man a few days ago and it blew up in her face. She must heal and forget that before she can move on completely. "

"She will make us stronger. We need her sooner rather than later. The war is coming. We can't keep going on with this distraction."

"I know but what do you want me to do? Pin her down, take her unwillingly and mark her while screaming. It isn't who we are. It is what separates us from Alpha Justin and his ruthlessness."

I heard a noise from her room sounding like a window opening. I opened my window quietly. Thank goodness for wolf hearing. I leaned out slightly peeking from behind a curtain, so she wouldn't see me if it was her. Sure enough, I saw her climbing out of her window. There was a balcony below us on the 2nd floor that was currently empty. I sighed and left the room heading down to the balcony to meet my escape artist mate.

"Are you sure you don't want to club her and drag her kicking and screaming back to our cave? You can blame me if you want, she doesn't have a wolf for me to talk to anyways." Titus muttered.

"Don't put it past me at this point." I fumed.

Titus went back into the depths of my mind as I went out to the balcony to await her. I waited in the shadows. She was oblivious to my location as she concentrated on scaling the wall. Her feet gently graced the wall as she shimmied down a sheet she had tied together. I couldn't believe she even attempted this. Were we in a movie now? The Moon Goddess must be having a grand laugh at my expense and this crazy mate of mine. However, she is making it down safely, so I guess I am slightly impressed although I am also livid. Where does she think she is going? She has no real plan. My packhouse is guarded well and we have patrols all over the territory especially heightened due to potential war, not to mention it is almost an hour back to civilization. She jumps down onto the balcony and as she turns to look around to take in her surroundings, I step out of the shadows. "Where to next love?"

She practically jumped out of her skin. Knowing she was caught, she raised her arms and put her wrists together like I was a cop who just arrested her, and she was holding out her hands so I would cuff her. "Don't tempt me." I snarled. Then motioned for her to go inside and back up the stairs. She stopped at her room door waiting for me to unlock it with a frustrated expression on her face. I walked next to her and looked her in the eyes.

"Let me tell you something about me. My wolf's name is Titus, and he is extremely strong but also very compassionate to those he cares about. He is possessive and would love nothing more for me to carry you over my shoulder back to my room and mate you and mark you to show the world you belong to us. I am the only one keeping him at bay but each time you defy me and go against me, I lose a little bit more control of him." When I said the last part, I let Titus come forward flashing my eyes a golden color then back to their normal brown color.

She gasped a little and looked away from me. I picked her up over my shoulder and carried her toward my room. Her heartbeat started to flutter faster, and I knew I was scaring her, but being nice wasn't working. I entered my room and shut the door behind me, then took her over to the bed and tossed her onto it. She shimmied back towards the headboard, and I climbed in next to her. "Scoot over." She moved to the side, and I climbed in under the covers, then covered her and slid her down from the headboard and into my arms spooning her. I whispered in her ear "it's late. I need to get some rest and I cannot sleep thinking you are going to attempt to escape all night. You are staying the night with me here. If you are a good girl and go to bed, then I will not let Titus do as he wishes with you. Goodnight." I pulled her body close to mine making sure she couldn't escape my clutches and drifted off to sleep in a matter of moments while listening to her heartbeat finally calm down and reach a normal rhythm.

Titus' POV (sexual content)

I smelled our mate's breathtaking fragrance and couldn't take it any longer. Jason had fallen into a deep, peaceful slumber. He rarely slept and when he did it was always a light sleep. This little one had no idea the impact she was having on him and me. I felt us become rock hard when brushing up against our mate's butt. I had to have her now. With Jason asleep, control of our body was all mine. I smiled contently.

I took control and slowly rolled her over, removing her bottoms while she slept. She woke up just as I removed them from her feet. By the time she realized what was happening, I had already pounced on her, grabbing her hands, and pinning them beside her head. Her eyes met mine. She froze completely and her heart started beating triple time while I stared at her with golden eyes. She for sure knows it is me and not Jason. I leaned down and nudged my face into her neck caressing her with my face and then kissing her leaving hickeys in my path. She was mine and everyone was going to know it. Tears started to form in her eyes.

"Little one, I am not going to hurt you. I want to satisfy you and enjoy you. You are my mate; you need not be afraid of me and what you want." I started rubbing my manhood against her crotch while holding her in place as I looked back into her eyes. After a short while, I could smell her arousal and feel some of her juices soaking through my boxers. I maneuvered her hands above her head so I could hold them in place with one hand while I removed my boxers. She remained frozen on the spot. I leaned to her eyes and kissed her fallen tears from each eye. At the same time, I went back to holding each hand with mine on the side of her head, locking my fingers with hers. I positioned myself at her entrance. I was incredibly hard and needy. I looked into her eyes once more and slammed myself into her hard and deep maintaining eye contact with her the entire time. I could hear the slap of our skin meeting and a slight moan from Mikayla. I wasn't quite sure if it was pain or pleasure, but I know she wanted it as much as I did. Jason started to wake up and try to take control, but it was too late. She was mine and I wasn't going to stop until we were both finished.

I continued to thrust in and out of her, hard and deep. The slapping getting louder and more frequent. She was tensing and squirming under me. I never left her eyes. She was enjoying this and was reaching the edge, about to climax and I stopped immediately. I could see a sense of longing and questioning in her eyes as she stared back at me. She had stopped trying to get her hands away from me a while ago, but I continued to hold her in place.

"Beg me" I commanded her.

"What" she replied.

"Beg me for your release" I repeated.

She hesitated in silence as we stared at each other. She broke her eye contact and whispered, "please."

"Please what?"

"Please keep going."

"Tell me what you want."

"I want you to give me my release." she whimpered. As those words left her lips, I thrust back inside her again. Pounding her wet, core. Savoring every moment of her juices around my hard member.

"Is this what you want?" I asked her.

"Yes," she screamed.

"Do you want me to stop?"

"No" she moaned.

I released her hands and smashed my lips onto hers, dancing my tongue into her mouth claiming every piece of her, tasting her, feeling her, hearing her, and touching her. She reciprocated the feeling as if she couldn't get enough of me, nor I her. The passion was warm and inviting and I wanted this moment to last. I felt her release and as my release ensued, I gave control back to Jason. The three of us were at a height of ecstasy, sparks flying, and so much built-up tension and anxiety evaporated at that moment.

Mikayla's POV

His eyes turned back from golden to brown and I knew it was Jason again. He stayed inside me and brushed my hair from my face and smiled down at me.

"Good morning love" he whispered.

"I won't be sleeping in your room again, since you cannot control your mutt."

"I may have been asleep for part of it, but pretty sure you were begging for it. You didn't beg me. I am a little jealous. Do you want to go another round?" he raised an eyebrow with a smug smile on his face.

I sighed, pushing him off me, and jumped out of bed. While pulling my pants back on, I looked toward Jason. "Give me the key to my room. I need a shower."

"A cold shower?"

"Are you done?" I was starting to feel embarrassed and wanted out of his sight like five minutes ago. He reached into the drawer by his bedside table and pulled out the key and handed it to me. I snatched it and turned on my heels to head out the door.

As I closed his bedroom door, he yelled, "you know where to find me if you need any help."

"Unbelievable" I mutter to myself but hearing him laugh afterward I know he heard me with his wolf hearing.

I walk next door and head straight for the shower.

I turn on the water and look in the mirror. "What is he doing to you? You need to be stronger than this giving into your desires. Have some self-respect."

She stepped into the shower. The water rolling down her body felt amazing as she forgot about her troubles. She couldn't help but picture Jason and his physique. Her body trembled at the thought of him. After a few minutes of remembering this morning's events, she continued to wash profusely. Jason couldn't control Titus. She more than ever needed to escape this place.

Jason's POV

"Thanks a lot, Titus, now she is pissed at me, and I didn't even do anything."

"No problem. It was worth it wasn't it to hear her beg for more and feel satisfied now? I would do it all again."

"Precisely her point and now she is not going to stay here with us anymore. We were taking steps in the right direction and now we are stepping back again. She isn't like the other women we come across. She isn't going to stay because we have money, or the sex is good. She wants trust, communication, and love. You must control yourself or you will push her away and she will reject us."

"She will be back. She was absolutely into it."

"Now I know how she feels dealing with me." I shake my head and go to take my shower.

After getting dressed, I go to Mikayla's room and knock on the door. She yells "come in" so I enter.

"Ready for breakfast. A wolf told me you worked up quite the appetite this morning," I teased her.

"Oh, it is you - stalker turned kidnapper turned rapist. Your informant was misinformed - I am not a breakfast person and am not hungry. You can go without me" she retorted.

"Unfortunately, you are not staying here alone unattended. Besides, yesterday you let the pack know you will be out and about making an appearance to prove you were not kidnapped, so you will get the opportunity today."

"I will," she said way too enthusiastically.

"Don't get too excited. I am sending two warriors to mirror your every movement, so don't get ahead of yourself. Besides, we are miles away from the city. There are shortcuts but you don't know them. If you go the wrong way, you could end up in the Full Moon Pack which would not be wise. You called me some very harsh things, but your safety and happiness are important to me. Alpha Justin would not show you any kind of courtesy." I warned her.

"Fine," she said in a huff and then walked out the door and towards the stairs.

Everyone showed up for breakfast and to be honest it was boring. I kept sneaking peeks at Mikayla and smiling and winking at her. She shifted in her seat like she was uncomfortable. Her attempts to ignore me were futile. I caught her glancing my way a few times.

I mind-linked two of my warriors who were trained as guards to escort Mikayla around the grounds. They appeared within minutes.

"Mikayla, this is Sean and Rick. They are two of our guardian warriors and will watch over you while you move freely around the pack territory. They will let you know what is out of bounds if you venture too far out. She can essentially go anywhere within the territory; you cannot leave the territory. Have a good time. We will see you back here at lunchtime in four hours. If you need me, they can mind-link me to find out where I am."

Jacqui interjected, "Can I please come with you, Mikayla? I still haven't seen much of the territory either and would like to earn your forgiveness."

Mikayla shrugged "It's up to you." She got up from her seat and started to walk towards the door.

Chapter 14: The Training Grounds

Mikayla's POV

Stepping out of the packhouse was a breath of fresh air. It was a beautiful day. The sun was shining, and the air was crisp but warm with a summer breeze. The area was surrounded by trees and a forest was within the distance. The green of the open field and trees contrasted with the blue sky and white clouds. Flowers of all colors were surrounding the building with red mulch to accentuate the colors. There were some paved sidewalks and some gravel paths leading away from the pack house. People were all a bustle already at 9:00 in the morning. I saw a mother pushing her baby in a stroller. The gardener was watering the plants. Some people were entering the pack house and some walking in all different directions. I wonder what they were all doing so early in the morning. I guess they all had their jobs to do. I never really gave it much thought. I was pulled out of my thoughts when an older man walked by into the pack house and said, "Good morning, Luna". He walked by and Jacqui nudged my arm, "he was talking to you."

"Oh, sorry sir, good morning to you. I was lost in my thoughts. Hope you have a joyous day."

I continued to walk down the steps and noticed a map of the area. I went to look at it and noticed water in one spot. I loved being near the water with the sound of the waves crashing into the rocks or beach and listening to the birds fly freely about. There was also a huge garden with a fountain. The one I could see from the dining area. There was a common area like a park which had trails going in and out and a playground, along with the training facilities nearby. "Is anyone training today?" I asked Sean and Rick.

"Training is daily but with different groups of people. We rotate groups every two weeks so we can train with other people, so we don't get lazy. There is a training session going on now. Luke is probably there leading it" answered Sean.

"Please lead me to the training grounds. I would like to see it for a few minutes and then walk through the garden, leading out to the park and lastly to the water by the cliff. It should almost be lunchtime by the time we make it through all of that."

"This way Luna." Rick pointed.

We walked for about fifteen minutes until an arena-type building came into view. It had a retractable roof from the appearance which was currently open. I mean it looked like a football stadium. How much money was in this pack? It had to cost a fortune to build and maintain. We took our seats in the bleachers and watched as the warriors sparred. I could see Luke walking around watching and talking to each set of sparring partners. He noticed us immediately and waved in our direction. It felt rude not to wave back so Jacqui and I both did a quick wave back at him.

There were 30 extremely fit and muscular males paired off and I was surprised to see 10 females there as well. All of them were throwing punches, landing kicks, tossing each other, or shielding themselves from blows. It was quite the sight to see. I would see someone get knocked down and they would do a flip to get up or a backward roll into a standing stance. I only wanted a quick glimpse of their training, but I found myself mesmerized. After about an hour of watching, everyone took a break. They all walked to the side benches and were drinking what I can only assume was water from this distance. Then, I saw some of them taking off their shirts as if the testosterone wasn't already in the air. However, they didn't stop at their shirts. Everyone was taking everything off. I looked at Sean and Rick. "What is happening" I questioned in shock.

"They are getting ready to train in their wolf forms. Most wolves aren't very modest when it comes to being naked. We bare it all and then quickly shift. We are all used to it so no staring or weirdness comes of it. No different than those who frequent a nude beach." Sean informed me.

By the time I looked back at the field, it was covered in wolves. Large, furry, snarling, biting at each other wolves. I had heard of werewolves through my education and training as a child, but the books did not do enough justice to the training site in front of me now. I couldn't turn my eyes away as I took in each wolf. They each had a uniqueness about them. My brain was telling me I should be scared, but all I could think was how beautiful they looked under the sunlight, sparring with each other. They looked like they were having fun and playing like dogs would at a dog park. If I was going to be stuck here longer, I was going to for sure make another appearance here to watch the training. After another hour, they took another break. They all shifted and put their clothes back on. Some shook hands, some patted each other on the back and others waved. The session ended, and they were all leaving. As they left the arena, another group of people entered including Jason and Matt.

Rick advised, "the next training group is the elite warriors of our pack. They have the most training and expertise at fighting both hand-to-hand combat and as wolves. They would be the Seal Team of the Pack. I used to watch them train as a boy. It was always my dream to train with them. It finally came true a few months ago."

People started to fill the bleachers. It was not crowded or full by any means, but busy compared to only us watching the last group.

I watched in awe as they all went into pairs and started sparring. Jason and Luke sparred together, and Matt and Kirk sparred together. I didn't know who anyone else was yet. I had never had official training growing up. I took a few self-defense courses along the way but nothing like what I was seeing now. I wish I knew what type of martial arts they were displaying. Their attacks and defense were both scary and beautiful at the same time. They were so fast and calculating. They must have years of training to be able to do what they are doing.

The onlookers would clap and cheer at the display. It was quite the show. Jacqui stood up and whistled loudly drawing Matt's attention. He took a huge kick to the face whilst being distracted. She cringed a bit while yelling, "my bad" in his direction. He smiled back up at her while Kirk helped him to his feet, and they began again.

They took their first break. I could see Jason looking in our direction with a smug look on his face. I wasn't going to give him the satisfaction of staying and watching any longer, so I motioned for everyone to get up and leave.

Chapter 15: The Park

We only had one hour of the four remaining after leaving the training grounds before Jason expected us back for lunch. I asked Rick and Sean to bring us towards the playground area, then we would head for lunch. After lunch, we could walk through the garden and then out to cliffs and water area, since they were in the opposite direction of the playground and training grounds. I was quietly following them taking in our surroundings. It was a truly scenic community. Everything was lush and vibrant. The people were happy, practically skipping and whistling down the street. Several greeted me with a head nod, almost a slight bow, before proceeding past us.

Rick led the way with me and Jacqui walking side by side and Sean walking behind us. Jacqui looked at me and then forward again. I could tell she wanted to say something all day but couldn't find the words.

"Jacqui, you are my best friend. What you did hurt me, but our friendship will survive it. I am still a little annoyed. I know it came from a good place and that even though you went against my wishes, you were doing what you thought was best for me. I am willing to forgive you if you promise to talk to me first if it involves me. I get Matt is your mate and there is some super strong bond that makes you do things against me, but please let him know that I am off-limits, and you are not going to lose me because you keep interfering and intervening in things that pertain to me without discussing it with me first."

"I am so sorry Mikayla. You are the best and I promise to always be open with you moving forward. I should have come to you in the beginning and maybe things would be different now. I was afraid I would lose you once you found out I am a werewolf."

I stopped and hugged Jacqui and then let her go and punched her in the shoulder. "You deserve that, and you owe me one girl's night."

She smiled, "you got it!"

We arrived at the playground area where lots of little children were playing and having a great time. The older kids were playing tag and the little ones were taking turns on the swings and slides. I heard someone shout "Luna, Luna" and I turned to see a little girl running towards me with open arms. She wrapped them around my leg and gave me a huge hug. I knelt and asked her what her name was.

"My name is Lucy. I can't believe you are here. I am going to write in my journal tonight that I hugged the Luna." I smiled at her and opened my arms, which she jumped into without hesitation, and I gave her the biggest hug I could and then told her "I love hugs and anytime you see me, you can give me a hug and I will hug you back." She smiled from ear to ear then ran off calling for her mommy.

Another child had heard what I said and asked if he too could have a hug and then it all snowballed from there. I ended up giving hugs to every child in the playground. There was a lineup of kids waiting to see Santa at Christmas, but it was only to see me. I was thanking my lucky stars it was only a hug they wanted from me. They were so excited to see me and hug me. It warmed my heart and honestly of all the Luna talk and things that I wanted nothing to do with, this was the one thing I would love to hold on to. It felt so great to make these kids smile and it was an easy thing to do.

Jason's POV

Does no one respect me anymore? "Rick and Sean, you were supposed to be back for lunch twenty minutes ago. Where are you?" I mind-linked them both.

Rick responded, "we are at the playground, Alpha. Luna is refusing to leave before she greets everyone who lined up to meet her. I am sorry. We have been trying to get her to leave and return."

"Matt and I are on our way."

"Matt, let's go get them or we will never get to eat," I grumbled.

"Where are they?" he questioned.

"At the playground."

"Why?"

"I don't know, something about Mikayla refusing to leave until she greets everyone who came to see her."

It took Matt and me ten minutes to get to the park where we saw a long lineup of children. At the front of the line was Jacqui motioning for a child to walk toward Mikayla. Mikayla was sitting on a bench, holding her hands out in front of her. The child jumped into her arms and Mikayla lifted her onto her lap and embraced her in a big hug, then started to talk to her.

As we made our way to the front of the line. I could hear the children whispering as we passed them.

"It's the Alpha and Beta."

"I hope we didn't get the Luna in trouble."

"Are they going to make the Luna stop meeting us?"

"Don't look them in the eye, it is forbidden my dad told me, and a sign of disrespect."

Matt snickered a bit as he turned to look the children in the eye. "Stop teasing them," I said to him. They will have nightmares for who knows how long looking at your face.

"They are more scared of you than they are of me, Jason," he reminded me.

"Rick and Sean, thank you for your service today. Go and get some lunch. Matt and I have it from here." They both nodded in unison and sauntered off toward the dining hall.

"Jacqui, Mikayla, do you mind telling us what is going on here?" I asked.

"We were checking out the grounds and when we got to the playground a little girl, named Lucy, wanted me to give her a big hug. It meant a lot to her, so I told her if she wanted a hug in the future from me, all she had to do was ask and I love hugs. A little boy overheard and asked if he could get a hug too and before we knew it all the kids were lined up waiting for a hug," she smiled warmly.

"Sorry Jason, it got a bit out of control, but it made them all so happy. We tried to leave twice, and they looked so dejected, so we got Mikayla to sit on the bench and she is hugging and greeting all of them." Jacqui explained.

I looked at the lineup which I would estimate still had about 40 children awaiting their hug from the Luna. I looked back at Mikayla, and she shrugged, motioning for the next child to come forward. I rolled my eyes thinking I was never going to get lunch.

"Children, it is time for us to have lunch, but we want everyone to get a hug. Are there any children here who would like a hug from the Alpha or Beta instead of the Luna, so we can get to lunch? The Luna is tired and hungry," I proposed.

A small girl close to the front of the line raised her hand slowly, as she peered out from behind the doll in her hand. I walked over to her and kneeling beside her asked, "do you have a question, sweetheart?"

"Can I really get a hug from you today, Alpha Jason?" she asked curiously.

I opened my arms and she smashed into me wrapping her tiny arms around my neck and squeezing with what I imagine was all her strength. I stood up closing my arms around her and rocking slightly back and forth, gently squeezing her back.

Matt chimed in, "doesn't anyone want to hug the big, bad Beta?" His eyes went up and down the line of kids before a kid raised his hand. Matt walked over to him. "Do you want a hug?"

The boy smiled and said, "if I hug you, can I still get a hug from the Luna? I felt bad no one wanted to hug you, so I thought you might need a hug, but I want to hug the Luna."

I heard a fit of laughter. As I turned to look, both Mikayla and Jacqui were chuckling trying not to be too obvious but failing miserably. With that, I couldn't contain my laughter either and started to belly laugh while hugging the girl in my arms. Soon all the kids and the adults nearby were all chuckling with us.

Matt swallowed his pride and told the boy while he respected his candor in sympathizing with another person, they couldn't break the rules and give him two hugs or it wouldn't be fair to everyone else, so he should wait for the Luna to be free.

I put the girl down next to me on the ground and went over to where Mikayla was sitting on the bench. "Okay children form two lines, one for a Luna hug and one for an Alpha hug. We need to go soon but we don't want to miss anyone since you have been patiently waiting." I turned to Jacqui and Matt, "you two can go ahead and get lunch. Mikayla and I will walk back together once we finish hugging all these children."

Matt and Jacqui held hands and walked back down the trail toward the dining hall. They were lucky to have found each other. I was envious of their relationship and how easily they came together. I stood next to the bench looking down at Mikayla and she smiled at me. Her first real smile since coming to our territory. Maybe Matt was right. I needed to show her what living in the pack could offer her.

We finished hugging all the children. It was about a fifteen-minute walk to the dining hall. Mikayla and I were alone walking along the path. She didn't say anything for the first five minutes and then she finally spoke, "it is well-kept and beautiful here. Your pack is happy."

"I am sorry Mikayla things have gone the way they have for us. I want you to stay with me and start a life with me in the pack. My wolf, how you make me feel, the war, Elliott trying to kidnap you, seeing you unconscious, my emotions are all over the place and I guess the one thing consistent through all the negative and positive is I want you by my side and safe. I can't say I would change my choices if I could do it all over again, but I would probably communicate it better to you. The entire pack is mind-linking about how happy their children are coming home from school today after getting to meet the Luna and the Alpha. I am very busy lately trying to protect my pack, I don't always make the time to enjoy the pack, so thank you for this afternoon."

"Can I please do more exploring after lunch? I wanted to see the cliffs," she pleaded.

"Matt and Jacqui have other plans for you after lunch and I couldn't agree more. How about Rick and Sean take you to the cliffs tomorrow after breakfast?" I countered.

"I guess it depends on what those two have planned for me. Do I get a choice?"

"I am okay whether you go with the plans or whether you go to the cliffs, but it is on you to convince Jacqui you don't want to do what she has planned. It is a battle I cannot win."

"I see. Cliffs tomorrow then it is," she grinned.

We entered the dining hall and got in line to grab our plates of food.

Chapter 16: A Night to Remember

Mikayla's POV

Today, I only had one regret: skipping breakfast. Hugging all those children gave me a euphoric feeling and has been the highlight of my week. I failed to notice how hungry I truly was until we entered the dining hall and the aroma hit my nose. The food here was excellent so at least there was that going for me.

Once we had our plates of food, Jason led me down the hallway. He opened a door, and we went inside.

"This is my office," he remarked.

"Why are we here instead of the dining hall?" I questioned.

"The rest of them all ate already. The two of us don't need to take up an 8-person table, so I thought maybe we could eat lunch together here and have a real conversation."

He motioned for me to sit at a 4-person table in the corner of his office. We ate in silence for a bit. Frankly, I was scarfing my food down to pay attention to the time.

"You were hungry," he said.

"Maybe a little bit," I sneered.

"Tell me how you met Jacqui. You both seem close and able to predict the other person."

"I thought I could until recently anyways. We had a class together. We were assigned as partners on a class presentation. We instantly clicked. We are complete opposites but complement each other well. I would've never guessed I would be friends with someone like her, but after two and a half years, here we are. She is like a sister to me. I love her dearly. How did you and Matt meet?"

"Matt and I grew up together, along with Kirk and Luke. Matt's father was the former Beta, so our parents had several meetings together and we spent lots of our childhood together. Training, learning, and getting into trouble. When my father stepped down, his father did as well. They told us at the same time. It was early for them to do so, but we were of age, and they felt we could handle it. Of course, they were always there for advice to help guide us."

"It must be hard to be responsible for so many people. Do you ever wish things were different?"

"We are all dealt a hand in this life. I was meant to be Alpha and I have trained for it my entire life. I wouldn't change it for anything. Although, there are days when it becomes a lot and I need a break from the stress of it all. I am sure I will have gray hairs by my 25th birthday at the rate I am going."

A knock on the door interrupted our discussion.

"Come in," Jason beckoned.

The door opened and Jacqui and Matt came strolling in. She was wearing a sundress and had her makeup done up. Matt looked a little dressed up as well.

Jacqui asked me, "are you done eating yet, Michaela?"

I responded, "not quite, why do you ask?"

"I have planned a double date for us all for tonight and it starts in an hour. I need you to come with me so we can get you ready," she demanded.

"Do I get a say in this?"

"You can say what you want, but you know it won't matter. Once I have a plan, it happens, so you can come willingly, or I can pester you until you change your mind. Your choice."

"Doesn't sound like much of a choice to me."

"Mikayla, trust me that I have your best interest at heart, will you?"

"Okay fine, I give. Who is going to be my date?" I glanced up at Jason.

"You think you are funny, don't you?" he replied.

"Maybe just a little bit," I sneered.

With that, Jacqui grabbed my hand and pulled me out of the room and upstairs to her bedroom to do my hair and makeup. She pulled out another sundress for me to wear and some slip-on shoes. She grabbed a bag she had packed by the door and led me out of her room. We headed back downstairs and down a long corridor. At the end of the hall, we went inside a large double door that opened into a huge theatre room. The screen took up one side of the wall and had paired-off seating spread throughout the room. In the corner was a snack bar with popcorn popping, a fountain soda machine, and bags of chips and candies. The lights were already dimmed and there were blackout curtains from floor to ceiling on the sides of the room.

We walked to the snack bar grabbing what we wanted and then she motioned for me to go and sit in the double reclining seat next to Jason while she sat next to Matt. She waved her hand in the air and the lights dimmed even further and the screen lit up with previews. Then she sunk into Matt's arm which was already engulfing her.

Jason and I surprisingly had similar snack choices. I grabbed a pack of Twizzlers. They were stuck together as I tried to pull them apart the crinkling noise got loud. Jacqui shushed me a few times until I finally got one out. As I was about to bite a piece of it off, Jason snatched it out of my hand and took a bite himself.

"What the hell? It took me a few good minutes to get that one out of the pack," I complained.

"I know, the entire theatre knows. You made me want one too. I doubt you would offer me one," he responded.

"There is an entire snack shop in the corner with multiple packs. I don't have to share. Get your own," I answered.

"Oh really! I didn't know you were so possessive of your snacks. Come on, let me have some too."

"No way, these are mine." I proceeded to snatch the one back from him he had taken from me and chomped on it quickly putting the entire thing in my mouth so he couldn't take it back. My cheeks were all puffed up, as I chewed on it triumphantly.

"That's how it is going to be?" he raised an eyebrow.

"Mine," I mumbled. Then Jacqui threw some popcorn at us and shushed us both again. I turned around about to give her a piece of my mind when Jason wrapped his arms around my body and pulled me close to him.

He whispered in my ear, "you can have the Twizzlers, but you are mine. Watch the movie."

The tingles went up my shoulders where his arm was touching me. I again felt that warm, fuzzy feeling from

101

the core of my stomach. I slowly let myself relax in his arms continuing to eat my Twizzlers and watch the movie. Occasionally, I would hold one up to his mouth for him to take a bite. I must admit this was peaceful.

The movie ended and Jacqui was right on point. "Next part of the date is coming up, follow me everyone," she gleefully stated. We left the theatre room and walked into another side door close by which smelled of chlorine. Jacqui grabbed my hand and led me into the ladies' washroom while Jason and Matt proceeded into the men's washroom. She pulled out a string bikini for the both of us. I looked at it and asked her where the rest of it was. She laughed hysterically and told me to stop being so modest.

After changing into the bathing suits, she led me through the door marked pool. The guys were already in the water. Jacqui walked out with her towel over her shoulder while I had mine wrapped around me hiding the practically non-existent strings of fabric. She set her towel on the bench and then dived to get into the water. No way was I going to dive in. I swear the impact of the water would make my suit disintegrate. Matt swam after Jacqui. I proceeded to walk over to the bench to take off my towel and then walked over to the stairs to get in the pool. It was cool but refreshing. Jason swam over towards me.

"Are you coming in or going to stand there all day?" he teased.

"It was fine until I got to my waist but it's cold now. I will get in eventually," I whined.

"Okay, take your time then," his eyes glazed over slightly.

"You are mind-linking someone." I guessed.

I didn't even see Jacqui come up from the side of the pool when she cannonballed in front of me sending a huge wave over my entire body. I brushed my face off, then dove into the water after her.

"It is shallow water, Missy. What are you thinking?" I reprimanded her.

We continued splashing around the pool and then played a bit of volleyball with a beach ball, then Jacqui and I played chicken while on Jason and Matt's shoulders. Of course, with wolf strength, Jacqui kept winning and knocking me off Jason. It was unfair. After horsing around for about an hour, we went and warmed up in the hot tub. We chatted about the movie and whether we liked it or not. After fifteen minutes, we exited the hot tub and then got dressed.

Jacqui led us back to the dining hall where we exited the French doors leading out to the balcony and into the garden. We walked past the fountain. There were so many beautiful flowers. The fragrance was astounding. After a few turns, we entered a central area that was shaped like a square with hedges for walls. There were stone benches around the outside of it and water that flowed underneath the ground which had stone arched walkways raised slightly above the water. There were lined lights around the outside of the perimeter. In one corner of the square, a lady wearing an all-white A-line gown was playing the harp. I could see fireflies soaring in the early evening sky lighting up from time to time. The sky was clear with a crescent moon and the stars shining brightly. In the very center of the square was a table set for four. Jacqui led the way and we all sat down. A cart was being pushed up the stone cobbles interrupting the tranquility of the evening. It stopped when it reached our table. Four spring salads with a raspberry vinaigrette were placed in front of us, along with a small bowl of corn chowder. A basket of breadsticks was already in the center of the table.

Jacqui pulls out a game called Outrageous. She explains how it works and says, "I feel like having a good laugh tonight, so everyone must do their best to make me laugh." She proceeded to explain the rules and we had a fun-filled night laughing and carrying on while finishing our meal. It was getting late, and I was getting tired towards the end of the night.

Jacqui finally let Jason and I disappear as Matt insinuated; he had other plans for the rest of their night which was only for the two of them. Jason and I walked back to our rooms. As we approached my door, Jason slowed down and turned to look at me.

"Michaela, I know I don't deserve it, but I will be kicking myself all night if I don't ask you if you would sleep in my room tonight. I promise Titus will behave. With the mate bond, I have trouble sleeping when you are not close. Please," he pleaded with me.

"Let me get ready for bed in my room and then I will come and sleep next to you once I am ready. If Titus tries anything, I am out," I responded.

"Thank you, I will see you soon," he said. He leaned in and kissed me on my forehead.

I proceeded to get ready for bed, as did he. When I was ready, I went to his room and knocked on his door. He beckoned me to enter. As I strolled into his room, I noticed he was already laying in the bed, motioning for me to join him. I walked over and crawled under the covers. He turned the lights out with his cell phone, set it down, and then wrapped his arms around me holding me tight. He whispered, "goodnight, love." It was a perfect evening. Our lives felt completely normal for a few hours, and I felt like if we hadn't met the way we did and things were different, we could be a happy couple. I did feel safe and secure snuggled up in his arms. I thought about the day and slowly drifted off to sleep.

Chapter 17: The Cliffs

The next morning, I awoke in Jason's bed, but he was already gone. He left me a note telling me the door was unlocked and I should meet him down for breakfast when I was ready. I went to my room, did my morning routine, and got dressed for the day. As I started to head downstairs, I ran into Jacqui who was also headed to breakfast. She was all smug with herself and her date night planning.

Jacqui gloated, "I worked up quite the appetite last night after we left you two. How did you all end the night?"

"You probably already know, so why are you pretending you don't," I replied.

"Jason did tell us you stayed in his room last night, but he would tell us anything else, so here I am to get the full story from my bestie."

"We just went to sleep Jacqui. He was a perfect gentleman. I feel refreshed after yesterday and it is probably time I go back to my life," I reminded her.

"You cannot leave yet Mikayla, we are still trying to find out Elliott's motives and he knows your entire routine. Even if he doesn't come after you, he could send someone else."

We met the guys for breakfast. Jason had arranged for Rick and Sean to give Jacqui and me the tour of the cliffs after breakfast while he and Matt finished off some more work they had to complete. I couldn't wait. Everything here was serene, so the cliffs had to be out of this world. Other than the garden, the area appeared to be the nicest on the map. I was very excited.

Rick and Sean were waiting for us when we exited the packhouse. We started heading towards the cliff. It was gorgeous and more than what I expected. Some seagulls were flying overhead, and I even saw an eagle nesting on top of a tree in the forest nearby. The waves were crashing against the cliff side and the tide was way in. The breeze was a little cooler here, but I could smell the salt in the ocean air. The grass around here was a vibrant green and so fluffy. I had to take off my shoes and feel the grass under my feet and toes. I sat down first, and the others followed my lead. I closed my eyes and proceeded to take deep inhales and exhales. Letting all my worries wash away from me. In the here and now, it was the sounds of the water and birds and the warmth of the sun on my skin that I was focusing on. It was so relaxing to take it all in and enjoy what nature had to offer. It had been ten minutes, not nearly enough when Rick and Sean jumped to their feet.

Sean stripped his clothes making me blush and turn to look away and I could hear his bones cracking as he shifted into his wolf.

"We have to go now" Rick stated with a sense of urgency. "There are rogues entering our territory not far from our location. Help is on the way. Sean and I are going to head them off. The two of you need to run in that direction towards the pack house immediately. Do not stop, keep going."

Rick then stripped also yelling go now, just before shifting into his wolf and heading in the opposite direction with Sean. Jacqui and I looked at each other. I quickly put on my shoes and was up and running with her. She was so fast. I should have spent more time at the gym with her. I was regretting it now. She kept encouraging me to keep going and not to focus on how tired I am. She said several rogues are gaining on us, and we were too far from the packhouse to make it. They had captured Sean and he mind-linked to Jason, who could mind-link to the entire pack that they were after Luna. "Do we know what they want?" I barely was able to ask while gasping for air.

"They want you," Jacqui responded.

I could hear the beating of paws on the ground and glanced behind me, then looked forward to the pack house in the distance. I could see several wolves coming at us from the direction of the pack house, but it was more than a football field away from us. We were never going to make it. I stopped and told Jacqui to shift and get out of here to save herself.

She refused immediately saying she couldn't leave me; I am her Luna; she has sworn to protect and would be honored to die fighting by my side. I was beyond frustrated and then looked her in the eyes, "as your future Luna, I order you to shift and leave me here NOW". She started crying then turned and ran. I saw her clothes shred as they left her body and she shifted into a brown wolf charging toward the wolves headed our way.

I turned towards the rogues bending over with my hands on my knees trying to catch my breath. There were four of them and they were surrounding me within seconds of Jacqui leaving me. I was so grateful she had gotten away, and I was able to stall them. All I had to do was stay alive until the others got here. I hoped they wanted me alive that is. Why would they want me?

Two of them shifted into human form. Both pulled knives out of bags they had around their necks. "It is over for you Luna. We have orders to kidnap you. In the event we can't, we are to ensure your permanent demise."

The first man lunged at me with his knife. I dodged him moving to the side and used his momentum to throw him to the ground. I didn't know a lot, but I had taken some self-defense training classes in the past. A girl can never be too safe. My heart was pounding through my chest, and I felt adrenaline coursing through my veins. It was a burning feeling. Did I get injected again?

The second man moved at me with his knife and in my confusion, he got me. It went into my stomach, and he twisted it causing immense pain and damage to my insides. I fell to the ground with it sticking in me and the two wolves jumped at me and started clawing and biting me. I curled myself as much as I could into a ball knowing if they got ahold of my neck, I was a goner, but them clawing at me in a slow, agonizing death made me think I should bear my neck to end the pain quicker. I didn't want to die. Sure, life had taken a turn for the worst lately and nothing was going how I thought it was, but I didn't want to die. I needed to turn things around. How did I even get here? I felt myself drifting away when I remembered a spell from my early training. I had to try it. I mustered up the little bit of energy I had left, and a blue surge erupted from my body shooting out in all directions. Then, I fell into unconsciousness.

Jason's POV

Being an Alpha, Titus was faster than all the other wolves. I was leading several warriors with Matt slightly behind me followed by Kirk, Luke, and everyone else. I was so worried. The ground was moving so fast beneath our paws. With our wolf sight, I could see her ahead of us even though she seemed miles away. She was surrounded by four wolves when two of them shifted. One lunged at her and fell to the ground. Then the second one moved and then the wolves. They were tearing her apart. I could

109

hear her screams and I felt like I was dying inside. A blue light appeared from where she lay on the ground and shot out like a shockwave. It sent the four of them flying away from her body landing motionless on the ground. The blue light continued in a wave in all directions and was headed toward us. Titus kept going to get to his mate but when the blue light got to us, it sent us reeling backward. Titus shook his head, then got up and started running towards Mikayla again.

"What the hell was that?" I asked Titus.

"I have no idea. Whatever it was, it was strong, and it came from our mate" he responded.

We got to her first. There was blood everywhere. She was unconscious. I couldn't think straight. My mate. She was dying. Her heartbeat was faint, and her breathing was shallow. She lay there getting paler by the second. My warriors tended to the four rogues. They were dead. I can only imagine the impact of the blast on them given the magnitude we felt at 100 yards.

A jeep pulled up near us and Sylvia jumped out with her medical gear. I heard Matt yelling for me to move back and give her room. She saw the sight before us and knowing that Mikayla was human, she checked a few things, then looked at me.

"She is going to die. She might have a chance if you turn her, but you need to bite her now. You're an alpha so she will become a strong wolf and hopefully, it will be enough to save her. I can't be sure it will work, but I am sure it is her only chance at this point. She has lost way too much blood for anything else to be done."

I stared at Mikayla unable to react when I heard Jacqui yell "Don't watch her die. Do it, I cannot lose her. Not yet. Not when I left her."

I leaned in closer to Mikayla on the ground. I grabbed her arm. I could feel my canines going into her wrist. A person had to be intentional at wanting to turn someone into a werewolf when they bit them. Otherwise, they were just biting them to kill or maim them as the rogues had done. I sunk my canines into her. Her skin pierced and I felt bad adding another bite to the many she already had on her mutilated body. I removed them, then bit into my arm and gave her some of my blood into her mouth. She started to convulse slightly and then stopped and was limp again completely unconscious.

"Did it work?" I asked Sylvia.

She checked Mikayla over and then shook her head. "I don't know. All we can do now is wait."

Another vehicle drove up and two men jumped out grabbing a stretcher from the back. They went to Mikayla. It wasn't easy to pick her mangled body up and put it on the stretcher, but they figured it out. After a few minutes, she was loaded onto the truck. I could still hear her faint breath and heartbeat so there was hope. I had lost two great warriors: Rick and Sean. As the truck drove towards the pack hospital, I shifted back to my wolf. Titus howled in pain at the injuries his mate sustained and the loss of his friends. An Alpha could feel the death of any pack member as the pack bond in place was broken. It was a horrible feeling that I don't think I will ever get accustomed to.

I wanted to go with her to the hospital and I would later, but for now, we had to check our border and find out how the rogues got through in the first place. How did they make it so deep into our territory? I should have been notified as soon as they crossed over, but I wasn't until they were already well inside. Titus ran to the border with Bruno, Matt's wolf, running beside him. Jacqui had gone in the truck with Mikayla, so I knew she was in good hands until I could be free to stay with her. I hope she wouldn't hate me for turning her into a werewolf.

Matt, a few warriors, and I shifted back to human form. One of the warriors who had arrived before us at the border threw us all shorts to put on so we wouldn't be investigating naked given we shredded our clothes in our haste to get to Mikayla. Poor Mikayla. It was horrible what she went through, and it was all because I brought her here. I okayed her to travel the pack grounds. I shouldn't have let her go or sent more warriors with her. I knew Alpha Justin was crazy and willing to break all the werewolf laws.

Several of our warriors were laying on the ground. I knew they were still alive as I would have felt their connections to the pack break if they had been killed. Nick, our second in training with Luke, walked over to Matt and me to report his findings thus far. "They are all alive but unconscious. We found darts laced with wolfsbane. The darts had a capsule filled with wolfsbane with some sort of time-release that keeps pumping it into the warriors to render them unconscious. We have removed the darts. They should all be able to wake within the hour." He then pointed over to the tree line near our border. "We found traces of several men having gone into the trees over there. We assume they shot the darts from the trees. They could have stayed and killed all our men, but it is clear they had a mission to go after the Luna and only her. They simply stopped anyone in their path to reaching their goal. We did find some tracks heading toward the Full Moon Pack.

My men didn't follow them across their pack border. It is no question they came from there. What do you want us to do Alpha Jason?"

"We have been training additional warriors so that we can increase the patrols. The time to increase is now. Matt and Kirk will be putting out new patrol groups starting tomorrow, which will have the new recruits spread evenly amongst the groups and one lead warrior for each group. Patrols must now include checking the land between our two territories on the Eastern side. For now, we can leave the other mid-areas alone until we can get more warriors trained. Collect the darts for testing purposes. Nick, you are to go to the tactical store, bringing a dart with you, and locate something the patrols can wear to protect against the darts. The Dark Moon Pack members will still have parts of the body we will not cover but we will minimize it as much as possible. There will be more to come. Matt, Kirk, and Luke meet me in my office to discuss Project Immunity."

I walked away heading back to the packhouse.

Chapter 18: Mia's Space

Mikayla's POV

I woke up in a beautiful field of flowers. There were so many different types, and I could see them as far as the eye could see in three directions. In the last direction, there was a sparkling lake with a Willow tree nearby. The sky was a cyan-blue color with the fluffiest white clouds I had ever seen. I felt the sunshine warming my body. The scent of the flowers filled my nostrils. It was so nice and surreal here. I had to be dead. How else could I be in such an amazing place? I started walking towards the lake so I could dip my feet in the water. As I got closer, I could see the edges of the lake which had white sand leading from the greenest grass I had ever seen into the water. I was wearing a white cotton dress that had spaghetti straps and draped down to my bare feet. I felt the crunch of the flowers under my feet with every step I took toward the lake. Then the soft green grass flattened and then springing back up as I stepped closer. Eventually, I could feel the warm, soft sand between my toes, and I let the water rush up slowly, allowing my feet to sink further into the sand.

"Mikayla" I heard someone say. I turned around to see a small, grey wolf staring at me. I continued to look around to see if I could see anyone around. No one was around so I looked back at the wolf.

"Hi Mikayla, my name is Mia" the wolf spoke.

I was utterly confused. "Hi Mia, where am I?"

"You are in my space which I created for myself. I pulled you here to keep you from dying, but I am not yet strong enough to send you back to your reality. You survived your attack; however, you need to heal."

"How did I survive that attack? I felt so much pain. There were four of them and Jason and the others were too far away."

"Don't be mad."

"Great! That means you are about to tell me something I am not going to like; well, I cannot promise not to be mad without knowing what it is."

"You were dying. In a final attempt to save yourself, you released a magic spell killing the rogues that attacked you. Using that spell made you extremely weak. You had lost a lot of blood by the time they reached you and were continuing to lose more. You were too far from the pack hospital for a transfusion and for the doctor to attend to your wounds. There was only one way to save you. There were no assurances it would even work."

"What are you trying to say?"

"Jason being an Alpha has better than the normal werewolf healing abilities. If he were to bite someone to change them into a werewolf, they would inherit his alpha healing abilities. His back was up against the wall Mikayla. You cannot be mad at him for choosing life for his mate. He had no choice to ensure your survival."

"Wait…. are you saying?"

"You are a werewolf. I am your wolf, Mia. Since I only came into existence yesterday, it is going to take me a few days to become fully grown. It will take precisely four days which is the next full moon. Normally a turn isn't done this close to the full moon to allow the wolf to grow a bit slower, but for obvious reasons, it could not be avoided. I was just a pup a few hours ago and I guess I would be around a teenager now. Even as a pup, I could pull you into this area of your mind that I created based on things you like. I tried to send you back as soon as Alpha Jason and Titus came, but I don't have the strength yet."

"Jason is here now. How do you know?"

"I can speak with Titus and if you concentrate on your body, you will feel a presence on your arm. It is Jason stroking your arm. He and Titus are begging you to forgive them for doing this to you without asking for your permission. They had not intended to turn you ever. He is torn up about not protecting you and everything that transpired. Do you think you can forgive him?"

I walked towards Mia and sat down on the grass next to her under the willow tree. "I am tired Mia, and this is a lot of information to absorb. I am going to rest for a bit and mull everything over." I laid back on the grass curling into the fetal position with my hands under my head for a pillow. Mia lay down next to me and said nothing else.

Jason's POV

We were in my office and all I could think about was getting to Mikayla. My mate was severely injured, how could I be thinking of anything else, especially how to defend against an attack? I was doing the best I could to concentrate.

"What is the progress of project immunity?"

Kirk reported, "there are 20 participants. Researchers started injecting them with diluted wolfsbane. All respondents showed an immediate response on the first dose. After 5 years in the program and eventually undiluted wolfsbane injections, all the participants can

116

have wolfsbane enter their systems without any effects. We have only tested the dose up to one plant and one full injection needle. We have found that 50% of the participants show aggressive wolf behavior the first time they shift after the injection. It appears it is just the wolves needing to let off some steam after having to deal with the wolfsbane. It still impacts the wolves, and they can feel it, even though it doesn't hinder them or stop them in any way."

"We have 100% immunity," Matt said shocked.

"It appears so. I mean we only have 20 participants, so it is a small test set and no control really for the experiments. All 20 were injected last week with a full syringe and all of them not only survived but also showed no signs of being injected. You wouldn't even think they were wolves if you had seen them receive the shots." Kirk replied. "We are quite pleased with the results, although it has been a long 5 years."

"Remind the participants and the researchers of their NDAs and let them know what happened today. I want one participant assigned to each patrol group. In the event of an attack like this again, they will be able to warn us via mind-link instead of being immediately silenced. It was a strategic attack. They hit everyone at the same time, so no one could warn anyone. By the time we were alerted, it was too late. This cannot happen again. Work on the new patrol groupings, adding a participant, new recruits, and experienced warriors to each one." I ordered.

There was a knock on the office door. I nodded at Luke, who was closest to the door, and he opened it. Dylan walked in. "I have information you are going to want to see now, Alpha."

117

"Luke and Kirk, start working on those patrol groups. Matt and I have other business to conduct. Let me know when it is posted for the warriors." I instructed.

"Come in and sit Dylan." I motioned.

Luke and Kirk exited my office closing the door behind them and Dylan came over to the couch to sit. I rolled my chair towards the couch and Matt took a seat in the chair. Dylan handed me a file while he started to speak. "Mikayla was born and raised until the age of 10 in the Light Magic Coven. She was a very talented sorceress even at a young age. My contact indicated there is a prophecy involving a sorceress, who will lead the witches in a great battle between light and dark witches. Any child who shows any promise of greatness has ended up dead or in a deep coma, unable to be reawakened. Mikayla was scheduled to be moved to reside in the dwelling with the elders, where they would protect her from her fate. However, a week before she was scheduled to show; her parents and her disappeared. I couldn't find a trace of her for two years, but at the age of 12, she turned up in the foster care system. She remained in foster care until she was 18. No word of what happened to her parents from my contact.

She lived in the human world and there is no indication she continued practicing magic. My contact said she was the best magic student she has ever witnessed and had she continued practicing, she might well be the strongest sorcerer or sorceress to walk the earth. However, since her magic has been dormant for such a long time, she would need to practice it to harness its full potential again. It would take time for her to control it and perfect it so that she could be powerful. If she continues to study magic and practice, she will again draw the attention of both the light and dark covens. Both would be after her power for

118

themselves or ridding it if they are not the recipients. You need to be very careful and tread lightly. If she is the one from the prophecy, they will eventually come for her; and she will be unable to escape her magic even if she so wishes. My contact said she can set up some blocking spells and protections for Mikayla so she can get stronger without being noticed. Magic usage is a beacon to those who are constantly searching. If she doesn't use her magic, they won't find her. It is all in the report."

"Thank you for getting this so quickly for us. This is extremely thorough. Can your contact be trusted with the information about Mikayla's existence?"

"She is a long-time friend of mine and I trust her with my life."

"But do you trust her with Mikayla's life? Is she of the light coven too?"

"I do and she is. The light coven wants to live in harmony with humans and other supernatural beings. The dark coven are the ones who believe they are superior and that all races should bow down to them. They believe werewolves are dogs meant to serve them as pets and protectors and nothing more. If you need her help, I will summon her to come here. She has already offered. Mikayla was special to her."

"I will keep that under advisement. Mikayla suffered an attack from rogues sent by Alpha Justin. She is recovering now, but it will take her some time to heal. I will address her magic with her when the time is right."

"I will take my leave then Alpha Jason. Oh, I also found the Elliott guy you were looking for. He vacated his residence, but he still goes to work. He runs a business downtown. It's also in the file."

"Thank you, Dylan. Matt will transfer your fee to you by the end of today."

Dylan left and closed the door behind him.

Matt stood up and walked over to the bar, "what's your poison today? We need a drink."

"You don't say. Can you keep up with all of this? I mean a week ago, I knew an imminent war was coming. I find my mate who happens to be engaged to someone else, who then cheats on her, she breaks it off, we have an insatiable night, she ditches me, I find her, her ex attacks her, I sneak her off here, only to find out she is a sorceress, she almost dies on my watch, and I turned her into a werewolf. You can't write this. How did my life become so complicated? I wasn't trained for this in my alpha training. They tell you; you will meet your mate, sparks will fly and she will make you stronger, not she will run for the hills and want nothing to do with you and then you take her against her will and wait for her to come around. What is going on, man? There isn't a drink strong enough for this." I shrug in defeat.

"Okay, so I will admit this hasn't been the fairytale mating you were led to believe, but Mikayla is special, and she is your mate. Now that you have turned her, she will feel the mate bond and she will not be able to ignore it as she has been as a human, or I guess sorceress. It was all part of the intricate plan by the Moon Goddess. You must trust you are on the right side of this even though it isn't being handed to you on a silver platter. How boring would that be anyways? You like a challenge. Admit it." He retorts.

"Not this kind of challenge. What if she never forgives me for turning her?"

"You saved her life. She has a wolf who like our wolves will not let her ignore the mate bond and will continue to harass her until she gives in. That is what they do. She will come around."

"I am going to stay with her. Let me know if anything comes up needing my attention."

Chapter 19: Meet and Greet

I left the office. After grabbing a new set of clothes in my room, I headed to the pack hospital. Upon entering Mikayla's room, I could hear beeping machines. The air was sweet with the smell of multiple bouquets. My pack already adored their Luna and were already showing how much they cared for her. There were fruit baskets and chocolate boxes, cards on the table and so many flowers. The room was full. I saw Mikayla on the bed. She wasn't pale anymore and I couldn't see any sign of the attack on her face and arms. The rest of her was covered with an electric blanket to keep her warm. Those were not usual here, so I assume it was another gift from a thoughtful pack member. I pulled a chair next to her bed. I kissed her on her forehead and sat next to her holding her hand with one hand and stroking her arm with the other. Her skin felt incredible, and I already felt some of the stress dissipate. "Mikayla, please forgive me for turning you. I love you. It was selfish of me. I couldn't help myself. I needed you to live." Titus started bouncing around excitedly in my head.

"Titus, why are you so happy?"

"Jason, they are alive. Mikayla and Mia."

"Who is Mia?"

"Mia is Mikayla's wolf. She is still young but aging quickly to catch up to where she should be if Mikayla had a wolf all along. I can talk to her, and she can talk to Mikayla."

Titus POV

As soon as Jason touched his lips to Mikayla's forehead, I heard a voice.

"Hello mate," she said.

"Mate? Are you Mikayla's wolf?" I answered.

"My name is Mia and yes I am her wolf." She replied.

"Are you both going to survive?"

"Mikayla and I are talking right now. She is alive and will be okay. She cannot awaken until I am a little bit stronger so we both need a little time."

"Will she forgive us?"

"I asked her the same question and she didn't answer. I did tell her the tingling she was feeling on her arm and hand was because Jason was touching her. He was there by her side awaiting her return. I could feel she was happy when I told her that. I hope she will come around with time. She has been through a lot. The Moon Goddess told me when I was created that Mikayla's journey isn't over yet, and she is going to need me to be strong and supportive when what comes to pass transpires. I got the impression she wasn't talking about her healing now. Mikayla knows you are her mates, and she can feel the pull now too. Even if she tries to deny it, she can only resist for so long."

"We are hers and you are both ours. She will come around and forgive. I am going to update Jason, he is losing his mind with guilt and wondering why I can be so happy at a time like this."

Mia laughed and bid me goodbye for now mate. The sound of her calling me mate was reassuring and alluring. I wanted to meet Mia right now. Thinking of her shifting and us being able to run through the woods together had

123

me even more excited. Then, it occurred to me. She had to have her first shift. The next full moon was only a few days away. I heard Jason ask me why I am so frigging happy.

"Jason, they are alive. Mikayla and Mia."

"Who is Mia?"

"Mia is Mikayla's wolf. She is still young but aging quickly to catch up to where she should be had Mikayla had a wolf all along. I can talk to her, and she can talk to Mikayla."

"How is Mikayla?"

"Mia said Mikayla is fine. She needs more time before she can awaken. Mia said she must be stronger before Mikayla can return to us, but it should be a few days. She told Mikayla she is now a werewolf and Mikayla is resting now and trying to process everything that has happened. She and I both believe she will come around eventually. Mia also said Mikayla can feel the mate bond now."

Jason rubbed his hands down his face, and I knew he had a tear or two slipping from his eyes, he was now trying to cover. He couldn't hide it from me though. He was falling apart. I had never seen him this vulnerable and broken. After telling him about Mia and Mikayla, I could feel a light warm inside him. He was getting hopeful and felt reassured he made the right decision to save her. His mate was going to be okay.

A knock came at the door and Sylvia peaked her head in. "Can I take a look at the patient now?"

Jason's POV

"Yes Sylvia, please come in. I have news."

She walked in and over to Mikayla checking the machines while she waited for me to continue.

"Titus was able to speak to Mia, Mikayla's wolf. They are both alive and well apparently but need time to heal more before Mikayla can wake up."

"I am so glad to hear that. She has been stable since this morning and we could not find a reason for her to still be asleep even though it was a major trauma, her body has healed nicely thanks to your alpha blood."

"Doctor, Titus reminded me a full moon is in three days. Mikayla will be forced into her first shift. Mia doesn't know if she will be awake by then or not. Do you have a way we can help the transition whether she is awake or still unconscious?"

"Hmmm... we do have some drugs we can give her to help ease the pain of the first shift, although given she is healing from the trauma, I don't think I would recommend using them. We all must go through the first shift and manage to come out unscathed even though it is painful. It isn't nearly as painful as what she went through yesterday afternoon. If she is still unconscious, then I don't know if she will even feel the pain. We are in unchartered territory right now. Mikayla is the test subject."

"Thank you, Sylvia, Titus, and I will work with Mia to try to determine if Mikayla will be awake or not during the process and get her through the first transformation. Given she is medically sound except for being asleep, can I take her back to the pack house?"

"Let me observe her for another few hours until it is 24 hours since the incident and healing process and then we can unhook her and move her. I will leave one of my most reliable nurses to stay in the packhouse so you will have medical staff close by to monitor things. I will want her to check on Mikayla's status and vitals every 4 hours for at least 24 hours and if everything checks out and continues to be normal, then we can stop and wait for her to wake up."

"I will have a room in the packhouse prepared for the nurse immediately."

Sylvia left the room. She was in the process of closing the door when Matt and Jacqui arrived. Jacqui had tears in her eyes and ran to the bed to hug her friend.

"Jason, blame me for making you turn her. She deserves to be happy, and I was the one who told you to do it. You were in shock. I wasn't ready to lose my best friend. I am so sorry. It is all my fault" she cried.

"Jacqui, you pulled me out of my frozen state, but you didn't force my hand. It was ultimately my decision, and I was selfish in not wanting her to leave yet when I had just found her myself. I hope that she will forgive me one day. I don't regret my decision and would do it again if it meant saving her life." I soothed her.

She was a good friend to Mikayla, and I could tell she was hurting just as much as I was at Mikayla's current situation. Jacqui was able to react when I froze. I had never frozen like that. I was always in control. Mikayla was my Achilles heel. I didn't want to live without her. I barely knew her and the more I find out the more intrigued I am. The more I want to claim her as mine and keep her safe.

"Titus can communicate with Mia, Mikayla's wolf. Mikayla and Mia are both doing well. They need to regain some strength and they both will be with us. It is going to take some time though. We are unsure how much time. Mikayla is aware she has been turned. She has Mia now which has brought her comfort. Mia said she is still processing everything but knows that Mikayla can now feel the mate bond as I can. This is all good news for our future. I am going to be hoping she will forgive me."

"Mikayla is going to be okay, and she has a wolf," she screamed and went over to where I was sitting and gave me the biggest hug. I felt a little uncomfortable as Matt gave me an evil eye at touching his mate. I shrugged my hands, wiped the shocked look off my face, and hugged her back while smirking at Matt.

He abruptly crossed the room to us and told Jacqui to let me save my PDA for Mikayla. It is so easy to get under his skin.

"Matt, don't worry, I only have eyes for Mikayla. Sorry Jacqui, Matt will have to do." I laughed.

She realized she was upsetting her mate and wrapped her arms around his waist while we all discussed Mikayla and what we should do to help her with her new life. Provided she let us of course. She could be quite stubborn.

Chapter 20: She Awakens

Mikayla's POV

I have no idea how long I was asleep on the grass under that willow, but I could still feel the warmth of the sun on my skin. Surprisingly, I wasn't sore at all having slept on the ground for who knows how long. I looked around to find Mia and spotted her running in the field of flowers towards me. When she got close enough, she said, "Good afternoon sleepy head".

"How long was I asleep?" I questioned, noticing she had grown considerably larger since I had drifted off to sleep. Her voice was more mature as well.

"You were asleep for about 30 hours. I guess you needed a recharge."

"What? Are you kidding me?"

"Nope, I tried to lay with you so I would be here when you woke up but then you kept sleeping and sleeping and sleeping. I needed to do something, so I went for a run – three times. I even went into the lake a bit splashing around hoping the noise would wake you."

"I cannot believe it. I feel well rested but certainly don't feel as if I was out for that long. You seem older now. How come the sun feels the same as when I got here? Shouldn't it be dark now?"

"I have grown, and we only have one more day until the full moon. This is a space that I have created in your mind for us. I know you like the warmth of the sun so I have left it up, but I can easily change the landscape into something else. It is all a figment of our mind and is not real. How are you feeling about things?"

"I cannot change what has transpired so I need to try to accept it in my way and my own time. Are you strong enough to wake me up yet?"

"Yes, I believe that I am. Are you sure you want to go now?"

"Will I still be able to see you if I go?"

"You will hear me and can talk to me in your mind. We both can feel each other and our feelings. I can see what you see as you go through life. You will never be alone again. You are also stronger than you have been in the past. You will need to prepare for our first shift though. Please let Jason and Titus help you. I have been communicating with them over the last two days. The first shift is always the worse and I won't lie to you, it hurts. You will get used to the transformation the more times we shift. It will not be as painful as what you recently endured. Once we shift, you will be able to see everything I am doing like how I see you, but I will have control. Are you sure you are ready to go back? You can stay here longer."

"I need to go back. Thank you for helping me."

"Always" Mia whispered. The scenery started to fade away and darkness took over. It no longer smelled of flowers. It smelled like an ocean breeze mixed with trees and grass after summer rainfall. I felt a tingly feeling on my forehead and heard my name "Mikayla? Are you awake?"

I opened my eyes which felt like I was prying them open after a long while. The sleep caked in my eyelashes and the dim light in the room felt like I was looking into an eclipse. My throat was sore, and I felt incredibly thirsty and hungry. I saw Jason leaning over me with so much hope and love in his eyes. I couldn't reciprocate those feelings; at least not yet. "What's a girl got to do to get a drink and some food around here?" I muttered with a slight smile on my face. He smiled back then pulled me up and into a long embrace. I honestly wasn't sure he was ever going to let me go. He took a huge whiff of me which I cringed at. No way I could be smelling good after a few days. I felt gross all over and he sniffed me again like he couldn't get enough of me and then he nuzzled his face into my neck. I didn't know how to get out of his hold which was making me both excited and apprehensive. I couldn't help but turn my head to smell him. It was him that smelled like the freshness when I awakened. Whatever cologne he was wearing was extraordinary. I would need to find out the brand. It was intoxicating. A part of me wanted to ravage him right here and now until I came to my senses. What the hell am I thinking? I pushed him away from me and asked again for a drink.

"Sorry, here you go." He reached on the nightstand and grabbed a bottle of water removing the cap, he handed it to me.

I guzzled it down like it was the end of the world. Normally, I loathed water, but this was the best bottle of water I had ever tasted. Almost like it was sweet nectar. "Do you have another please?"

He smiled and walked to the other side of the room which had a mini refrigerator and pulled out another bottle. "The other was room temperature. You may want to go slower with this one."

I nodded and took a big gulp and then paused.

"How do you feel?" he asked while glaring all over me like he was assessing any damage.

I moved my arms and legs, removing the blanket from over me. Then sat up completely, rotating my legs over the side of the bed. I set the bottle of water down on the bedside table and went to stand up. Jason reached for me with a hand under my shoulder in my armpit and helped me stand, then cautiously let me go when I nodded reassuring him. I raised my legs one at a time and then stretched my arms to the ceiling. "I feel great," I said surprised, "except for hungry".

"I have already mind-linked for some food to come up and let Matt and Jacqui know you are awake."

He barely finished his sentence before the bedroom door was swung open and Jacqui came running over to me arms wide open. She slammed into me so hard that we both fell back onto the bed. "Oh, my Goddess, I am so sorry Mikayla" and she proceeded to hug me while laying on top of me.

"Jacqui, I am fine. Can you let me up already?" I complained. Matt and Jason laughed. Jacqui slowly got up from me like she was going to break me. She should have thought of that before she lunged at me and tackled me to the bed. She spends too much time at the gym.

"Welcome back Mikayla," said Matt, "I am so glad you are finally awake. These two grumps have been super annoying without you around." Jacqui hit Matt's shoulder and Jason growled slightly at his comment.

I sat up on the bed with them all staring at me in complete silence. None of us knew what to say. I broke the silence, "So, I hear I am going to have the first shift tomorrow evening at the full moon. Anything I should know?"

They all looked at each other and shared a glance. I could tell Jason was mind-linking with them. "I am right here, please don't do that in front of me when it concerns me. I am a big girl and want the truth. Otherwise, I will leave and deal with it on my own with Mia. I am sure she can guide me through it."

Jason responded, "Sorry Mikayla. You are right. The first shift is the worst, but it is something we all have gone through. Your bones crack and then shift along with your joints and muscles into your wolf form. Eventually, you get used to the feeling. Like if you started working out at the gym after never going and your muscles are sore and you feel the burn, but after continued workouts, you feel relief and your muscles no longer feel the pressure. For those that turn later in age, it typically eases the pain to have your mate with you. With your permission, I would like to take you back to my villa where we spent our first night together. There are woods in the back. You can have your first shift there away from everyone. Matt and Jacqui will come with us and meet us in their wolf forms once you complete your first transformation. Titus, Bruno, and Ruby are all excited to meet Mia and go on a first run with her. Mia and Titus have been communicating for the past two days. Because we are mates, they can communicate even though I haven't marked you and you are not officially a part of our pack."

"I'm a rogue!" I yelped. Realization dawned on me that I didn't belong to a pack unless the Alpha accepted me, and I accepted the pack. I didn't want to be a rogue but was too embarrassed to ask Jason to let me join his pack. I mean, he wanted me to be his Luna and mark me and I would be his mate for life. I barely knew him. Wouldn't this be getting his hopes up? I still wasn't sure about all of this and if it was truly where I belonged.

Jacqui answered, "yes you are a rogue since you are unassigned to a pack. Don't worry, I was a rogue for years. It doesn't have to be a bad thing."

"Thanks for your help, Jacqui" muttered Jason sarcastically. "If you don't want to be a rogue, you can always join our pack and then you can mind-link with us all too. It is your choice."

I stuttered not knowing how to respond when Matt chimed in and saved me. "You don't have to decide right now Mikayla. Let's focus on getting you through your first shift and then we can move on from there."

Jason's POV

Mikayla needed some time alone to freshen up she called it. She didn't have to make me leave my room. I've been a gentleman up to this point unless you count Titus' blemish, but she ended up enjoying it. I don't think she holds it against me. She doesn't know how crazy she is making me.

Matt and I were going over things with Kirk so he could watch over the pack and territory while we were away for a few days.

Luke just arrived. "Luke, I need you to take four of our best fighters and one tracker to this establishment." I handed him an address. Elliott works there during the day. Grab him and bring him to the dungeon. We have questions and something tells me he can give us some answers. Besides, he might still be a threat to Mikayla, so he needs to be neutralized. Matt and I will be leaving for a few days to assist Mikayla through her first shift. Under no circumstances is anyone outside of our pack to discuss that Mikayla survived the attack or that she is now a wolf.

I want to keep it discrete for as long as we can. It may have implications we don't know yet.

Luke nodded his head in agreement. As he left the office, he wished us luck with Mikayla's first shift.

Kirk, Matt, and I finished up the last touches on our plan for defense, training, and security measures. Kirk was an excellent Gamma, in fact, he probably could be a Beta. Matt, Kirk, and Luke always had my back. We all grew up together looking after each other and even though we all saw things from different perspectives, we came up with some great ideas supporting and growing them with each of our specialties. The pack was thriving. We were the second-largest pack in the area and the fourth largest in the world according to records. Alpha Justin's pack was only larger due to the recent takeover of two packs he had conquered and acquired their members, resources, and land. However, I was pretty sure we were still the strongest pack given our training methods. Even women and children received a certain amount of training. I never wanted anyone to be completely defenseless. You never know what psycho was lurking around the corner.

It was clear Alpha Justin was ramping up so that he could take us out, but he was in for a surprise if he thought that was going to happen. I wasn't wanting to start a war between the two largest packs, but if it came down to it and I was pushed, I would switch from the defensive to the offensive and take him down. I had heard rumors of his cruelty, and from first-hand accounts of those who had escaped to our territory, I was starting to believe all of them were true. Trevor and his family were terrified. He gave us ample information on how Justin ran things. Justin was calculating and ruthless. He would lie, cheat, and steal to get what he wants, and it has given him everything he needs. He cannot be trusted, and I had an ominous feeling when I thought about the future. I couldn't prove it, but it was clear to me Justin wanted my Luna gone. He knew what additional strength an Alpha has by having a Luna by his side and it would make it more difficult for him to take over my pack. I wonder if he knows how powerful Mikayla is after all. Dylan was able to get quite a bit of information on her. Alpha Justin may already know of her. Mikayla did manage to kill all her assailants, but she also ended up in a life-threatening situation forcing me to turn her. I'm unable to trust that she can protect herself yet. I must keep her close and somehow limit her movements around the pack when we get back from the villa. I have no idea how to convince her. She is so stubborn. She will be a strong Luna for sure. My lips curled into a smile thinking of us running the pack together and how strong we would all be when Jacqui mind-linked Matt and I they were coming downstairs and were ready to go.

I glanced in Matt's direction and noticed he was eyeing me peculiarly. "What gives man?"

"Nothing" he smirked, "just funny watching you think of Mikayla."

"What?"

"You get a ridiculous smile on your face whenever you are thinking or talking about her. It is hilarious. I didn't want to interrupt your happy moment."

"You're a dick. You get a stupid grin when you are thinking about Jacqui too you know."

"Touché!"

With that, we went out into the hall and met Mikayla and Jacqui.

"Ready to go ladies?"

They both nodded and headed towards the door with their bags in tow. Matt and I ran after them with our bags, we had left by the door waiting for them, and promptly grabbed their bags from them. We packed up the SUV and were off.

"Who's up for stopping for lunch on the way? I am starving."

Collectively, they all agreed.

Chapter 21: Wolf Abilities

Mikayla's POV

Jason drove, I was in the passenger seat and Matt and Jacqui were in the back. I could feel Mia with me which comforted me but also weirded me out a bit. It was going to take some getting used to having her there with me permanently, but I was grateful to have her.

"I am glad to have you too Mikayla and you will get used to having me around," Mia said.

I must've been startled a bit because Jason asked if I was all right. I nodded to him and let him know Mia was talking to me and it surprised me. He also indicated I would get used to it.

"You can hear my thoughts," I asked her.

"We are two entities Mikayla, but we are connected in every way possible. You will feel and hear my thoughts and vice versa. Once you complete the mate bond with Jason, you will also be able to feel him and Titus. However, they will not be able to hear your thoughts as I can. Ours is the strongest bond possible. They will feel you though when you are happy, sad, or scared, or aroused. Wolves' senses are so much more than a human, or I guess a witch's in your case. They can even smell when you are aroused."

"They can?" and I glanced at Jason, who looked over quickly and then back at the road.

"What is Mia saying to you?" he asked.

"She was telling me about the bond she and I share with hearing thoughts and feelings. She also indicated if we complete the mate bond, you will feel what I am feeling too but cannot hear my thoughts. Lastly, she said you can sense when I am aroused." I told him.

The car swerved slightly as he glanced over at me with a shocked look. Then Jacqui piped in from the backseat. "Yes, we can all detect when someone is aroused through smell, but it isn't something we talk about openly. Yes, we all know you are attracted to Jason and want him at times as much as he wants you."

I was so embarrassed. I could feel my face turning bright red and an equally shocked look come on my face. Jason had regained his composure and decided to tease me. "That is why Titus took over the other night and well you know what happened after he gained control," he said. I could hear snickering in the back seat from Matt and Jacqui, as I grew an even deeper shade of red which I wouldn't think was possible. Mia thought in my head "oh yeah, I would love to get some of that action" and instantly I felt myself craving their touch. I meant to yell at Mia in my head but inadvertently yelled it out loud in the car, "MIA!" It was too late. The images of Jason and I and Titus and I together ran through my mind, and I could feel myself longing to be touched by them again. I closed my legs tight and turned to look out the window hoping it would go unnoticed when Jason asked "are you sure you want to go grab some food? I can take you straight home to our bedroom if you prefer?" I turned towards him and slapped him on the shoulder. "Are you enjoying this?" I responded. He smiled and replied. "Of course, I am enjoying my mate and her wanting to be with me." Instantly, I was able to smell his arousal too. I glanced down and saw the bulge in his pants, then looked up at him. He twitched his eyebrows at me and then winked. I guess our conversation inspired Jacqui and Matt also as the car filled with their scents as well. I rolled down my window for some fresh air.

"Well Mia has more control over me than I realized, but I have lots of self-control too. Where are we going to eat?" I changed the subject.

Jason's POV

The rest of the ride to the restaurant was quiet with a bit of snickering here and there from the backseat. The Broken Diner was one of my favorite places to go. It was close to the villa and my parents took me here every Friday night for dinner. It was our special thing to do when I was a child.

My parents have been traveling since I took over as Alpha three years ago and they would make appearances every few months to check on me. We had weekly chats to catch up on everything that was happening. They were pretty much on the plane when I told them not to come back yet. The threat of Alpha Justin going after my parents was too much to add to my plate with everything else going on. They wanted to meet my mate and help with taking care of the pack. They made everyone in the pack a huge family, knowing everyone's names and interests. They were impressive and taught me everything I know. I asked, no begged them to give me some time with Mikayla to get her to come around to the bond before they came. The calls with them were more frequent but I kept them in the loop. My father may not have been Alpha anymore, but he was still an Alpha wolf and was going to help us when the time came. My mother against my better judgment was refusing to stay away much longer. I was able to get some photos of Mikayla and send them to my parents to appease them ever so slightly. After updating them on Mikayla being a witch, they decided to reach out to a few of their confidants to get more information. They had heard rumors of the prophecy discussed at the meeting of the Alphas, an annual event in which all the Alphas joined together to discuss issues within the packs, the world, new pack rules, or anything else of relevance. My parents promised once they got the intel they were seeking, they would be back and there was nothing I could say about it. I sure hope Mikayla comes around before they get back. They are already calling her their daughter and asking when they can expect pups. As if I didn't have enough pressure on me right now.

We pulled into the parking lot of the Broken Diner. After proceeding inside, Mikayla went to the restroom with Jacqui before making their way to the booth. Matt had this ridiculous grin on his face staring across the booth at me. "Do you have something to say?" I asked.

"Me? No. What would I have to say?" he answered.

"Then stop staring at me with that dumb smile on your face." I threatened.

"Or what?" he rebuked.

"Or we will go outside, and I will help wipe the smile off your face," I smirked.

He laughed, "I can feel the sexual tension." I threw a bun at him they put on the table which with his wolf reflexes he caught instinctively, then took a bite of it.

Mikayla and Jacqui returned and sat next to us.

"All freshened up," Matt said more of a statement than a question. Jacqui punched him in the shoulder.

Glaring at him, she said "shut-up or you will remain fresh all night." Matt's smile came off his face instantly and he picked up a menu as nothing happened.

"So, what is everyone going to order?" he asked.

We all grabbed our menus. I knew what I was going to order but sometimes they added new items which were always seasonal and worth a try. The waitress came over. "My name is Angel, and I will be your waitress today." I noticed she was only talking to me and not looking at the others when she added, "what can I get for you today sweetie?" It annoyed me that she was looking at me like a slab of meat given Mikayla was right there next to me. She had audacity but I guess we did look like maybe we were just friends. She wasn't sitting close to me in the booth at all. I decided to flirt back with Angel and see Mikayla's reaction. Titus growled angrily in my head as soon as I thought about it. "It will be fine Titus. A little jealousy is healthy." I smiled at Angel saying, "why don't you take everyone else's order and save the best for last Dear?" She winked at me and then proceeded to take everyone's order. While she was taking Mikayla and then Jacqui's order down, Matt mind-linked me, "you are playing with fire Jason." "I know what I am doing" I mind-linked him back. After Angel took Matt's order, she focused back on me. "And for you handsome?" I ordered three appetizers for us to share and then a steak and shrimp dinner for myself. Angel smiled back and said in a sexy innuendo, "I thought you might like to eat. I'll save some dessert for you for later." She walked away to place our orders in the kitchen.

"She was friendly" I stated attempting to spark a conversation.

Jacqui piped up, "she was blatantly flirting with you, while Mikayla is right there. She has some nerve. What the hell is her problem?"

141

Mikayla spoke up, "Jacqui, it is okay. Wait staff frequently flirt with their clients to get larger tips. I have done it plenty of times and it works. Besides, Jason was encouraging her, trying to get a rise out of me. I guess being an Alpha of a pack has a lot of responsibility, so he must remain childish in some area of his life."

"Wait, what?" I spoke.

Mikayla started laughing. Jacqui and Matt were sitting silently staring from her to me waiting for a response and unsure what to do. Mikayla added, "thank you Titus for the warning. Jason, if you listen to Titus, I think you have a better chance at me becoming your mate." She gave me a huge smile.

I smiled back and started laughing muttering "traitor" out loud so everyone could hear it. We all laughed; and I put my arm around Mikayla's shoulder and slid her closer to me giving her a pouty face and looking her in the eyes, "you like Titus more than me?" I added a whimper for pity.

"Still playing games I see" she stared into my eyes. Before she could say anything else, I leaned forward quickly pecking her on the lips, then moved back slightly to look into   her   eyes.

"I didn't know you were into games, but I can oblige." I raised my eyebrow at her and waited for her response. However, Angel came back and slammed our drinks down on the table drawing all our attention. We all looked in her direction. Mikayla pulled back from me. I rested my arm on the back of the booth behind her without moving it completely away. "Thank you, Angel."

"I'll be right back with your appetizers" she almost seemed to whisper, then turned on her heels and went towards the kitchen.

"Oh great! Now she is going to spit in our food," Mikayla remarked.

"No way, did you spit in peoples' food?" Matt interjected.

"Of course not, but I also wouldn't openly flirt with a guy who had a woman sitting in the booth with him. Both are morals and ethics in the same category," Mikayla retorted.

Angel brought our appetizers. "Everything looks amazing," I told her staring at her and not looking at the food at all and giving her a wink.

She smiled back at me, "we take pride in things here."

I took my arm from behind Mikayla leaning over and then grabbing a wing from the appetizer platter she just brought. "I can see that" I replied and gave her an elevator look eyeing her down and back up again.

"The rest of your food will be out shortly," she said. Her eyes gleamed in the light as she eyed me back up and down and then her arousal hit me. I saw Matt and Jacqui get uncomfortable as they looked across the booth at Mikayla. I didn't dare look at her yet, at least not until Angel walked away. Suddenly, the glass of coke on the table tipped over and fell towards me. The coke and ice started to roll down the table as I shifted to the side when it took an unexplainable turn over the edge covering my crotch. Angel yelped, "Oh my goodness, let me get some more napkins." She ran off to the condiments stand in the middle of the diner.

I glared at Mikayla. "Are you serious?"

"No more serious than you are flirting with our waitress." She rebutted. "Besides, you needed to cool off and she needed to stop staring."

I laughed, "sounds like someone was getting a bit jealous."

She laughed, "sounds like someone wants to be celibate for the rest of his life."

Angel came back with the napkins. Mikayla grabbed them from her and almost in a scowl said "If you know what is good for you, you know that I can handle it from here. If you want a tip from us, then you should find us someone else to wait on our table immediately." Angel glanced at me and then walked away.

I asked Mikayla to let me out of the booth so I could go and change my pants, but she refused, saying I needed to think about my actions. I dabbed myself with the napkins picking up all the ice cubes that didn't fall to the floor and sat there quietly in complete disbelief. Matt mind-linked me "Mikayla did that on purpose. Her pupils had a blue light surrounding them before the coke spilled. She knows she has abilities."

Soon after, an older woman came to our table introducing herself and bringing us our remaining food and another coke for me.

I finally broke the silence. "Can we talk about something serious Mikayla?"

"What's on your mind?" she asked.

"Are you aware you are a witch?" I questioned.

"It is not a topic of discussion for a restaurant. Let's wait until we get to the villa. Enjoy your lunch," she smiled and continued eating.

Chapter 22: Cards on the Table

Mikayla's POV

We finished lunch and then headed to the villa. We left our bags in the foyer. Jason informed us that someone would bring them up for us and we could head to the living room to talk. I knew what he wanted to talk about. I wasn't sure how much he knew but clearly, he knew something. He grabbed a file from the side of his bag and showed us where to go.

The living room was huge. Large windows from the floor to the ceiling let in the afternoon light. The hardwood flooring was a dark brown with an area rug with a huge gray wolf in the center of it with green pine trees around the edge of the rug. There was a brown sofa, loveseat, and oversized chair. A gas fireplace surrounded by a brick wall with photo frames across the mantle. A tv was mounted above the mantle and I could see the surround sound speakers around the room. The crown molding and pot lights gave the room a newer feel. There were also two beautiful lamps on either side of the sofa which I could only assume gave a more relaxed atmosphere when used. A small bar was in the far corner. A wine rack was on the wall behind it, each slot filled with a bottle. I sat on the sofa, and Matt and Jacqui sat on the loveseat. Jason sat on the sofa but turned to face me.

"Yes, I am a witch and yes, I purposely made the drink spill on you and yes, I enjoyed your reaction and yes, I will probably do more things like that to annoy you when you are misbehaving. I guess I can teach an old dog new tricks," I laughed.

"Mikayla, stop shielding things by making fun. This is a serious matter. People are looking for you and they are not good people from what I can ascertain. Using your magic is only going to draw attention to yourself unnecessarily. I found you and I want to keep you alive and well," Jason said softly and directly with concern in his eyes.

I sighed, "when I used my powers to kill off the rogues, I didn't know what I was doing. My body knew what needed to be done. If I was going to die, I was going to take them with me. My parents left me books about my heritage and what I am. They were entrusted to me after my 18th birthday by a law company my parents had arranged before leaving me in foster care. There was a letter from my parents. The books had spells and incantations. Directions on how to perform them. The letter said I was a powerful witch and my abilities had been forced to be dormant by another witch. It said eventually, I would age to a point in which my natural powers would be stronger than the witch who made them dormant and they would return. The letter also indicated that if I practiced the larger spells, I needed to cast protection spells first to hide the magic from those who would be searching for the use of strong magic. The letter also stated a supernatural event could trigger my memories and abilities to return.

When my unconscious self saved me, everything came back. I had been studying the books left to me and memorized every word of every spell. I know how to do many things, but I have not practiced them. I wanted no part of this life. I wanted a simple, quiet life with a husband and children to raise. I thought I had that with Elliott. I was wrong. Finding out you are a werewolf and an Alpha, and I am mated to you and supposed to be your

Luna. All of that was very overwhelming and so far from what I pictured my life to be which is why I haven't agreed to it. I hope you understand Jason, I do have feelings for you, and I am attracted to you but the life you are offering is vastly new to me. I honestly don't know what I want now. I feel something bad is coming for me, something worse than has already come. I don't know what the future holds for me, but I know I need time to process. It has been a week and I lost my fiancé, who tried to kidnap me. I still have no clue as to why or what his intentions were or where he was going to take me. I then met my mate, was told I am to be a Luna, got attacked and almost murdered, then turned into a werewolf and unleashed my supernatural witch powers. Tomorrow night I am going to have my first shift. Excuse me if I am using amusement to cope with the events of the last week. It's a lot to absorb and accept."

Jason moved closer to me on the sofa and wrapped his arms around me giving me a hug. "It is a lot. You are not in this alone. I am your mate and together we will move forward and cope with everything coming our way. You are amazingly strong."

Jacqui chimed in, "Mikayla, we are here for you. Through it all, you will never be alone. We will figure it all out. I love you. You are my best friend and the sister I never had. I am sorry you have so much stressful change in your life, but I am happy I can be here for you and Jason is a great man to have by your side, even if he acts childish and jealous at times."

"Hey, uncalled for Jacqui." Jason still had a tight hold on me. I could feel the tingles going through my body and his positive energy flowing through me, warming me up and comforting me. I leaned my body into him and rested my head on his shoulder, wrapping my arms around him and returning his embrace.

Matt grabbed the file from the floor where Jason left it. "There is more to your story Mikayla we have discovered. There are gaps we will need to try to fill in and maybe the contents of the letter and your books have more information. Jason had you investigated after the shockwave you created killed those rogues and sent us all flying in the air. This is the file our investigator put together for you. You can read through it on your own, but the important part is you were a child prodigy in the witch world. At ten, you were stronger than many full-grown adults. Tales of your strength were starting to spread which your parents feared. A war is brewing between the light and dark magic covens. A prophecy tells of a sorcerer or sorceress that will have the power to end the war in favor of the light magic coven. Anytime someone shows superiority in magic, the dark magic coven comes for them. Some of them are murdered and some have ended up in a coma from which they never awaken. Your family clearly tried to protect you from being found out. You were put in foster care and your memories and magic were hidden and forced to be dormant for all this time. We all are concerned for your safety at this point. Besides the fact, we are pretty sure it was Alpha Justin who tried to have you assassinated so you could not mate and truly bond with Jason giving him more power."

"I don't understand. How can I give Jason more power?" I asked.

Jason spoke, "when an Alpha finds his Luna and they have mated and been marked, the Alpha and Luna both get stronger and more powerful, gaining the abilities and power of the other if it is their true mate. If I bonded with

148

you as a human, I would gain some power. If you were a werewolf or a witch or vampire, then I would gain more power than if you were just a human. We don't know for sure if the gained power is equal to the supernatural. Regardless, completing the bond adds more power to any leader. Alpha Justin is gunning for my pack. To become the Alpha of our pack, I need to relinquish the Alpha position to him by choice or he must kill me. With the rumors of his ruthless and dictatorial style, I will never give him control. He will have to kill me. He has his Luna already so has gained additional power. I don't think he could take me in a fair fight even though we haven't bonded yet. He wouldn't want to take the chance that I gain more strength."

"I see. Will you be able to use magic when we bond then?" I asked curiously.

"Don't you mean IF we bond?" he teased.

I rolled my eyes. The thought of him being killed by another Alpha pained me down to my core. I could hear Mia in my mind whimpering and practically begging me to let him mate and mark me as soon as I completed the first shift. Shutting her out of my thoughts so I could think wasn't easy so I had a minor slip of the tongue, and wouldn't you know, Jason was all over it.

"All of you keep implying it is inevitable for us to be together, so excuse me if I had a slip of grammar when I am trying to understand why?" I fumed.

Jacqui piped in now, "Mikayla, when you couldn't feel the bond, there was a possibility you would reject Jason. You can reject him right now if you want."

Jason growled in anger at her words, and I swear if looks could kill, she would be dead.

Jacqui continued, "as I was saying, you can accept or reject the mate bond. The Moon Goddess has reasons for forming true mates and Jason is your destiny. We all know you are attracted to him since you met him at the club. Since becoming a wolf, you will feel the desire to be with him even more. Your wolf will constantly be nagging you. Your body will defy your outright denial and give away your true wants. You and Jason are a perfect match. You can end the pull of the bond by rejecting Jason now, but let's be real and honest. We all know that is not what you want. If you reject him, there is no going back and changing your mind. If you accept him, there is no going back and changing your mind. You are either all in or all out. You should decide sooner rather than later. If you are going to reject, then it will be better to rip the band-aid than get any further invested and if you are going to accept, then you should embrace it and enjoy the life you were meant to live. Jason, I know you and Titus are probably debating ripping my throat out right now, but Mikayla deserves to know the truth, the whole truth, and accept you knowing everything. I will support any decision that she makes, even if it is the wrong one." In the last part, she looked me dead in the eyes.

Jason was still holding on to me. His grip tightened and I could feel his entire body tense as Jacqui told me about being able to reject him and end this now. She had a point though. I needed to consider everything and decide. No need to draw it out and make things more difficult for us all. All their eyes were peering at me, waiting for me to respond but I honestly didn't know what to say. I didn't know I could say no to all of this and grasping it all was making my head spin. It was a life I never could have imagined and still trying to figure it out was tedious. I wanted to melt away into the floor and come up for air when I was ready.

"Please stop looking at me like I am supposed to make a life-altering decision after a 30-minute conversation. It may seem like a no-brainer to all of you. I get it. You are all for me accepting and embracing our future. You are asking me to uproot my entire life and ignore what I saw for myself. Not only that, but you are asking me to do it and then become matriarch to a pack I don't know and be a leader during a war I want no part in. Give up my school, my friends, my job, and my home so that I can be happy with Jason. I thought I was happy with Elliott and in a matter of seconds, everything came crashing down on me. Jason, you are wonderful. If I had to choose between accepting and rejecting you right now and had no other choices and I knew it would be saving your life, I would accept you. This is way more than just me accepting you though. I would also be accepting a new life, a pack, a leadership role, relocating, and a war. The list goes on and on. I only wanted a family and a white picket fence. You have a pack house and a villa, and a nightclub, and God only knows what else."

Jacqui interjected "Goddess."

"What?" I asked.

She elaborated. "You mean Goddess only knows what else."

I was in the middle of a rant, and she halted to correct me. Wolves had the Moon Goddess, but I only turned wolf recently and hadn't even shifted yet. Was I supposed to change things now? Ridiculous. "I am going to go and take a long bath. I need to relax and think things over." I stood up out of Jason's arms and started to walk out. Turning around to look at him, I asked "are you coming?"

Jason promptly rose and started to follow me. "I didn't think you would want me to come with you."

"How else would I know where to find a towel? You wouldn't happen to have any bubble bath, would you?" I responded.

"Right, towel. Follow me."

He led me up the stairs to his bedroom. It was familiar and the memories started coming back of our night together. I followed him through his room and into the bathroom. He went into a cabinet on the back wall of the bathroom and pulled out a towel. He turned around and looked at me, then smiled. "Are you sure you want to take a bath and maybe not do something else?" Damn arousal giving me away again. Then I was alerted to his arousal as well.

"Jason, I was recollecting some fond memories which may have slightly aroused me. However, at this very moment, I am tired and want to relax without any pressure of mating or accepting a bond," I sighed.

Jason's POV

Mikayla had been through a lot these few days. I would give anything to make it easier on her. She was so stubborn fighting everything the entire way. She did have her reasons though and it did make sense how she explained them. I was thrilled she didn't reject me, and she said she would accept me if it was just me and not the package deal. It was a lot to take it. Hell, I had a tough time dealing with it all some days and I was raised and trained to be prepared for it. After Mikayla had her rant, it dawned on me how daunting all this must be for her to be thrown into it all. She looked worn out, not to mention, she had recently woken up from a coma and almost died, so no doubt she was tired. I walked over to her in the bathroom, setting the towel on the countertop. I didn't say a word and grabbed her hands and motioned for her to come with me back into the bedroom. Much to my surprise, she didn't question me or hesitate. Maybe she trusted me enough or maybe she was all out of fight. I walked her over to the bed and pulled the covers back, then had her sit down. I took off her shoes and swung her legs up. She leaned back on to the bed and I pulled the covers up tucking her in. "Get some rest Mikayla, then take your bath when you wake up. The towel is there now and there is some bubble bath under the sink. It might be a little toward the back though. I don't take many bubble baths." I leaned down and kissed her on her forehead.

As I started to pull away, she smiled up at me, then said "will you lay with me and hold me until I fall asleep? You make me feel calm when I am in your arms."

It was difficult to keep a straight face. "Sure." I turned around to walk around to the other side of the bed and I know Matt would be making fun of me right now if he could see the smile on my face. After removing my shoes, I climbed under the covers, putting my arm up and Mikayla slid into it and nestled her head onto my chest. Her hand rested on my chest and her warm body was pressed up against me. I was aroused again, and I knew she could tell. She closed her eyes and after a few minutes, I could hear her steady breathing and the beat of her heart. She was already asleep.

I lay there holding her. Smelling her intoxicating scent. Everything about her was amazing. Her acceptance, if and when, she finally decided upon it would be so much more than accepting the mate bond. She would be excepting me and our future life. I always assumed it would be easy once I found my mate, we would be together, end of the story. She is literally weighing all her options and making sure she has no regrets and choosing this life for herself. Even with pressure from her friend, her mate, her wolf, my wolf, Matt, and the bond itself. Does she even know how strong she is to fight for her choice?

"Earth to Alpha Jason!" I heard through mind-link. I guess I had dozed off for a bit as well. "What, Matt?"

"You need to come downstairs" he replied.

"We are sleeping, you woke me up. You handle it. I am sure you are capable."

He cut me off "your parents are here."

My eyes shot open, and I glanced down at a sleeping Mikayla in my arms. She looked so at peace right now. I didn't want to disturb her by moving, but my parents were not something Matt would be able to handle. Hell, I didn't know if I could handle them. Why are they here? I ask for a little time and can they oblige, nope. This is where transparency got me. I shouldn't have updated them but how could I have left my mate out given the attack was on her and I turned her myself? Ugh! I palmed my forehead and dragged my free hand down my face. Then slowly tried to remove my arm gracefully from around Mikayla. It was a failed attempt. As soon as I started to move my arm, her eyes opened, and she looked up at me.

"You are so comfortable. I feel so much better now. Thank you for staying with me," she grinned.

"Believe me when I say the pleasure was all mine. I fell asleep also, but Matt woke me up in a mind-link. I need to go downstairs and take care of something."

"Your parents are here!"

"How did you know? Titus!"

"Don't be mad at Titus. He wants to keep Mia and me well informed of things that you should be doing by the way. Stop with the secrets and hiding things from me."

"I am not trying to hide things from you. You don't understand."

"I am all ears waiting for you to explain it to me then. Isn't any good relationship based on trust and communication?"

"My parents know you are my mate. They know of the attack and your transformation. Aside from wanting to reach out to the cohorts to get information about you and Alpha Justin, they only have one thing on their mind."

"What might that be?"

"Grandchildren!"

"You cannot be serious. We don't even know what the future holds for us. How do they know they will even like me? How can they be talking children already? Did you tell them we slept together? Oh no, I am in your bed right now."

"Calm down Mikayla. See why I didn't say anything. I am not ready for kids yet either, but it won't stop my mom from referring to it every chance she can get. Don't take it personally, she has been on my case about finding my mate and giving her grand pups for years now."

"The apple doesn't fall far from the tree."

"What is that supposed to mean?"

"I mean ever since you found out I am your mate; you have been pressuring me to accept you and the bond. Every chance you get to slip it into a conversation, there it is. Front and center."

"Forgive me, if I have been waiting my entire life to meet my true mate and finally find her and want nothing but to spoil her rotten and take her into my arms every night. The bond pull is stronger with Alphas, and I have had Titus in my head telling me to mark you already and deal with the consequences later, but he is the good one right. The one who keeps you in the loop and doesn't hide anything. Wake up Mikayla. Everything I have done has been for you, my true mate, the one that I love and want to spend my life with, however long or short it may be. I need to go downstairs and greet my parents. Despite them adding some pressure, they are the best parents I could've hoped for, and they are also a part of the package deal you need to accept or reject. It's 5:30 now and Miss Flint serves dinner promptly at 7:00. If you want to take your bath, feel free, but please don't be late for dinner. It upsets her when she has prepared a fantastic meal and we let it get cold."

I left the room slamming the door behind me before she could say anything.

"Way to go Genius, now she hates both of us," said Titus.

"She doesn't hate me, but she knows the truth about you now. You shouldn't be playing her against me and passing information to Mia then to her. It stops now." I huffed while making my way down the stairs to the living room. Titus went to the back of my mind and said nothing else on the topic although I could hear his thoughts saying I was grumpy because I wasn't getting laid. Annoying mutt I thought and could hear him growling in my mind.

As I passed through the foyer, I saw all my parents' luggage which meant they were here to stay. Why did I pick the villa to bring Mikayla to? Did I tell them I was bringing her to the villa for her first shift?

"Hi, Mom... Dad."

"My baby boy. Jonathan, he has aged so much in the last two years while we have been traveling. Don't worry baby, we are here for you and are not going anywhere until the threats are neutralized and you and Mikayla are okay to have pups," my mother promised.

"Mom, I am not a baby, please don't refer to me as your baby in front of Mikayla. It's bad enough that you did it in front of Matt and Jacqui. If either of you speaks a word of this, there will be hell to pay." I reprimanded my mother. She laughed it off and wrapped her arms around me squeezing me tight so I could barely get air.

"Nonsense, you will always be my baby. Now, where is Mikayla? I am dying to meet my daughter-in-law," she responded.

"She is upstairs taking a bath. We need to talk before she comes downstairs. Please sit down." I gestured to the couch. My parents shared a glance with each other and then proceeded to sit down. Matt and Jacqui were still sitting on the loveseat. I sat in the chair then continued, "I haven't told you everything. You know Mikayla was human or so I thought. It turns out she is a witch with memories of her magic blocked. You also know that she was attacked and to save her life, I had to turn her. The part you are missing is that she has yet to accept me as her mate. I figured if I delayed you meeting her and coming here, she would accept everything, and then I could introduce you all. I am sorry I kept it from you. I didn't want you to worry and come rushing home," I apologized.

My dad spoke up first, "Jason, you know your mother and I are here for you and there isn't anything you cannot tell us. We still want to meet this young lady that has

157

captured your heart. By the way, we are going to call you baby in front of her." Matt couldn't contain his laughter.

Mom looked at me intently before saying, "Son, why has she not accepted the bond? You are a great catch."

"It isn't me, Mom. It is everything that comes with me. The pack, her being Luna, giving up her current life, an impending war and so on. It wasn't what she pictured for herself and with her almost dying, turning into a wolf, going through her first shift, realizing her memories were blocked, she is now a powerful witch and potentially multiple people are trying to harm her, accepting our bond isn't something she wants to rush into. I don't blame her given all of it started the night she met me." I confessed.

My parents were silent as they took in my explanation of events and Mikayla's hesitation.

Chapter 23: The Parents

Mikayla's POV

I had come down the stairs and heard Jason explaining things to his parents. I took a step back wanting to retreat but then realized at this point, I had nowhere to go. I was very anxious about my first shift and nothing anyone said was making me feel better about it except for having Jason nearby. His aura seemed to give me a sense of calm and a feeling of power that I could make it through anything. It was a great feeling, and I knew I was getting closer to him. Although now I wasn't sure if it was getting to know him or the mate bond that was doing it. It was a little disconcerting. Guess I must put on my big girl pants and meet his parents eventually so might as well do it now.

As I entered the room smiling as if the conversation hadn't impacted me, I spoke, "now everyone is up-to-speed, I am famished. Can we eat?"

Jonathan stared at me looking as if he wanted to say something but couldn't. Allison glanced at him and then at me. She stalked over to me and without warning wrapped her arms around me and embraced me in a huge hug. "Welcome to our family Mikayla. Everything is going to work out for the best. You are a beautiful, strong, willful, and resilient woman and we are incredibly lucky to have you as our daughter. A daughter we can be proud of and the daughter we always dreamed of joining our family."

Her words took me off-guard. My knees went weak, and I grabbed onto her for support returning her embrace. Tears prickled down my cheeks. I never realized how badly I wanted to be accepted and how much the love of a mother I was missing in my life. This woman whom I just met seemed to know what I needed to hear and all at once everything hit me like a ton of bricks. I sobbed uncontrollably. I willed it to stop but I couldn't. The waterworks kept streaming and I held on to her tightly unable to let go. She reciprocated whispering "it is okay. We are here now, and you will never be alone again. You are going to be okay. Let it all out. It isn't good to bottle up these things. You will feel so much better. Release it all into the world and onto my shoulders sweetheart."

I kept thinking to myself how safe and secure Allison was making me feel. I wanted to hold on for longer and didn't want to be torn away from her hug. I needed it. The more I thought of holding on to her; the more I sobbed. It was like we were the only two there. My eyes were closed so I didn't realize anything strange was happening until I heard Mia reaching out to me.

"Mikayla," she said.

"Yes Mia" I responded in my head, surprised that even in my thoughts I had a sniffle in my words after all the crying.

"You need to let go of Allison. You triggered your powers and there is some sort of protection bubble around the two of you. The others are worried as they do not know what is happening and you are blocking their voices out. They cannot touch you either. Titus was able to reach out to me to ask if everything was okay."

I opened my eyes and there was a translucent bubble surrounding us. Allison slowly released me smiling and also looking at it. She reached out to touch it and her hand went through it. However, Jason and Jonathan were on the other side trying to reach in and it acted like a barrier. They were unable to reach past its walls. Allison stepped

160

outside the bubble completely. She was able to step back inside it without it blocking her out. I stared in awe wondering how I had conjured up such a thing. Did I really do it? It must've been me, but I didn't even know I could do it. I certainly didn't mean to do it. I thought about how to get rid of it and it wasn't necessary and after a few more thoughts of trying to figure out how to make it disappear, it vanished into thin air. Allison, Jason, Jonathan, and I all tried to reach out to where it had been previously and nothing. It was completely gone, undetectable as if nothing has been there before. What the hell?

"Incredible! I have read about protection barriers before in the history of some battles, but I never thought in a million years I would get to see one. It was everything the books described. Those inside the bubble could move in and out of it, but anyone outside could not penetrate it. They used them to protect those who couldn't fight during wars, like children and the elderly. Truly amazing! You are quite powerful. I could feel the strength in the room. You didn't even realize you were doing it. It was effortless to you," Jonathan spewed excitedly, then came to give me a hug. He stopped with his arms mid-air and then said, "maybe leave it at a handshake for now" as he held out his hand.

We all laughed at his comment. "I am so sorry. I had no idea I was doing that and don't know what came over me. How embarrassing and such a great first impression." I sulked.

"Are you kidding? You created a bubble in the middle of the living room we could not break or get through or anything. Justin can come after Jason all he wants. If you are by his side, it is futile. Besides, the memory of seeing you glow blue and emanating unimaginable power is better than a great first impression." Allison stated. Did she always know the perfect thing to say?

Jason came over and put his arms around me. "You could have cried on my shoulder you know."

"Are you jealous?" I asked.

"Isn't it obvious?" he smiled.

Miss Flint entered the room, "dinner is ready. Come and get it while it is hot everyone." She stalked towards the dining room.

We all followed with Jason leading the way. As soon as I got a smell of the food, my mouth started to water profusely, and my stomach let out a loud growl I am sure everyone heard. The dining table was already set with glasses and silverware but no plates. We all sat down. Off to the side of the room, Miss Flint had a stack of soup saucers, she was filling from a huge pot that was on a trolley. She placed a saucer in front of each of us and wished us a good dinner indicating there were four courses. Pretty sure in unison all of us said thank you and then started in on our soup.

The soup was warm and appetizing. After all the crying I had done, I still had a sniffle here and there I tried to stifle but this soup was heating me up to the core warming my insides with every bite engulfed. Apparently, it was a lobster bisque, which I had never had, but goodness would I love to have it frequently. It was smooth and creamy. It could have been satisfying because I was so hungry, but I will never know. The soup was followed by small salad plates as another appetizer, then the main course was an assortment of steamed vegetables, a medium-rare, cooked steak, and creamy garlic mashed potatoes. I used to hate having even a smidge of blood on my plate from the steak. Sure, I liked it pink, so it was succulent and not like beef jerky being well-done but for some reason, this medium-rare had me salivating. I wanted to delve into the meat and ask for ten more. "Mia" I called.

"Yes Mikayla, you are craving the meat because you are a wolf now. We typically like to eat more meat and potato type meals as opposed to veggies and such being carnivores and all."

"Makes sense and I have no complaints at this moment. I would die a happy woman if this was my last meal."

After the main course, dessert was brought out – an apple caramel pie with whipped cream and a side of vanilla ice cream with caramel drizzle. Thank goodness wolves have a greater metabolism, or so I heard, than the average Joe. I can't imagine how big my butt was going to get eating Miss Flint's meals. I don't know where they found her, but her culinary skills are truly magnificent. She and Pop could share a few recipes. I missed Pop. I wonder how he is doing. He's probably worried about me. I need to go back to my life.

After dinner, we all departed to turn in for the night. I was worn out from all the crying still and after filling my belly to the brim, needed to relax for a bit. Jason's parents had traveled a long way to get here so quickly and were jetlagged. Jacqui and Matt, well they just agreed to go to sleep as well. They were quiet for the afternoon and evening. I did have a few mental breakdowns so it may be the reason they were treading lightly around me for now anyways. Jacqui always had a way of speaking her mind and telling me straight. I admired that about her and knew she was always a true friend. She would give it to me good or bad and let me know when I was being a complete idiot. She was so sure I should end up with Jason and accept everything happening. I wish I had her assurances. I didn't know which life to choose. My old one or my new one. To be honest, they both seemed to be in shambles and need of a pick-me-up. These thoughts all continued running through my mind until I was ready for bed. I had done my nighttime routine in the bathroom and came out to Jason who was already laying on the bed on top of the covers. He got up, walked over to me to kiss me on the cheek then said, "Finally" and went into the bathroom closing the door behind him. I shrugged my shoulders and then went to the side of the bed I had slept on earlier. I didn't want to talk to Jason tonight. I wanted to sort out my thoughts on things. It wasn't long before I drifted off to sleep again. He hadn't even come out of the bathroom yet.

Chapter 24: Transition

"Mikayla, wake up. Earth to Mikayla. Time to get up." I woke up and looked around but didn't see Jason anywhere. I stumbled to the bathroom got myself cleaned up and dressed in my morning routine. "Mia, did you wake me up?" I thought.

"Yes, Mikayla. You need to get ready for our shift. It's late. Hurry up."

I dragged my body out of the bathroom and then the bedroom. My brain was telling my body to go, but I was like a zombie. My feet were dragging, and, in my head, I swear I was moving at a much faster pace than my body was moving. I felt so sluggish and lethargic. As I protruded down the staircase, Miss Flint walked by. "Good evening sleepy head, come to the dining room. Dinner will be served shortly."

Wait, what? Did she say evening and dinner? What the hell time was it? I walked into the dining room. Everyone was seated already eating what looked like nachos. They all stared at me as I walked over to my seat next to Jason. "Did I die and forget last night?" I muttered. There was a collective laugh in the room.

Jason leaned over kissed me on my cheek, then informed me "it is normal to feel completely rundown before the first shift. Your body starts preparing early. Our meal tonight is fortified with lots of carbs. You are going to need your energy for the shift, so eat up."

"Is it evening already, I slept through morning and afternoon. It only felt like a couple of hours at most. Why didn't anyone tell me I would easily pass as an extra on the Walking Dead? Aren't you supposed to be helping me through this transition?"

Jacqui responded, "we were discussing whether we should wake you up or not when we heard you moving around up there. Feeling groggy and sleepy is normal right before the first shift, but as usual, you take everything to the extreme and slept for 22 hours. It's all good."

I reached out and grabbed a blob of loaded nachos placing them on my plate and attempting to eat slowly, pretending like I didn't want to devour the entire plate in front of me. Hungry didn't even cover it. My body doesn't feel like it is me anymore. All these changes are going to take some time to grasp. These nachos were spectacular. I had to have more. As I stretched out my arm to reach for the platter, my stomach had a huge shooting pain. I retracted my hand and grabbed it releasing a tiny scream in discomfort. The entire table looked at me, then at each other. My entire body started to tingle and felt like it was being stretched out like I was strung up to four horses and they were each pulling a limb in opposite directions. The skin on my face felt like it was growing tighter and in my peripheral vision, I could see my nose and mouth growing larger on my face. I scooted my chair back forcefully away from the table and fell to the floor crying out in pain.

"It's time. She's early. Everyone, help clear the dining room, and move the table, and chairs out of the way. She is going to shift here. There isn't time to move her elsewhere." Allison yelled.

"Agh!" I screamed. Bones from my arms, legs, and ribs started cracking. I could feel my muscles pulling in different directions. My face was continuing to contort

166

and the area on the floor seemed to be getting smaller or no wait. I was getting bigger. I could hear furniture moving and footsteps all around me.

Jacqui grabbed my hand. "You are going to be okay Mikayla. Scream through it if you need to. It will be over in a few minutes."

Minutes, this felt like an eternity already. How long had it been? "Agh!" I screamed some more.

Jason's POV

Mikayla had finally joined us. In another five minutes, I would have run and gotten her. It was taking all my willpower to let her sleep. I knew she needed her rest, but this was pure agony. She walked into dinner, and all seemed fine, except she was still complaining about being drained and none of us telling her. We would have but she never woke up so we could walk through things with her. In hindsight, we probably should have told her earlier. She screamed out in pain and the next thing I knew she was on the floor and my mom was screaming at us all to move the furniture out of the way, she was starting her shift. Jacqui dove to the floor with Mikayla and grabbed her hand whispering in her ear.

Then, I noticed her eyes were starting to glow blue. I had no idea whether this was a good thing or a bad thing. When those rogues attacked, she blasted them to their deaths not knowing what she was doing and when my mom hugged her, she built that protection bubble not knowing what she was doing and now her eyes were blue again. Something was about to happen, and I didn't know what.

"Everyone, get out now. We will meet you outside when she is done shifting." I ordered through my Alpha command. Now that I was the Alpha, even my parents had to obey a command without hesitation. I didn't like using it, but I wasn't going to risk them. I had no time for arguments or maybe I did. I had no idea when whatever Mikayla was conjuring would surface but I wasn't taking chances with those I cared about most. I dropped to my knees next to Mikayla and grabbed her hand. Tingles ran through my hand as our bond grabbed hold of each other. She turned her face to me our eyes meeting and gazing into each other. The blue slowly subsided back to her natural dark brown color and her aura which exuded so much power also had calmness and tranquility in it. Her eyes softened and she stopped screaming out. I felt her hand start to turn into a paw in my hand and fur grew from her skin. The final crackling sounds came to a halt like how you hear lots of popping when you are making popcorn and then it slowly fades as only a few more are left until it completely stops when they are all done popping. Typically, the first shift takes hours, but Mikayla transformed in a matter of minutes. I released her paw and in front of me on all fours stood the most beautiful wolf I had ever seen. Her coat was a midnight black color. It shined in the lights from the chandelier above us in the dining room. Her eyes were no longer her dark brown eyes, but they were a topaz blue glistening from the tears she had spilled while shifting. She moved forward and nuzzled her nose into my neck indicating she was okay – they were okay.

"Hi Mia, it is great to finally meet you." I stroked my hand down her head, neck, and back. Titus was flipping out in my head.

Miss Flint walked in with the next course of the meal. "Sorry Miss Flint, we had an early shift." She looked at Mia, rolled her eyes, and walked back into the kitchen.

"Mia, can you follow me outside please, and then I will shift? Everyone else is already waiting for us and then we will go on a run through the backwoods."

Mia nodded. I stood up and walked her out the back door. We had woods lining the back of our home which wasn't a huge forest like our wolves loved to run through for hours on end, but it was big enough for us to have some fun and it was secluded enough that we wouldn't run into any humans. Once we got back to our packhouse, there were plenty of woods to run carefree through on our territory.

Outside everyone had already shifted, so I went behind the side of the house, removed my clothes then shifted. Titus walked us out and playfully circled Mia hitting his nose at her from each side, when he made it back to the front of her, Mia jumped at him and pinned him to the ground licking his face. "She's a feisty one Titus, you have your hands full just as much as I do with Mikayla." I laughed in his head.

Titus laughed back, "Mikayla is feeling mortified right now at Mia's action. Other than that, she is okay and enjoying the feeling of the evening air in her fur. She is asking when we are going to run."

"Well, what are you waiting for then? Don't you want to keep our mate happy?" I asked.

"Mia is our mate too and is enjoying slobbering all over me. Are you jealous? I am getting more attention from Mia after five minutes than you've gotten from Mikayla after five days." He teased.

Then he rolled over, so he was pinning Mia. After giving her a quick lick on the face, he jolted for the tree line. Everyone followed behind him.

169

Mikayla's POV

Mia watched as the others started to disappear into the trees in front of us. I asked her, "are we not going to run as well?"

Mia replied, "I am giving them a head start. There's no fun without a chase."

If I could roll my eyes I would, but Mia had complete control. She bolted for the tree line. I watched as she sprinted into the trees following the others. They had a good lead on us, but I didn't care. Even though I had no control over our body right now, I sensed everything. It was twilight still, so seeing wasn't an issue, but I could hear everything from who knows how far away. Birds were chirping away. A babbling brook was nearby. It sounded like a small steady stream trickling somewhere nearby. I listened to the beat of our paws pounding the ground. Mia was swerving in and out of trees and bushes and around rocks and some fallen trees. Light came through the gaps in the leaves illuminating the pathway and I could see the others moving similarly ahead. A warm breeze graced our fur as we whipped through the woods. I closed my eyes letting in the warmth of the evening sun, the sounds of the animals and water, the feel of the air on my body, and the smell of evening dew and the approaching nightfall. I leaned back and relaxed opening my eyes and watching Mia take us wherever she wanted to go. I had given her complete control and trusted her unconditionally. I could feel her happiness as she too felt everything this run had to offer. It was rejuvenating, to say the least after everything the last week had forged on my shoulders.

Mia started to surpass the others moving her way closer and closer to Titus who was in the lead. After about 15 minutes of running, she finally caught up to him. The two were running in tandem. It reminded me of the final leg of a marathon. Both pulled away and pushed themselves to run faster. It was clear they were racing each other for the lead trying to assert some dominance. I could feel Mia. She was enjoying the challenge Titus was giving her and equally challenging Titus right back. Occasionally, depending on how the woods were presented, Titus would take the lead, only to fall back and Mia takes the lead. I could see him when he got ahead of us and feel Mia's frustration as she surged forward faster, only to feel her delight as she overtook him time and time again.

Mia and Titus started to slow up. I could see the edge of the treelined homes a little further ahead. Mia informed me, we were turning around and heading back. Humans would be close. We didn't want them scared thinking a wolfpack had taken over the woods. It would only lead to chaos for them and take away their free reign in these woods. They both turned around and started to casually walk back side-by-side. I could tell they were talking back and forth but since we hadn't marked each other, I wasn't able to hear what they were saying. Jason would have been equally in the dark unless Titus was updating him.

"Where are the others?" I questioned Mia.

"They couldn't keep up and decided to turn around and go back. As Alpha's, Titus and I, are faster than the others," she replied.

I thought about what she said and how Jason's parents were Alpha's, when Mia spoke again "yes they are Alpha's too and they might have been able to catch up with us, but apparently, Allison told Titus she didn't feel like having a pissing contest tonight and was heading back to give Miss Flint the heads up we would be returning and help us prepare something to eat or warm up what was already prepared. This run and the shift are going to leave us famished, especially since we slept so long prior and didn't have much to eat. I feel it already."

She was so right. I wish she had never mentioned food. It is all I could think while we walked back ever so slowly back to the villa. A few nachos weren't going to cut it and now we expended all this energy running through the forest. Until she mentioned food, I was enjoying every second of our excursion.

"Calm down Mikayla, we will be home soon so you can eat." She laughed.

She heard a noise up ahead and to the left. A twig cracking. Her ears perked up and she looked in that direction. Titus also went on alert. Then two wolves walked out slowly from behind an enormous tree.

Mia was happy. She told me they were Ruby and Bruno, Jacqui's and Matt's wolves coming back to join us on our walk back. They could talk to Titus and Jason through mind-link and only Titus could talk to Mia and her to Titus. I will admit, it was irritating to me I could not hear the conversations I knew were happening around me. My list of pros and cons of accepting Jason and this new life was getting out of hand, but this would go into the pro column. Or would hearing everyone be a con? Maybe too early to tell, but a pro in this situation.

The four of us headed back to the villa. I have no idea what they continued to talk about. Mia stopped passing the messages along pretty much after telling me who the wolves were so I wouldn't be frightened. Running through the woods was so much more exhilarating than this slow-paced walk. I swear the hungrier I was getting, the slower they were moving. I wish I could command them to move faster. It was dark now as we approached the villa. The full moon was out shining brightly in a clear sky. It was easy to admire its beauty and the moonlight beams adding serenity to an already beautiful landscape. I am a werewolf. I have a wolf. The Moon Goddess matched me with an Alpha, a super strong sexy Alpha and he wanted me. All of me to be his and nobody else's to give me everything he could from this world. He had gotten mad at me yesterday for not letting him. What was my problem? Becoming a werewolf was the best gift Jason could have given me. I didn't know it at the time but would accept this change to my life whole-heartedly. I loved Mia. I loved this evening, except for the painful shifting, although it was less than I thought it would be. "Mia please don't tell Jason any of this through Titus. I want to thank him for giving me you and saving my life when we are alone later." I pleaded.

"My lips are sealed, Mikayla; and I love you too." She replied.

The others all darted in different directions around the side of the house. Allison came out with a blanket and throwing it over Mia and then I shifted back into me. How come it was so easy to switch to me? I barely felt a thing other than the cold breeze against my naked body. I needed more than a blanket to block the evening air.

"Thank you, Mrs. Bloodright." I spoke.

"Please call me Allison and you are very welcome. Run upstairs and put some clothes on then head to the dining room so we can finish dinner," she instructed.

"You don't have to tell me twice," I yelled as I dashed into the house and headed to the stairs. I could hear her giggling at my reaction.

It took no time at all for me to get to Jason's room. I had to use the bathroom first, but when I looked in the mirror and saw myself and then dropped the blanket and looked over myself some more, I realized I better have a shower. Being out in the woods was a dirty business and I certainly needed to freshen up before going to dinner.

By the time I got to the dining room, I was the last one again. Seriously, why am I so slow. I swear I was hurrying. Miss Flint started serving the plates before I even made it to my seat, and I noticed a glare coming from her. I remembered Jason telling me she loved to cook but hated when it got cold, and people didn't take the time to enjoy it. Well, she was going to know that I was going to enjoy every minute and every taste of this meal tonight.

Chapter 25: The Past Returns

Jason's POV

Never have I seen a human, werewolf or anything eat as much as Mikayla ate tonight. I better have the pack doctor check to ensure she doesn't have a tape worm. I am clueless as to where she put everything and with every bite she hummed and hawed like it was the best bite of food she ever tasted. She made me eat more well after I was full because she made it seem even better than it already was with Miss Flint's excellent culinary skills. Miss Flint was smiling as she kept replenishing the food. Everyone at the table except Mikayla had finished eating a good 30 minutes ago, our bellies practically protruding out of our bodies. When Mikayla polished off the final pieces of the last dish, she leaned back in her chair looking utterly satisfied. Then Miss Flint announced dessert would be served in five minutes as she ran back into the kitchen. This woman is a culinary mastermind. I have previously thought about renovating our old-fashioned home into a more open concept style primarily so I could watch her cook and see her skills at work. She had to have help or be bringing it in the back door or something. She was one woman, and every meal was delivered and tasted to perfection. It was getting on my nerves how perfect at it she was. It would be nice to be able to cook like that for myself but who has time to learn with everything else going on? Maybe one-day things will settle down and I will retire the pack to our kids and then Miss Flint can show me a thing or two.

Mikayla looked genuinely excited about dessert. She practically jumped out of her seat. She was so cute like a child waiting for Christmas morning. How she got so excited over dessert was comical. Jacqui must've noticed it too and was very blunt with Mikayla all the time.

"Mikayla, how much are you going to eat? You're making my stomach full watching you. Even people who are starving don't pack away as much as you did and now you are bouncing in your seat like a kid on Christmas morning waiting in anticipation for Miss Flint to come back," she said. I knew great minds thought alike, but could she read minds, seriously, I was thinking the same thing. The others kind of nodded in agreement around the table waiting anxiously for Mikayla's response.

"Jacqui, I thought you were my best friend. I don't work at a diner because I can't eat a good meal when I see one. Besides, I was asleep forever, and are you telling me after you shifted the first time and ran a marathon, you were not extremely hungry, or was it just so long ago in your old age, you cannot remember?" I smirked.

"Only making an observation Mikayla, maybe it is because you are shifting later in life or you were turned or you are a hybrid, but you slept longer than normal, you shifted way earlier than normal and now you are eating exponentially more than normal. Checking my best friend to make sure you are okay, especially after your first shift." She smiled back at Mikayla holding her hands up in surrender.

"Yes Mikayla, how are you feeling about your first shift and everything now?" my mom interjected before Mikayla could say anything.

"I am feeling fine, better than fine. I loved having Mia in control. It was a welcome feeling relaxing and letting her take the reins and enjoying everything the run and woods had to give me." She responded.

"Mikayla, when you were shifting your eyes glowed blue. What was that all about? Do you know?" my dad recalled. Right, I was wondering the same thing but completely forgot. Again, we all looked to Mikayla for some epiphany to make sense of it all.

"My body was in pain, and I saw a flashback of me when I was younger practicing a protection spell. I guess we practiced a lot of protection spells as young witches and warlocks in case the war started, the adults didn't want to leave us defenseless. I have forgotten most of them, but the memory was recalled when the pain started. It was excruciating and the protection spell was meant to ease a painful experience. It would make the person's brain unable to send pain notifications throughout the body even though the pain was happening. I started to use the spell and then Jason also touched me when he commanded you all to leave the room. Tingles went down my arm where he was holding me and sparks in the hand he was holding. Without being able to feel the pain, the tingles and sparks seemed amplified and then everything was over, and I had shifted. I stopped the protection spell since I wasn't feeling pain anymore." Mikayla explained.

My father leaned in interested, "can you only cast the spell on yourself, or can you cast it on others?"

"It can be cast on others. It is a simple spell if you know the words and have the power. I wasn't drained in the slightest after doing it, although, it could also explain another reason for me to be hungry after tonight's events." She responded.

"Dad, how about we let Mikayla accept things before we start scaring her away even more with requests? I see where this is going." I stopped him from going further.

Mikayla smiled and grabbed my hand in hers as Miss Flint walked through the door with dessert. As soon as the smell hit my nostrils, I knew it was one of my favorites: chocolate lava cake. The outside was a moist chocolate cake, and the inside was a goopy mess of chocolate that oozed out like lava from a volcano when you sliced your fork through it. My mouth started to water even though my stomach was begging me not to add another bite. Mikayla's hand slid out of mine as she grabbed her dessert spoon and proceeded to cut into the cake. When she leaned forward to place the cake in her mouth, she slowly placed her mouth over the spoon, and I could tell she was savoring every taste of the dessert. She let out a small moan of delight which immediately took me back to our first night together and instantly got me aroused. To my detriment, everyone else noticed since they all glanced at me. All I could do was shrug my shoulders and pretend it was natural. I needed to control this infatuation I had with her. Women in the past could turn me on, but not during random everyday things like Mikayla could. She was enjoying the cake completely oblivious to what she was doing to me and Titus. He was also circling horny in my head wishing he was the spoon. He certainly wasn't helping the situation with all his dirty thoughts.

Luckily the cakes were small. We all retired to the living room for about an hour where we pretty much lazed about watching the evening news waiting for our stomachs to recover from the onslaught of food we had eaten. My cell phone started to ring. I looked at the caller id. Picking up the call, I asked the caller to hold on a minute and excused myself to the office. It was across the foyer from the living room so not too far. I motioned for Matt to follow me as I walked by, and he was on my heels in an instant. I closed the door to the office and told Luke to go ahead. "Hey Jason, we have Elliott. He is in the dungeons chained up with silver chains laced with wolfsbane. We haven't questioned him yet as per your instructions. Do you want us to wait or start without you?" he said.

"Leave him in there until morning. We will be returning tomorrow. Matt and I will talk to him first. Bring him a bottle of water every two hours but no food. He needs to know we are not in a hurry, and we can draw this out for as long as we need." I replied.

"Gotcha Bossman," Luke responded. We said our goodbyes and ended the call.

Matt asked, "what are you going to tell Mikayla?"

"We aren't going to tell her anything. He has caused her enough pain and that chapter of her life is closed. This is now pack business." I said sternly.

Matt nodded his head and said, "it's your decision, whether good or bad." Shrugging his shoulders, he walked towards the door and over his shoulder mentioned he would update Jacqui we are heading back tomorrow morning.

I thought about what he said but I truly wanted to protect Mikayla from any more trauma. It would most likely come to torture to get Elliott to spill about his plans and why he was planning on kidnapping Mikayla. The pit of my stomach was telling me it had to do with Alpha Justin. I had no proof, but the events of the last few days were too coincidental for me not to think the two are associated. I left the office and headed to the living room to grab Mikayla.

I walked in, "We will be heading back to the pack house tomorrow morning after breakfast. Mom, Dad, are you staying at the villa or coming back to the packhouse with us?"

"We will stay here for a couple of days until the jetlag dissipates and then head over to the packhouse" answered Dad.

"Sounds good, Mikayla, are you ready to go to bed?" I questioned.

She yawned as she nodded yes and stood up to leave saying goodnight to everyone as she walked towards the stairs.

I followed her to our bedroom. It was clear she was exhausted. She quickly got ready for bed and scrambled under the covers. Once I was ready, I slid under the covers and to my astonishment, Mikayla turned towards me giving me a slight glance and making eye contact as she proceeded to put her head on my chest and pull my arm around her. She nuzzled into me and closed her eyes. I felt myself fade away into the night with a smile on my face.

When I woke up the next morning, Mikayla was cozy in my arms. I could tell she was already awake. I looked down at her and kissed her forehead. She looked back up at me and said "Good morning. I would say sleepy head, but pretty sure I have the world record on file as of lately" and she gave me the widest grin I've seen on her. I loved her. This moment could last forever, and I would be content to ignore everything else in our world. She got up abruptly saying something about needing to pee, but I wasn't completely awake yet, and off in my head, so I missed it completely.

She did her morning routine and came out of the bathroom to get dressed. I went into the bathroom to freshen up while she dressed, then came out and got dressed. The last two mornings, she had already gone downstairs or was asleep, so it wasn't a big deal for me coming out with my towel and dropping it to get dressed. However, today, she was sitting on the bed ready to go waiting patiently. I wasn't sure if this was good or bad, but she gasped when I dropped my towel and started to get dressed. I had to tease her, "it isn't anything you haven't seen before."

"I know but it was different. I didn't know you at all and your intentions then and it was dark, not daylight. Just hurry up, I want to talk to you" She laughed and turned away.

Instantly, I felt my heartbeat pick up and felt extremely anxious. What could she want to talk about? She must've picked up on my tension. "It is nothing bad. A quick chat before we go. You cannot get stressed out every time we need to have a conversation." She smirked. At least she was in a good mood this morning so it must be good.

After getting dressed, I went and sat next to her on the bed.

She looked at me intently and then said, "about turning me into a werewolf. I honestly wasn't sure how I felt about it. I was incredibly nervous about the shift and what it all means for my life moving forward. It also occurred to me, I needed, no wanted, to tell you I am grateful you saved my life and I think you made the right decision turning me instead of letting me die. Last night was magical and for the first time in a while, things felt right. Like I was where I was supposed to be. It is going to take time to get used to Mia being around reading all my thoughts and deciding which ones to share with Titus and you and her responding to my private thoughts, but she is already a part of me. A part I wish I had sooner. So, thank you, Jason. Please don't feel any guilt over your decision anymore."

Today was already shaping up to be a great day. I pulled her close for a hug and whispered in her ear, "you are amazing". I held her tightly for a good while, not wanting to let her go when I heard Matt's voice in the hallway yelling through the door. Are you two coming or not?

I released her from the hug. "There is one more thing Jason. I need to go back to my life for a bit so I can think. After we get back to the packhouse, I am going to pack up some of my clothes and head back to my place and the diner. I know it is a little dangerous, but I have my magic and Mia. If anything goes sideways or appears dangerous, I will get back to the packhouse immediately. Please don't fight me on this. I have already made up my mind. I will keep in touch with you every day if it is what it takes."

"Ok," I replied. She had a look of shock on her face. I honestly wanted to grab her by the arms and command her to forget what she had said and forbid her from leaving my side. However, I had Elliott to deal with and frankly, I didn't know how to entertain Mikayla and deal with him without her finding out, so having her go away for a bit was probably a good thing. I figured she would want to at some point, either reclaim her life or tie off loose ends before coming back to me. She doesn't know but I borrowed one of the apartments across the street and would have rotating security on her 24/7 for her protection.

"Wait, what? Did you say okay?" she remarked.

"Yes, okay," I confirmed.

"I wasn't expecting you to agree so quickly. I had a whole speech ready to debate."

"No need. Take some time on your own. I'll text you daily to keep you abreast of anything new and likewise for you.

Chapter 26: Misunderstanding

After arriving at the pack house, Mikayla went upstairs to pack up her things to leave after lunch. Matt and I went to the dungeons to start interrogating Elliott. Luke and Kirk were also present.

Elliott was chained to the wall with limited mobility. It had been less than 24 hours and he already looked completely disheveled. We walked into his cell. His head was already raised and his eyes on the door to see who was coming. Disappointment fell on his face when he saw the four of us enter.

"Where is Mikayla? I will only talk to her and no one else," he warned.

"You do not get to decide whom you do and do not talk to Elliott. You attempted to kidnap my mate and future Luna. We need answers. We don't particularly like torturing wolves for information. However, if put to the test, we will pass with flying colors" I explained calmly.

"Torture me and you will get nothing. Mikayla is the only one who can understand. Please can she be here? She can reveal everything" he said.

"You have put her through enough. She is unaware you are even here. I will not endanger her life again."

"I wasn't putting her in danger, at least not intentionally. All your questions will be answered if I can please see her. You can be here as well, but it must be Mikayla."

Matt mind-linked me, "this is strange, but I think you should ask Mikayla if she wants to talk to him. If she finds out you are hiding Elliott from her and torturing him, it could backfire on your mate bond. She is extremely strong-willed. She needs to accept you, Jason. For your benefit and the packs. We need our Luna on our side. The best way to accomplish her acceptance is to include her."

Luke chimed in his two cents, "I can go and get Mikayla if you want."

I guess everyone agreed she should be here. "If you say anything to upset her, anything at all, I will end you, answers or not," I threatened.

"I wouldn't think of it, but when she discovers the answers to your questions, she may be upset" he replied.

"I will be right back, watch him." I motioned to the others.

I entered our bedroom as Mikayla was closing her suitcase. "All packed," I asked.

"Yes, I am ready to go." She replied.

"Can I ask one favor of you before you leave? You may not like it and if you don't want to, it is okay. I will find another way." I asked.

"Depends on what you had in mind," she said coquettishly.

"Not what I currently had on my mind although I would like to explore the option later before you go." I walked over to her and gave her an embrace.

Then while holding her I looked down into her dark brown eyes, wishing I could hold her now and never let her go. Duty called though and as much as I was hesitant, the conversation had to happen. "My warriors, under my instructions, managed to capture Elliott last night. He is being held prisoner in our cells so we can find out why he tried to kidnap you and what game he has been playing. I have come from there. He is adamant he will only talk to you and all our questions will be answered. You don't have to go if you do not want". She cut me off mid-sentence responding, "let's go. I want to hear his answers, not that it will make any difference."

I kissed her forehead, then selfishly asked, "can we come back and talk more about the other topic afterward?"

She shook her head in amusement, the seriousness of the Elliott situation falling from her face, as she leaned up and kissed me on the lips. I reciprocated her kiss, grabbing her closer to me and kissing her passionately like it was the last kiss we would ever share, and she was my entire world. After a few minutes, we broke away from each other out of breath. She headed to the door, and I followed.

She walked straight to the dungeon. I asked her, "how did you know how to get to the dungeon?"

"After I woke up from the attack before we went to the villa, I took a picture using my phone of the site map in your office. Still shaken from the attack, I figured I should know how to get around the territory and know when I was getting close to the edge of it, so I studied it at the villa and memorized it."

We went down the steps to the cells and I pointed to the door at the end. "He is in that room. Are you sure you are up for this?" I asked anxiously.

"To be honest, I don't want to see him, but I need to know what the hell happened. It was two years of my life. I thought I could trust him, and he broke my trust in so many ways. It will help me move on. I hope."

We entered the room and he looked at Mikayla immediately. "You are a wolf?" he questioned.

"It's a long story, but it's your story bringing us here today." She replied. "Tell me, what do you want from me?"

I admired how straightforward she was making sure he kept on topic. Power was emanating from her as she glared at him waiting for him to spill everything.

He started, "First Mikayla, I am sorry for the role I played. I need you to know I am not a bad guy. An Alpha can command his pack members to do anything he wants whether against their will or not. When I found out you were a witch, I did some research. In my wallet is a spell that will allow you to investigate my mind and see the past. You will see the truth and gain all the answers you need. I cannot answer anything you ask."

It all was beginning to make sense. Why he had asked for Mikayla and why he said we can torture him all we want but he still would only give the answers to her. His Alpha must have put commands in place to stop him from revealing events and their reasons. It is a complete abuse of power to force pack members, but given the rumors, I wouldn't put it past Alpha Justin. I use my command occasionally, but I never like to have to use it and only when it was warranted like when I thought Mikayla might hurt those around her when she was shifting. Never for my direct benefit. My suspicions were more than likely on point. Elliott needed to confirm it though.

Elliott's things had been placed on a table on the opposite side of the room from him. They did see the paper with the spell but hadn't known what it was. Luke grabbed it handing it to Mikayla.

"How do we know this spell will do what he says, and it won't harm any of us?" I asked.

"Let me take a look at it," said Mikayla. She silently read over the words in her head. Then she started to mumble something at the words and the sheet of paper started to glow green. She then looked back to me and indicated she verified the spell would not cause harm but is unable to verify if it will do what it is intended until she tries it.

Hesitantly, I gave her the go-ahead and instructed Matt and Luke to be ready for anything.

Mikayla moved closer to Elliott. She placed her hands on either side of his head which had Titus upset saying it was more intimate and her hands should not be touching another man. I rolled my eyes at it, but it did also irk me. She recited the spell. Her eyes turned blue again with a magic hue glowing around them. She stared into Elliott's eyes, and he stared back into hers. It was almost like she could see right through him and was looking past his eyes and face. I called to her, but she didn't respond. Her breathing got more erratic, and her heartbeat picked up. Elliott started to sweat profusely, and his heart also began to race. I was starting to regret my decision to allow Mikayla to come down here and see him. It felt like my first mistake and letting her conduct this spell my second. What was I thinking? He tried to kidnap her. Titus was flipping out in my head, and I was losing it. I started to go to her to stop what was happening. I had to try; she clearly was in agony. I could see it on her face, in her breathing and her heartbeat. The only odd thing was Elliott appeared to be having the same emotions and reactions. Matt stepped in front of me.

"You need to trust she can do this. We must find out the truth. She is your mate, so if you need to leave the room and calm yourself, we understand, but you cannot stop her. You have no idea what will happen if you stop her in the middle of the spell. This is way out of our league." He warned.

I hated to admit it, but he was right. "I am not leaving, but I will give it a few more minutes," I stuttered out angrily.

Mikayla's POV

Placing my hands on each side of Elliott's head, I peered into his eyes. He reciprocated staring right at me which felt a bit awkward now. It never bothered me before. I wasn't sure if it was because of how things went between us, or the fact Jason was staring at us. I quickly started to recite the spell and as soon as I spoke the last words, it felt like my mind left my body and flew into his mind. He was concentrating on a memory, and I was pulled into it. He was talking to himself in the mirror, "Mikayla, if you are hearing this now, it means things have gone sideways for us. It never should have gone as far as it did, but I had no choice. Please forgive me for everything. What you are about to see may astonish you so brace yourself?"

Instantly, we flipped to another memory. He was with two other wolves. They were both muscular in build and tall. Elliott spoke to them. "Please Alpha choose someone else. I recently found my mate and want to be by her side. I cannot do what you are asking of me," he said.

"You are the one for the task. Your mate will understand," the larger one said. The door to the office opened and a woman was dragged in by two other wolves and let go on to the floor. It was the woman from the club in the bathroom. She was crying and had bruises which were healing quickly. The larger one motioned to the other wolf. "Grab her."

The other wolf grabbed her and helped to stand her up. The larger wolf walked over to her and ran his fingers down her face and then her arm. "Such a beautiful she-wolf. You will do as we ask of you for the sake of your pack. Your pack comes above all else. If you cannot put the pack above your lady, then we will put your lady below all the unmated men in the pack. She will be pillaged every night by a different wolf and will cater to all and any of their demands. I will command she obeys their every whim and desire. You will feel her torment through the mate bond every night. Don't worry, I will not kill her, she will be ours to play with until her natural death. Is that the life you want for your mate? Are you clear on what you must do and what will happen if you do not?" The man let her go and she ran to Elliott, her mate. He wrapped his arms around her and apologized to her.

"I will do as you have requested Alpha Justin. Please let my mate go and give us one more night together before I leave in the morning. I beg of you to grant me this one mercy," he pleaded.

Alpha Justin walked over to his desk acting like nothing had happened and replied, "take your woman home and enjoy each other. You will be in my office promptly at 8:00am or she will suffer. Do not defy me, Elliott."

The two of them left the office together. Her sobs could be heard down the hallway.

****

Another flash and we were in another memory back in the office. It was light outside so I assume it was the next morning.

"I command you Elliott to fall in love with Mikayla. You will imagine she is your mate and pursue her until she falls for you. You will watch her and report back to me

190

daily," he started. He continued placing command after command into Elliott's head of what he could and could not do and what he could and could not say. What to do if Mikayla ever found out the truth or something happened to deter him from his plan? The commands went on for about 20 minutes as he read them out of a journal he was holding. The very last commands were around his capture. He could not reveal anything to his captors and as soon as he was able, he would commit suicide.

****

Next, we were in his work office. I hadn't been there often but occasionally to meet him for lunch. His mate was there crying again. "Why are you marrying her? I am your mate. The Alpha has gone too far. Why can't we run away together and leave this life behind. Are you going to have children with her too? What about me?" she sobbed.

"You know I don't like any of this. Lisa, you are my one and only. Mikayla is a nice girl, but she doesn't mean to me what you do. You are my mate and what my wolf and I crave. If I defy Alpha Justin, he will have you raped every night. He has promised me this will not go on forever. The time will come when we can be together peacefully, but the pack needs me to keep tabs on her every move and no better way than as her significant other. It is you I love with my whole heart," he responded as he pulled her in close for a kiss.

****

Alpha Justin yelling, "what do you mean you ruined everything, and Mikayla has left you? I command you to tell me what happened."

"She was supposed to be out with her friends, so I went out with Lisa. It was to a posh club which was difficult to get into without connections. I never thought I would run into her there. She caught us in the act and ran off. I tried my best to run after her and talk to her afterwards, but she refused my advances. The best I was able to get was her to agree for me to pick up my belongings tomorrow from her apartment." Elliott explained.

"Idiot. I should have Lisa punished for your stupidity and ruining my plans. It took years to get you placed," complained Alpha Justin. He started throwing things around his office. The other wolf who was with him previous shook his head. I am guessing he was his Beta since he was there each time Elliott was in the office, but I wasn't sure. He continued, "all is not lost yet. When you go to her apartment tomorrow, you will tell her you want to take her out one last time and explain everything to her. Tell her she shouldn't throw away two years for one discretionary act and you are sorry. If she agrees, you will take her here to our pack house and we will deal with her from there. If she disagrees, then you will give her this injection. It will knock her out so you can bring her here unconscious. Either way, she needs to be here. Do not fail me again."

****

"Alpha Justin, I couldn't get Mikayla. Alpha Jason and Beta Matt came rushing into the room. It was all I could do to escape and keep them from getting me. I followed them as far as I could. They took Mikayla to their territory." Elliott recalled events for him.

"Elliott, you have disappointed me time and time again. Go home, we will discuss your punishment tomorrow," Alpha Justin indicated.

Elliott walked home slowly and when he got to his home, the door was open. He ran inside and the whole place was turned upside-down and everything inside was destroyed. Furniture was thrown around and wrecked. He ran around frantically calling out for Lisa when a man came from the back of the house. "They took her," he whispered. His face had bruises and cuts on it which were healing. He looked defeated.

"Who took her," Elliott asked.

"The enforcers came and destroyed the house looking for Lisa. We had gone on a run, and they were waiting inside when we returned. I tried to fight them off, but they took her. What the hell happened Elliott," the man questioned.

"I lost Mikayla. Everything fell apart and Alpha Justin is angry. Where did they take her? We must get her back." Elliott cried out and fell to the ground.

"What's wrong Elliott?" the man asked running to his side.

"Dad, they are hurting her. I can feel her fright and then pain through our bond. Alpha Justin said he would have her raped repeatedly if I didn't agree to help him with Mikayla. What am I going to do? I cannot do nothing." He angrily yelled.

"He won't kill her. You are going to have to be strong for her. Try to mind-link her and connect with her and find out where she is right now. Where did they take her?" he instructed.

"She won't tell me. She said they will kill me if I come, and she cannot live without me." He shifted into his wolf and ran trying to follow her scent as he sniffed all around.

****

Elliott was holding Lisa in his arms. She was gone. He cried out to her. "Lisa, my Lisa. You did not deserve this life and me as your mate. I am so sorry. I failed you. I am so sorry. Alpha Justin is going to pay for this and then I will join you in the afterlife my sweet Lisa," he promised.

****

I awakened from my trance with tears in my eyes. Elliott also had tears in his eyes. I couldn't stop sobbing at the lifeless body he held in his arms crying out for her. It was horrible. Alpha Justin did unspeakable things to get me, but none of the memories indicated why.

Jason ran to me, and I fell into his arms. His warmth making me feel better he was there to comfort me but worse knowing this was gone for Elliott and it all had to do with me. If I never caught them in the bathroom, Lisa would still be alive. If Matt and Jason hadn't come to my rescue when Elliott drugged me, she would still be alive. I felt a bit guilty even though deep down, I knew it was all Alpha Justin's fault.

Jason asked, "are you okay Mikayla? What happened?"

I thought for a minute and then told Jason, "Elliott has to join our pack."

Both Jason and Elliott yelled in unison, "what?"

"It is the only way he will be able to talk to us. I have more questions and we need more information from you Elliott. You want to avenge Lisa against Alpha Justin, then you need to get out from under him and help Alpha Jason. If you sever your ties to Justin, then his commands will no longer work, right?" I asked. "Jason, he has been commanded to keep things from us and it is a very detailed, well thought out, long command. If we don't do this, then the first chance Elliott gets, he will be forced to commit suicide."

"No wonder he asked us to restrain him completely," Luke recalled.

"An Alpha's commands can transcend packs though, so rejecting his pack and joining ours will not remove the commands," Jason explained.

"But if you command him to ignore all of Justin's commands, it might work. His Alpha's commands should negate those of another if contradictory, in theory. I don't know if it has ever been tested," Matt shrugged.

"How do we know this wasn't part of Alpha Justin's plan and Elliott isn't leading us astray?" Jason asked.

"They had his mate ravaged and beaten to the point she couldn't live with herself and look at Elliott so she ended her own life so it wouldn't continue further. I saw his memory of him holding her body in his arms and his vow to seek vengeance. Despite being commanded to form a relationship with me, he was always kind to me. I believe everything he has shown me. We can tell you in detail once he is a part of our pack and you cancel the commands from Alpha Justin. You don't have to trust him but trust me." I asked.

Jason looked to me, then Elliott, and the other three in the room, Matt, Luke, and Kirk. Then he turned to Elliott and asked him, "do you agree with Mikayla's proposition? Is it what you want?"

Elliott spoke, "you would even consider it, makes you a better Alpha than Justin. He is a tyrant and many of us are forced to do unspeakable things. I will reject him if you agree to accept me. I will do everything I can to aid you in this war against him so I can see him fall. After he falls,

195

I would like you to release me from the pack. I will remain as a rogue and leave this life behind me."

"Before you agree to this, you need to know I still don't trust you. I will accept you into the pack and attempt to negate the other commands with my own commands. You will have to be monitored at all times. We will give you a room in the pack house for now, but it will be a room we control the locks. You will be permitted to walk freely with a guard around the territory during hours dictated by me for the time-being, until you have earned my trust. I will not waiver on this condition. I must protect my pack and ensure you are faithful to us moving forward." Jason waited for Elliott's response.

"Having a guard and remaining under lock and key is far better than what I was living under Alpha Justin. I promise to do everything in my power to help you take him down. I will gain your trust. Thank you, Alpha Jason, for giving me a chance. I am fully aware; I do not deserve it. I will do what I can to make up for my indiscretions towards Mikayla, however, long it may take." Elliott promised.

Jason looked at the others and they all nodded in agreement. He looked back at Elliott, "Reject your former Alpha and pack first. Then I will ask you to accept me and our pack. Once it is done, I will command you to disregard any commands previously given to you by any other Alpha. Lastly, we will remove your restraints and see if it worked." He looked over to Luke who pulled a knife out of a sheath hidden in his shirt and placed it on the table.

Elliott completed the rejection. Then, Jason and Elliott completed the acceptance. Jason then revoked the other commands. Matt and Luke proceeded to release Elliott from his chains. Elliott shook his arms out and then proceeded to say, "Alpha Justin was behind everything. For the record, seeing if I could tell you, it was Alpha Justin is a much better test than seeing if I commit suicide." He shook his head in disapproval, but with a smirk.

I couldn't help myself. I had to laugh out loud. They all looked at me. I raised my hand apologizing but couldn't stop myself from laughing. Then, Jason started to laugh as well, "I guess it was a better way." Instantly, the tension was gone. We all left the dungeons, heading to the dining hall to eat. Luke escorted Elliott to a room where he was going to be staying and could freshen up.

Chapter 27: Let Her Go

Jason's POV

Once we all grabbed our servings of food from the buffet in the dining hall, we went into a private room so we could eat and talk, where the rest of the pack would not be able to hear Elliott's account of events. Elliott described in detail everything from Alpha Justin forcing him to pursue Mikayla to the untimely death of his mate, Lisa, taking her own life. As he told his story, I had to feel bad for the guy. I couldn't even imagine being forced to be with someone other than Mikayla now that I found her and then having her raped by my pack members at the orders of the Alpha. Occasionally, I glanced at Mikayla for her to confirm she had seen the memories he was describing. It did make sense he wanted revenge. I don't know if he would ever recover from the trauma he had been dealt.

After he told his story, he asked how Mikayla became a wolf. We told him about the attack, her almost dying and turning her. He was visibly guilty and angry at the same time. His expression changed into concern. He looked at Mikayla like none of us were there, which frankly made me angry, and said "I am so sorry Mikayla. It is my fault Alpha Justin knew you were here. You could have died because of me. I already killed my mate. I could not go on if I lost you too." I felt Titus perk up. He was trying to take over wanting to assert his dominance over Elliott and tell him to back off his mate when Mikayla replied to him.

"Elliott, it was not your fault what happened. All the blame is on Alpha Justin. For the record, yes, I was devastated when I saw you in the club. However, one thing led to another. Jason coming into my life took all the pain I felt away and now I have Mia, my wolf, by my side as well. I have found my magic and have started remembering things I had forgotten. What happened had to happen so I could get to this point in my life. I am still confused at why Alpha Justin was using you to keep tabs on me though," she confessed.

"Mikayla, I didn't want any harm to come to you. You must believe me. You may not have been my true mate but spending as much time together as we did and being who you are, of course, I would develop some feelings for you. I would always choose my mate over you, don't get me wrong, but I wanted you to be safe too. I regret I couldn't be there for Lisa or you in the end. I hope to prove myself in the future. Thank you for giving me this chance," he continued. "Alpha Justin knew you had magical influence. How he knew, I do not know, but I know he knew this. He wanted me to watch for your magic to activate. He said it was dormant and that one day it would come back. He had hoped to use your magic to aid him in his quest for power. When he found out you were Jason's mate, he wanted you dead. He knew the magic would help Jason instead of himself. He didn't want Jason to gain any more power than he already had against him. He is determined to take over this pack so he can officially be the Alpha of the strongest pack. Alpha of a pack isn't enough for him. He is power-hungry and wants to reign over everyone. He is starting with the wolf packs, but I guarantee he is thinking bigger. In his office, he has a list of all the wolf packs. When he takes over one, he crosses the packs name off the list, like he is wiping it from existence. Those who fight him, he has killed. The remaining are accepted into the pack and must do his bidding or face the consequences. I wasn't in his pack from the beginning. He took over my pack about 5 years ago. He assigns each wolf a position within the pack from the warriors down to the cooks. Wherever you are told to

199

go, it is where you stay until he says otherwise, or you die. It doesn't matter if you like it or not or want to be somewhere else. I always wanted to train to be stronger, but he refused. He said he needed me to remain soft and businesslike for the pack. He sent me to work every day at his office downtown, but I did nothing while I was there. I was a figurehead, sitting in the office, bored day in and day out. Lisa and Mikayla are the only things I looked forward to in my pathetic life. Lisa and I wanted to figure out how to get away, but he always had her guarded. She couldn't go anywhere without her guard, and he was very loyal to Alpha Justin and his cause. Jason, you need to know, he rules by placing his Alpha command on those who are disobedient. A lot of us want out and want nothing to do with him or his war, but he makes it impossible for us to leave. The security around the pack territory is just as much to keep people in as it is to keep them out. Whenever someone escapes, he tortures and sometimes kills the guard who was supposed to be the closest to the escape location."

Mikayla placed her hand on my leg and squeezed ever so slightly to get my attention. I guess it was obvious Titus and I were having a battle of control. I turned to her, and she said, "Jason, you can talk to Elliott more later or tomorrow. I want to get going back to my apartment. Can you arrange for someone to take me if you want to finish talking to Elliott?"

Elliott interjected, "you cannot go back to your apartment. He will have people there on the off chance you return. He wants you dead Mikayla. It isn't safe."

"There are things I need to take care of back at the apartment and in my life. I cannot uproot everything because of a threat. He tried to kill me once and I survived.

I am more powerful now with Mia and my magic. It isn't up for debate. Jason?" Mikayla asked.

I could completely understand Elliott's hesitance. I was feeling it too. Mikayla was so frigging stubborn when it came to her old life versus her new life. I could sense she was coming around to the notion of this was meant to be her life and that she belonged here with me and the pack, but something was still holding her back from letting go of her old life. I had to let her go. She would come back, right? The whole if you love something let go and it will come back to you. I wanted to lock her up and throw away the key but what good would that do me?

My eyes glazed over as I mind-linked two of my warriors. "Let me help you grab your things, and a ride will be waiting outside in ten minutes to take you back. I am going to talk with Elliott more about Alpha Justin. I will text you later to check up on you. Please keep in touch with me or I will send an army to bring you back," I threatened.

"I promise to check in with you regularly Jason to confirm I am all right," she agreed.

We went up to grab her bags from the bedroom. I faced her, putting her hands in mine. "Are you sure about this? Even Elliott is worried about you going there. Alpha Justin might be waiting for you." I asked.

She gazed into my eyes and much to my surprise she leaned in and up to kiss me. Sparks shocked me into acceptance as my entire body tingled with warmth. Our eyes closed as my tongue pushed past her soft lips and tasted her, playing with her tongue as we wrestled for dominance. Then to my surprise, she bit my bottom lip and sucked on it hard. It aroused me and distracted me, so she won our battle of tongues. A smile graced my face and she slowly pulled away from me. "It will be okay. I must go back. Thank you for understanding and agreeing," she said. She stepped away from me grabbed her small bag and headed out the door. I grabbed the larger bag and followed her out to the front of the packhouse.

"Mikayla, this is Chris and Scott. They are twins. Sean was their older brother. They will escort you to your apartment and look around your apartment and area before heading back to the territory. Not only are they at the top of the warrior class but they also have exemplary tracker training giving them the bonus of being strong and aware. Chris, Scott, this is Mikayla." I introduced.

"It is a pleasure to meet you both. I hope I am not taking you away from too much driving me back to the city. Thank you for your time," she said holding out her hand to shake and greet them.

They looked at each other a little shocked. She was their future Luna, should they be shaking hands with her. Reluctantly, Scott reached out his hand first and responded, "it is all our pleasure to have been bestowed the task of protecting our Luna. Nothing we could be doing would be more important."

"I didn't know Sean for long, just a few hours really before the attack. He was quite impressive in those few hours. I regret not getting more time with him. I am sorry for your loss and that it was at my expense. Please accept my condolences," she said.

"Sean was over the moon excited to be your escort that day. You made all his dreams come true. Protecting the Luna is a great honor. He worked hard to get to where he was. We would have expected nothing less from our big brother than to throw down for his Luna. He was bragging all day to us. We were incredibly jealous. We miss him, but he died doing what he felt he was born to do," said Chris. Scott nodded in agreement.

Mikayla practically lunged forward and wrapped her arms around them both. Their heads went into her shoulder, and they both looked over at me not knowing what to do. I shrugged at them both equally surprised. After an awkward minute, she released them, hopped in the back seat, then glanced in my direction waving goodbye. They grabbed her bags and slid them into the back of the SUV, then told me she was in good hands as they got into the driver and passenger seats. I watched as the SUV pulled out and slowly drove out of view.

Mind-linking was easy with those in proximity, but it got more difficult the further away a person was from the territory or me. Being the Alpha, I could mind-link further than anyone, but Mikayla's apartment was too far away. I pulled my cell out of my pocket and dialed. "They are on their way. Are you ready?" I asked.

"We have the surveillance in place. The three of us will take shifts watching from across the street. The couple whose apartment we took over was excited you offered them a free stay in your hotel downtown with room service and spa treatments. We told them it should be about a week but might be longer and we would be in touch," he spoke.

"Why did you tell them we needed the apartment?" I asked.

"We told them we were filming at the diner across the street and needed an angle for the cameras from this building. If they didn't want to accept our offer, we would move to another apartment in the building. They immediately accepted and packed up their things. We drove them to the hotel yesterday and checked out the area around the diner and apartment today. Nothing out of the ordinary. We also went into the diner to eat a couple of meals already in case anyone else was watching," he confirmed.

"Excellent, if anything remotely out of the ordinary happens or you feel anything no matter how small might be off, I want you to contact me or Matt right away without hesitation regardless of the hour," I instructed before ending the call.

Since I had my cell out anyways, I sent Mikayla a text saying I missed her already. Her response came back quickly which excited me. However, it merely indicated she wasn't even out of the territory yet and I needed to get a life. She added three emojis: shrugging, shaking my head, and laughing. I chuckled at her response as I walked back into the packhouse knowing she was going to be back.

Elliott was locked in his room until dinner. He said he needed some rest since he didn't get much being hungry and tied up in the dungeon. It made sense and turns out he is not such a bad guy. I was still going to be on alert near him but given Mikayla could collaborate with most of his story by seeing his memories, it seemed he was done more wrong by Alpha Justin than any of us. His recount was testimony to the lengths Alpha Justin would go to; there was no end to his tyranny. I didn't want a war. If Alpha Justin decided to bring it, then we would not remain on the defensive for long and we would take an offensive position. If he challenged me, I had no choice but to take him down.

Mikayla's POV

My apartment did not come as close to nice as the packhouse, but it was my home. The ride seemed to last forever. I swear everyone purposely got into accidents to disrupt traffic to delay my arrival. Why did it seem the world was against me sometimes? Maybe it was a sign I should have stayed with Jason at the packhouse. The drive should have been one hour, but it ended up being two. When we finally arrived, I offered them some food at the diner, my treat, but they declined to indicate they wanted to get back and it had taken more time already. I must admit, it surprised me Jason didn't force me to have a permanent bodyguard following me around the entire time I was away from the packhouse. My spidey senses made me think something was amiss and he was watching me in other ways. What a stalker! I giggled as I walked up the stairs to my apartment. Before realizing Elliott wasn't a bad guy, after all, Jason had the locks changed in case he had another key made since he had his key for a while. I opened my apartment door and to my astonishment, everything was orderly. The very last book was put into place on the shelf. I remember having a book out before Jacqui had arrived and Jacqui had told me about the scuffle she and Elliott had in the apartment, but how was it so tidy? I dropped my bags down at the entrance and proceeded to look closely around the apartment. Jacqui had slipped a nanny cam in there before to watch me and Elliott from the bedroom, which in hindsight turned out to be a great idea or who knows where I would be right now, but it was also very intrusive, and I wasn't about to let another one stay there. I searched everything on the shelves. Turning up empty, I again laughed at myself for how paranoid I was now with everything that occurred.

I decided I needed to relax. I ran a bath and before I could get in and soak my anxiety and stress away, there was a knock at the door. I went over and peeped through to see Pop standing there trying to look through the peephole. Why do people do that anyways, you can't see anything from the outside. I opened the door and he looked mad, then he took a step forward and wrapped his burly arms around me. "Where have you been Mikayla? I have been worried sick about you wondering if I should call the police or the hospital to find you. I hugged him back and when I let go, he continued holding on. I started to feel awkward and felt I needed to apologize. "I am sorry. I had a medical emergency and was in a coma for a few days. They were able to fix me up good as new though and I am fine now. I came back as soon as I was able. Jacqui told me she let you know I was okay" I responded.

"She did but then your apartment was broken into, and some strange men came and changed the lock and were up here. I came to see if you were here when I heard steps from downstairs, and they said you were not there and you would be in touch. What is going on Mikayla? Are you in some sort of trouble?" he asked concerned.

"Pop, it is the opposite. I did have a medical issue which is now resolved, but I am in good hands. I came back to see you and apologize for missing shifts so abruptly. It must've left you scrambling. Can I make it up to you?" I questioned.

"Mikayla, you are the daughter I wish I had. You have always helped me, have a good head on your shoulders, and are genuinely a nice person. I always thought you would take over the diner from me one day with all the effort you have put into making the customers happy and the buzz you helped me create for it," he indicated.

"Pop, you know I was going to school and when I finished, I would be moving on to my next adventure. I would always come to visit you though. You have done so much for me. I was simply trying to pay you back as much as I could, but it will never be enough. You have given me a job, a place to call home, and a family," I said trying to hold back my tears of happiness for this man who was like a father to me over the last two years.

"You are going to leave, aren't you?"

"I have a choice to make between what I have grown to know and love and a new life I never imagined for myself but seems to be drawing me into it. I honestly have not decided yet."

"Mikayla, sweetheart, you were always meant for a better life than this one. I knew it was inevitable from the first day I met you. You seemed so sure you were happy in this life. You are so much more. I hope you can see it now. It appears you have grown in the last few days you have been away. Don't hold on to this life because it is what you know, and you are afraid of another life. Search your heart and decide which life belongs to you. It should be an easy decision for you. I think you have already made the decision. Please keep in touch with an old man. I'm getting grumpier by the day and only you put up with me now," he smirked.

"Thank you, Pop. You know I love you right?"

"What's not to love? Now, forget all this heartwarming stuff. My old heart cannot take it. Are you going to come downstairs and bail me out of a jam one last time? Kate has called in sick again."

"Somethings never change. I will wash up quickly and be down in ten," I promised.

Pop retreated down the stairs with a smile on his face and a jump in his step. The old man was truly amazing. Any girl would have been lucky to have him as a father. She would have had him wrapped around her fingers though. I laughed at the thought as I closed the door and went to the bathroom to freshen up. A few minutes later I was downstairs waiting tables again, probably for the last time.

Chapter 28: A Surprise Visit

Jason's POV

It had been four days since Mikayla left for her apartment. I had lots to keep my focus on the first few days, but I was getting antsy with her being so far away for such a long time. Elliott was now free to travel the pack grounds with a guard. It was clear he wanted vengeance. He had been plotting for two years how he could take down Alpha Justin in case his situation went sideways, which it did. He got as much information on income and funding ventures helping Alpha Justin financially while he wasn't working at the office. He was able to provide ten different businesses and their locations. He helped draw a map of the main territory around the pack house. He couldn't give much information on security and training since he was deliberately kept at bay. Apparently in his old pack, before Alpha Justin took it over, he was training to be one of the elite warriors like his father and grandfather before him. However, Alpha Justin wanted to exert his dominance, so he made him a carpenter working on all the buildings in the pack territory until his assignment to Mikayla. Mikayla was the fun part of it. He had to go to the office every day pretending to be the CEO, but Alpha Justin didn't give him any information or let him do anything in the business. He would go into the office and stay there all day like he was busy but was bored out of his mind. This is what gave him time to research and plan against him.

He asked me yesterday if he could join our warriors in training. He said he spent time in the office exercising mostly and learning how to fight on you-tube and google. A war was coming. It was inevitable. Elliott wanted to be on the frontline in the action fighting against Alpha Justin and his followers. Most of his pack was gone. However, those remaining wanted nothing more than to escape his clutches. They were unhappy with their lives. His pack wasn't the only one either. Alpha Justin had conquered five different packs in the last six years. One of the packs was allies and was taken completely off-guard and never forgave him for backstabbing their Alpha. Three of the others mostly were upset at his takeover and their inability to choose their careers and the strict rules imposed on them. The last pack was grateful to him. Their Alpha was a weak leader and left them with little. The pack was barely surviving on their own and he didn't want to lead them. He was looking for an Alpha to take over his pack. Those members were the most loyal to Alpha Justin other than those from his original pack. He made enemies of a few here and there, but in most cases, he would have anyone who went against him killed to ensure no one would revolt. He would make examples out of anyone he caught going against him in grueling torture in front of everyone in a courtyard. He would take days to kill a wolf he claimed was selfish and not putting the pack's needs first. He practically thanked me for having him kidnapped and said I saved his life. It was such a twist I wasn't expecting.

Elliott was being sincere or at least it felt like it. I was still having trust issues, so I told him I needed to think about the warrior training. Matt told me to let him go. Jacqui having hung out with Mikayla and Elliott a lot was all about forgiving the guy and letting him atone for his sins. The two of them had been hanging out with Elliott a lot and mostly gathering information from him and providing it in a report.

Matt, Kirk, Luke, and I spent many hours with my top warriors, planning our defense. How were we going to protect the women and children? Each one of them was getting special training on defense. In case our pack was penetrated, I was hoping everyone could have a fighting chance if having to fend for themselves. I didn't want it to come to a child fighting for their life, but given what I heard of Alpha Justin, it seemed no pack member would be off-limits to his hostile takeover. We had security personnel running around the clock, and drones watching for any movement near our border or just across in the territory between our packs. In addition to the rounds, all our pack members were running on a 24/7 basis around the edge of our territory. We came up with a warning PA system with different sounds which would warn people to gather arms or retreat to areas so we could activate traps we had set up or protect ourselves from a weapons or poison attack. We had ordered more weapons which were to be delivered in the coming days. Food stores were being created with canned goods and other non-perishable items. Our territory came with loads of self-maintained crops in fields and greenhouses. They would be a target for sure during a war to cut off our food supply. At least, it would be one of the first places I would attack if I were him, but I wasn't. He was much more ruthless, so I had to think like him. Since the attack on Mikayla, things were quiet. It had me a bit unnerved and I wanted her here by my side so I could watch over her. Several pack members had been traveling and were living outside the pack. They had been recalled so we could increase our counts and so if war started, they would be here. Every member of my pack was loyal to our pack. I prided myself on catering to the needs of the people. I wanted them to be happy and therefore me happy. We had trained hard and made ourselves financially self-sufficient over the years. Planning and coordination took a while. Trucks of different supplies were arriving daily. We even had cement brought in and a secondary bunker was being built. The pack house was being upgraded into a fortress according to Luke's words. Fortified doors and window covers were installed. I have no idea what else he and Kirk were up to, but they were spending a lot of money. The purchase requests coming across my desk were insane, but they assured me, it was all necessary and to trust them. Luke sure was in his element. I may have been trained to be the Alpha, but my younger brother was trained to protect the pack using all means necessary. He loved his training and excelled in military tactics. He and Kirk graduated at the top of their class and have continued training at the top institutions, as well as traveling to other packs and bringing back their knowledge and training. Nick was also a trusted trainer and had his own set of fighting skills. After all the hard work the last few days and things starting to fall into place, I felt we were ready for an attack and would be victorious. I couldn't underestimate Alpha Justin though. He managed to take over five packs, so he was intelligent and knew what he was doing.

I was lost in thought when Matt entered my office. "Jason, when are you going to get Mikayla back here? Jacqui keeps asking me a hundred times a day. I had to forbid her from asking me more than once every hour. I am going to tell her to start pestering you instead of me soon," he complained while sitting on the sofa.

"Don't make Jacqui my problem, man. I already have my own strong-willed woman to handle. You are on your own. You can tell Jacqui I will be heading out in about two hours for a surprise visit to Mikayla's apartment."

"Finally. What took you so long?"

"You know the answer to that question. Why are you pestering me?"

"Mikayla always puts you in your place. She says what is on her mind and isn't afraid to say what we are all thinking."

"You're an idiot."

"An idiot you keep by your side to be your wingman and plan your every move. Sounds contradictory to me."

"Are you trying to give me a headache? Keep this up and I won't go for another day, so Jacqui continues to drive you nuts."

"Jacqui wants us to go with you for backup."

"I am not going to force Mikayla to come back. I feel confident she will come with me of her own free will. I want some alone time with her anyways. If all goes well, we will head back tomorrow."

"Tomorrow, oh you dirty dog. You going to blame Titus again."

"It was Titus' fault last time. Why do I tell you anything? Was there something else you needed? I answered your question I will be leaving soon enough."

"You sure you want to go solo? We got your back."

"I appreciate it, but I will be fine. I will text you when we are on our way back tomorrow. I need to finish signing this paperwork so I can head out. Is there anything else you needed?"

"Nope, get it done. If you are still here in two hours, I will come back and kick you out."

"You would kick me out of my own pack house."

"In a heartbeat."

Mikayla's POV

I had the music blaring, well as loud as I could with the diner open downstairs, dancing around the apartment and organizing things. It was midday, but I was still wearing my pajamas, a cotton tank top, and shorts. My hair was tied up on top of my head and a bandana covered my forehead as I worked up a sweat in the summer heat while sorting through some books. The windows were open in the kitchen and living room providing a soft, warm breeze. My phone pinged. I reached over in anticipation. Looking at the message, I felt a little disappointed it was Jacqui and not Jason. It had been four days and honestly, I was so sure Jason would turn up at my doorstep after day one ready to take me back to the packhouse. He sent me a couple of texts a day to see if I was okay. They were all surprisingly short and said a hello greeting, then asked if I was doing all right, and then a goodbye greeting. I am starting to doubt this whole mate bond thing, except Mia is jumping around in my head asking when we are going to go back to Jason several times a day and night.

"I wouldn't have to keep asking you if you would make the decision and go. You know you are ready to accept this new life with Jason. Why are you delaying everything?" Mia complained.

"You are worse of a nag than Jason pestering me to change my life. Listen to the music. If you cannot stop listening in on my thoughts, at least stop responding to them," I demanded as I continued sorting.

"What are these books anyways, Mikayla," Mia asked.

"These are the books I mentioned at the Villa, my parents left for me. They were held in trust at a law company and when I turned 18, a lawyer came to my door informing me who he was. He said he was there on behalf of my parents who set this up 8 years prior and showed me the two boxes on my doorstep. I had to sign for them, and he left. I never saw him again. I took the boxes inside and read the letter from my parents and it had these books. They are books of spells. I read them all over when I first received them and sometimes, I looked at them afterward. Nothing happened so I didn't believe any of it until now. Can you feel the magic like I can?"

"I feel the magic and I can feel your power. You are so strong, Mikayla. We are strong together and you and Jason will be stronger together, along with Titus."

I responded to Jacqui's text. She also kept asking when I was coming back. I guess everyone except for me knew I would be back. It wasn't a matter of if, but when. It was aggravating me into wanting to stay away longer to prove them wrong.

"Why would you not want to be happy to prove others wrong? We are all thinking it because it is meant to be and frankly, you should have decided a long time ago. You have had plenty of opportunities. Stop being defiant. You are only hurting us, all of us."

As her lecture finished, the phone rang. It was Jason. My heart fluttered and Mia started doing somersaults in my head.

"Mia, calm down. I can't concentrate when you are doing flips in my head."

I answered the phone, "hi, Jason. How are you?" For some reason, I was ecstatic he had called. Up until this point, he had only texted me. I was feeling almost giddy. What was wrong with me? I thought I was past this whole schoolgirl crush and oh he called me finally feeling. How does he make me feel this way?

"I am depressed. How are you?" he stated. My excitement shrank with his words. He sounded so pathetic and sad like something had happened.

"Why are you depressed? Is everything okay? Did something happen?" I asked starting to feel nervous that someone might have gotten hurt or worse.

There was a knock at the door at that moment. I was feeling angry someone was bugging me right now. I needed to know what had Jason down. I wanted to make him happy and soothe whatever was bothering him. I ignored the door and waited for Jason's response.

"I brought an early dinner for my mate, but she isn't opening the door to let me in," he responded.

I looked towards the door, then asked, "Mia, are you doing back flips in my head because you know Jason and Titus are nearby."

"Maybe," she responded.

"Whose side are you on anyways, Mia," I asked while walking to the door with my phone in my hand. Before opening it, I answered Jason on the phone, "my overbearing mate told me not to open the door unless I knew who was there and for what reason."

"Your mate sounds like a smart guy, you should start listening to him more often," he retorted.

I rolled my eyes and opened the door, "maybe he should ask nicely instead of telling me."

Jason's POV (sexual content)

Her words stung a little. Although she had a point. I never really asked her to be with me and choose me. It was always, we are mated, and it is fate. Did I ever ask her? I wasn't sure. I must've at some point. I am a jerk. The thought made me smile.

"You are smiling, so I guess the depression has passed," she said.

I took her in with her skimpy tank top and shorts. It was clear she wasn't wearing a bra and instantly I thought about grabbing her into an engaging kiss and carrying her off to the bedroom. It got me aroused and I saw her facial expression change as it was obvious, she noticed. "May I come in?"

She stepped aside holding the door. "Well, I guess the dinner and you are a package deal, so you both can come in."

"Very funny. Wait until you see what I brought for dessert," I said while winking at her.

She closed the door behind me. I walked into the living room. There were things everywhere around her apartment. It was a disaster. She ran to remove some items from the two-person dining set she had set up against the wall in the living room. I set the food down in the empty spot and then looked around her apartment again. "Did you get attacked again?" I joked.

She folded her hands over her chest and answered, "it is sort of like spring cleaning, but it is, I am leaving my old life behind, for a new life in a packhouse, as a werewolf with a mate, attempt at organizing, while leaving my wolf clueless because she has a habit of spilling the beans before I get to say anything."

"My wolf does the same thing to me. For clarification," I stepped closer to her closing the gap between us, then grabbed her folded arms, "Mikayla, will you be mine and come home to the packhouse with me?"

"Thank you for asking," she unfolded her arms and took a step closer looking me dead in the eyes, "you are mine and I am coming home with you."

It's all I needed to hear from her. I grabbed her in my arms and planted my lips on her plush lips. I could smell the sweat on her from the summer afternoon and I couldn't help but think of how much sweatier she was going to get. Her words, the kiss, and those thoughts were all it took to make me fully erect. I pressed my body up against hers feeling needy and wanting. Her arousal wafted into my nostrils and a low growl escaped me as I kissed her more passionately. She wasn't thinking of me as a one-night stand now and Titus wasn't seducing her into submission. She wanted this and I was going to give it to her. I lifted her and she wrapped her arms and legs around me. I carried her into the bedroom and laid her down on the bed falling on top of her. Continuing to wrestle our tongues together I trailed my hand down her body starting with her cheek, then her neck and shoulder stopping momentarily at her breast, and then moving down her sides to her hips and butt. Squeezing, she let out a cute little screech. I took the opportunity to shower her neck with kisses, slightly sucking and licking her neck tasting the saltiness from her sweat.

Her hands found their way to the bottom of my t-shirt and lifted it off me. Her soft hands roamed over my chest and shoulders sending electricity from her fingertips to my skin. I knew she was feeling the same tingles as my fingers touched her skin down her body. I pulled up her shirt and she leaned up so I could easily remove it from her. I tossed it over my head and smiled down at her angelic face. My eyes traced down her body until I reached her breasts. They were perfect. Not too small, not too big, and perky and smooth. I tilted my head towards them adjusting my body down hers rubbing my erection against her core as I moved down slightly. I heard her gasp as I moved across her and my lips stopped on her nipples taking as much of her breast into my mouth as I could. Rolling my tongue over her making them hard. She moaned arching her back and leaning her head back into the bed as I continued to rub back and forth against her. Her arousal was filling the room.

I reached my arms around her torso and rolled over, so she was now laying on top of me, making it easier for me to remove her shorts. As I started to slide them off, she shook her head no and then pinned my hands above my head on her bed. She then started to slowly place kisses down my body starting at my forehead, then my nose, my lips, and my chin. Moving down my neck and then my chest to my belly button and then she sat up looking at me smiling while she undid my pants and then continued kissing me down my pelvis until she reached my erection. She kissed the tip of it and then used her tongue to lick down the side of my shaft until she reached the bottom, then she licked back up again. Her lips went over me and took all of me in working her way back down this time with me inside her mouth. Her tongue moved down my shaft and then up again. When she got to the top, she swirled around the tip. It was driving me crazy. It had been a while since I took care of myself with everything going on, so I knew I couldn't last through this very long. I groaned equally in delight at how amazing I felt right now and at the realization, it wouldn't last. I already felt myself building up at her perfect movements. I wanted to finish inside her, not like this – at least this time. I sat up and grabbed her under her shoulders and pulled her on top of me, then rolled over so I was back on top again. "My turn" I smiled mischievously at her.

I gave up trying to pull her shorts off and decided I could buy her several more pairs like them. I grabbed them in my hands and ripped them off her. A shrill escaped her lips, but I could tell she enjoyed it. Copying her movements, I drew kisses down her body until I reached her core. My tongue licked at her core tasting her juices and stroking her gently while rotating over her sensitive areas. Her body twitched at my motions and her mouth gasped as the electric current passed from me to her. I moved two fingers inside her and began to move them in and out as I continued to caress her with my tongue. When I noticed her hands grasping tightly at her bed covers and her body arched, I got more aggressive with my movements until she reached her climax and had her release.

As soon as her body stopped convulsing, I was moving back up her and placed my erection at her core. I moved my pelvis around teasing her. After a few seconds which felt too long for me too, I moved myself to her entrance and slowly penetrated her as deep as I could get our bodies entangled as one. My eyes met hers and I slowly pulled out to the edge of her before thrusting back in hard and fast, then holding myself deep in her again, slowly pulling out. I did this a few times until she came close to the edge again before pulling back one last time. Then I thrust myself deep into her and continued fast moving in and out, hard, and deep. You could hear our skin slapping together. Our bodies melded together creating pockets of sweat in this summer heat. She started to tense and contract around me. As she climaxed and started her release, I banged her even faster and harder so I could join her. It was only a few seconds longer and I felt the flood of juices shooting from me into her. I pulled out and moved down slightly so my head was resting on her chest. Her fingers stroked my head gently.

I have no idea how long we stayed like that, but it was Mikayla's stomach growling which brought me out of my state of ecstasy and peacefulness. I raised my head, my eyes meeting hers. "Shall we have dinner, since we already had dessert?" I asked.

"How about a shower first, then dinner?" she responded. I had to admit with this summer heat, we were gross at the moment, but I didn't care in the slightest until she mentioned it. I rose from the bed, then put out my hand to help her up. We went to the bathroom together and she started the shower. Before hopping in she grabbed two towels and two washcloths from a shelf outside the bathroom. She climbed in, then motioned for me to follow her.

Mikayla's POV (sexual content)

Embarrassment was an understatement as we lay there coming down from our high together. It was so relaxing and then my loud stomach had to ruin everything and indicate how hungry I am. Whatever he brought smelled divine, and I had only been snacking on junk all day while sorting through my stuff. He asked if we should have dinner, but I needed a shower first. I was sweaty and disgusting when he got here never mind how I felt now. It was hot anyways, even after our release I needed a cooldown.

I climbed into the shower after grabbing some towels and washcloths. Jason followed me. I poured some soap into my washcloth and started to clean myself up when Jason's hand grabbed mine and took the washcloth from me. He started washing my shoulders, then moved the cloth down my arms one after the other taking the cloth across my neck and then down my chest and stomach. Then he turned me around and did my back down to my butt. After which, he got down on his knees in the bathtub and washed each of my legs and feet. He then used his hands to motion for me to spread my legs a little. He ran the cloth over my crotch from front to back cleaning up all the juices from both of us and then I saw a smirk come on his face. He rose to his feet and turned me around, so his front was against my back. I felt his erection against my butt and knew dinner was going to be delayed and I didn't care. His hands wrapped around me grabbing my breasts and he started showering me with kisses on my neck. Then he moved one of his hands down and lifted my leg as he pressed up against my core again. His erection entered me, but this time instead of slow and steady movements to start, he started hard and fast from the beginning. He lowered my leg now that he was nestled inside me, then raised his hands to my breasts again. He held on to them as he pounded me from behind. As I started to build up to my release, I started flexing myself around him squeezing his membrane each time he moved deep into me. My hands went out in front of me on the shower wall to keep myself from falling into it, his thrusts were so hard, jolting my body forward. It felt amazing and I could barely hold on anymore. Just when I thought I couldn't take anymore, he moved one hand down to my core and the other to my hip. He pounded me even harder and faster if it was possible and rubbed me senseless. I screamed his name "Jason" as he sent me to amazing heights and sensory overload. After I came, he moved both hands onto my hips and was thrusting himself into me. I was sensitive and soft, and his pounding was sending shocks through my entire body. It felt so amazing, I never wanted it to stop but didn't know how much longer my legs could hold me up with so much feeling being poured into me. I felt his release and he slowed his pace and then stopped engulfing my body in his hands once more and resting his head in the crook of my neck. I leaned my head back onto his shoulder. A sigh of relief escaped my lips.

The cool water from the shower was raining down on our bodies as we held our embrace for a few minutes. Remembering I was hungry, I moved from his arms and turned around to face him. I pecked him gently on his lips before grabbing his washcloth and pouring soap on it in front of him. I then proceeded to wash his entire body. After I finished his body head to toe, he turned me around and started to wash my hair. I loved going to the salon to have my hair washed by someone else. Feeling their fingers massaging my scalp and now Jason was doing it, but his fingers had little electric currents which sent tingles throughout my head. I couldn't help but moan a little and close my eyes. If I wasn't standing, I could surely endure this for an eternity. Jason brought me out of my escape when he reached down and turned the tap off. We dried ourselves off. I grabbed his t-shirt, and he grabbed his pants. I threw on a pair of panties also.

Gathering once again at the dining table, he started to take the food out of the bags. It smelled incredibly delicious now, my mouth was watering. He opened the first dish, and it was chicken chow mein. Chinese food I thought. Perfect. I grabbed two forks and he glanced at me puzzled. "I am too hungry to try to use chopsticks. It is a fork or my hands but one way or another the food is making it into my mouth sooner rather than later."

He laughed at me and continued opening the other dishes: beef and broccoli, shrimp fried rice, lemon chicken, black bean string beans, honey garlic ribs, garlic shrimp and veggies and sweet and sour chicken. Two boxes of plain rice were also included and then two fortune cookies and two cokes. My eyes were bulging by the time all the dishes were open. We couldn't even fit them all on my dining table, we had to put some on the kitchen counter. There are only two of us. He must've realized what I was thinking because he then said, "I didn't know what you liked and was hoping we would work up an appetite and need more later. I was not expecting you to throw yourself at me as soon as I walked in the door. I thought you would play hard to get."

"You are clearly confused. I didn't throw myself at you. I told you I was going back to the packhouse with you. You then dragged me off to the bedroom like a caveman," I glared.

"You told me to with your eyes and Titus has been begging me to carry you off like a caveman since we met at the club," he said.

"Oh please, you had me rolling my eyes since the moment you showed up. I am still rolling them," I responded.

"Mikayla, there is the truth and there is what you believe. Can we eat now?" he gave me a mischievous smile. I swear I wanted to reach across the table and slap it off his face. Unbelievable, I was going to have to deal with this child for life. I decided to let it go this time given I was hungry. I loaded my plate and started eating. He followed suit.

After we finished eating, we cleared my things off the sofa and snuggled together watching a movie. Unfortunately, I never found out what happened at the end of the movie. A sex scene came on about ten minutes into the movie and Jason was ready to go again. He turned off the tv and pounced me right there on the couch. We fell sleep afterwards in each other arms on the couch only to have him wake me up at some Godly hour in the night carrying me to the bed and having his way with me again before we drifted off to sleep. This man was insatiable.

He was already out of bed when I woke up in the morning. We were headed back to the packhouse. We spent the morning putting my things in boxes to either go to the packhouse, sell, or give away. My important documents and books my parents left me were kept in a fire resistant safe with a passcode entry. Before we left my house, I figured I should change it, since Elliott already confessed, he knew the code which is how he found the memory reading spell which saved his life from both Alpha Jason and Alpha Justin. Jason was going to send someone with a van to pick up my things for me, so we were travelling light with my two bags of clothes I brought back with me from the packhouse. During the night, Jason managed to wake up and finish off the Chinese food. How he isn't a gigantic marshmallow man is beyond my comprehension. We went to the diner to have lunch so I could say goodbye to Pop and let him know the apartment would be clear within the week for him to rent to someone else. After my stuff was picked up in a day or two, the keys would be dropped off to him. However, Jason paid him rent for the rest of the month and the following month for his trouble of having to find a new tenant and a new waitress.

Jason and I slid into the same side of a booth and ordered our meals. Pop came over and slid across from us. He extended his hand to Jason and congratulated him for seeing me for the amazing woman I am. Then he proceeded to threaten him if anything happened to me. Lastly, he thanked him for truly making me smile and look for a better life. Our food arrived and Pop started to get up. I stood up also and gave him a big hug, thanking him for being there for me and everything he had done. He was one of the things I regretted having to leave behind. I wanted to tell him I would visit but given the impending war and my new life as a wolf, I honestly didn't know if it was feasible, and I certainly didn't want him worrying about me or someone coming after him to get to me if I kept the connection open. Jason told me he would have some members come by occasionally to check on him and report back. I wanted to do so much more for him, but it would have to do for now. Maybe once the war was over, things could be different. He was a father to me, and I knew he was getting older. I wanted to repay him by helping him when he would need it one day given, he didn't have children of his own. Jason could sense my sadness or my traitor of a wolf, Mia, informed Titus who informed him, but either way he placed his arm around me and whispering to me everything would be alright made me feel better. After lunch, we headed out to the SUV and started for the packhouse.

Jason informed Matt and Jacqui we were on our way back. Jacqui texted me right away saying "atta girl." Now I am left wondering how much Jason disclosed to Matt. I haven't asked because I probably don't want to know. Jason reached over to grab my hand.

"I didn't tell him anything. I don't kiss and tell," he said.

"MIA!" I yelled. "Why don't you ask me what I am thinking instead of going this roundabout way to get our wolves involved?"

"Because Mia tells the truth, and you are cryptic and keep things to yourself."

"If our relationship is going to work, you are going to have to start communicating with me and not my wolf or both of you will be alone," I threatened.

"Okay, okay. Mikayla, you are my mate. You are not going anywhere. I am going to spoil and pamper you. We will have a few pups and..."

"A few pups?" I exclaimed.

"Well yes, don't you want to have children. We need an alpha heir to take over the pack when we are too old, and you know my parents are already buying clothes and wanting to decorate the nursery. My mom has been pressuring me since I found you."

I fell quiet at his words. Was I even ready for children? I didn't feel ready for becoming Luna and now I needed to produce and raise an heir. A war on the horizon. How could I bring a child into this and what if they try to go after my child? I better research protection spells. I wonder if our child will be a wolf or witch or both. My mind continued to go down a rabbit hole for a few more minutes when I was interrupted by Jason.

"Mikayla, we don't have to have children right away, but I hope you want to have them one day. I wouldn't want to have a child with this war happening. We need to take care of Alpha Justin once and for all first before I would want to consider it. Are you on birth control right now?" he asked.

"Yes, I am on birth control. Elliott and I didn't want to have kids right away. Of course, I can see why now. His poor mate having to go through seeing us together. I can understand how it would drive her mental. I don't want to see you with anyone ever," I responded.

"When you started to walk out of the club the first night we met, I almost killed the guy. All I knew was I had to leave with you. Thank the Goddess for Matt jumping in and offering the jerk VIP access and other women. It might've been a blood bath and then I would have had to kidnap you because you would think I was a murderer and it would be so much different right now," he grimaced.

"Everything you said is horrible and terrifying. I completely understand," I smirked.

"Glad it didn't have to come to it. You are everything to me, Mikayla. My heart belonged to you the moment I knew you were my mate. Titus wouldn't let me think or do otherwise even if I had wanted." Jason leaned over while pulling me closer and kissed me on my forehead before turning back to concentrate on driving.

I peered out the window watching my neighborhood and familiarities fade away from sight as we drove out of town. It would take a while before we got to the pack house. It was closer than an hour if we could drive straight through the forest, but we had to circle around and then back track to get to the pack territory. It was about an hour which was nothing, but I was tired from last night's escapades, so I leaned into Jason, resting my head on his shoulder while we held hands.

I jumped startled as Jason yelled my name, "Mikayla! Wake-up!"

"What is happening?" I said loudly as I looked around us. There was a pickup truck in front of us and one behind us keeping us at a pace.

"Something isn't right. These trucks came out of nowhere and are not letting me pass and are riding my bumper too closely," he said on alert.

Suddenly, a semi-truck came barreling towards us and smashed into my door and kept revving the engine. We were near an overpass and the pickup trucks and semi together were leading us over the edge to the drop below. It was about a 10-foot drop so it more than likely wouldn't kill us but was meant to disorient us so an attack could happen.

Chapter 29: An Act of War

Jason's POV

Grabbing the wheel, I did my best to maneuver the car so it wouldn't go over the edge, but it was futile. We were boxed in and were going over. We had to try to minimize any damage to us and run for my territory. "Open your bags Mikayla and pad your clothing around us, we are going over. Once we go over, we need to get out and make a run for it in that direction. I am stalling our fall for as long as possible and mind-linking the pack to get here."

"Jason, I can put a protection bubble around us like I did your mother to protect us from the fall."

"How long can you hold up the protection bubble?" I asked.

"I don't know. It drains my energy to keep it up and I am not yet strong enough to have it for a long time. I would guess around 20 minutes maybe a little more. Once I cannot hold it anymore, I will go unconscious," she responded.

"Can you put it up and take it down again?" I asked.

"Yes" she said.

"Okay, wait until we are already going over the edge. Try to put it up at the last minute to conserve your power. Once we hit the ground, drop it and we need to dash out of the car. We can shift into our wolves and run in that direction to our territory."

"I can't shift Jason. I cannot cast magic while in the wolf form. I must be in human form. We will have to try to make it on foot as far as we can and then I can put up the protection bubble. How long for the pack to get to us?" She asked.

"They are about 30 minutes from here. Matt will get here faster because he is a Beta wolf and Luke as an Alpha wolf. I will have to fight until they get here and hold off the attackers. There is a cliff we can have behind us just inside the woods. We need to make it there so you can be behind me, and I can protect you until the others get here." I planned.

"Your Alpha and Luna are being attacked. We are about to be thrown over the Whispering Forest overpass. We will be running on foot to the Blackened Cliff where Mikayla will protect us with a bubble for a time and then we will make a stand until backup arrives. If you arrive in time. Every capable wolf of fighting needs to come. I have no idea how many there are or will be yet. I will mind-link again when we get into the bubble. Those who cannot fight get to the bunkers in case the fight spills into our territory. Everyone move now!" I mind-linked the entire pack.

"Jason, we are on our way. Hold on." Matt responded immediately.

We were heading over the edge. I could see Mikayla's eyes go blue as I pulled her into a hug as close to me as possible. A clear bubble formed around us right before we impacted the ground and then disappeared.

"Go now," she said.

I pushed the door open on my side and I slid out from the car. It flattened a bit from impact and turned upside-down, so we had to army crawl to get out of it. I could hear howling in the distance. I grabbed Mikayla's hand pulling her from the vehicle faster and setting her on her feet. "Run!"

We ran toward the woods and headed towards Blackened Cliffs. It was a side of a hill which was said to once have volcanic activity in the area leaving it completely black. It was high and curved inwards so we would be protected from attack from the back and sides. The downside was we would be trapped waiting for the mercy of my pack members to arrive and save us. They were gaining on us since most of them were in their wolf forms. It was clear this was a well-planned attack. No wonder it had been so quiet at Mikayla's apartment and the diner. They knew I would go to get her and would bring her back to the pack. I should have brought backup with me and guards. It isn't typical for me to travel alone, but I wanted her all to myself. Since there was no activity, I took a chance and was regretting it. If we get out of this, I will never be so careless again.

The cliffs were in sight, but we were not going to make it. Two wolves were gaining on us quickly. "Mikayla, keep running," I turned to them and shifted in mid-air while lunging at them. Titus took over immediately ready to kill anyone in his path. He ripped the throat out of the closest one, then dodged the second one in time. A third wolf came out of nowhere and before Titus could move out the way, he was tackling Titus and a blue light that looked like a hand on the end of a rope extended from where Mikayla was standing grabbing the wolf by the neck and snapping it in one swift move. Titus rolled over and attacked the second wolf. After wrestling together, he was able to get his jaws on his throat and pulled back sending blood splatter all over. There was a small gap between the next wave and the two of them. Titus ran over to Mikayla.

"Mikayla, Titus said to keep running towards the cliffs," Mia said.

Mikayla turned. She and Titus ran towards the cliffs. The other wolves were on our heels, but Mikayla made it. "Titus," she yelled, "you need to come near me now. There are too many of them. The closer we are the less energy I use up."

Titus ran over to her, and she put up the protection bubble immediately. Two wolves who almost had them, lunged towards them and bounced off the wall of the bubble. Shaking their heads and standing up abruptly, they started pacing back and forth in front of the bubble. It was clear they were mind-linking someone. More wolves started to arrive, both shifted and unshifted. I counted about 20 so far. Titus laid down next to where Mikayla had sat on the ground to concentrate on her spell.

"Matt, how's the pack coming? Are you getting close? Mikayla and I reached the cliffs. There are about 20 wolves now. I hear more coming in the distance." We are in a protection bubble. They are unable to penetrate it, but Mikayla isn't powerful enough to hold it forever. She will lose consciousness and it will fall. I will take a few down but I cannot last against them all.

"Luke and I are about 15 minutes out. Chris and Scott were out for a run when you messaged. They should arrive right before Luke and I. The rest of the pack are about 5 minutes behind us. Some less, some more depending on their speed. Kirk is leading a group to flank them from the overpass since they followed you into the forest," he replied.

As I closed the mind-link, I saw him approaching on foot with a smirk on his face. He thought he had won already.

"Alpha Jason, a pleasure to meet your acquaintance," said Alpha Justin as he closed in on the bubble.

I shifted back to my human form opting to stay sitting calmly. First, I was naked and had no clothes, not that when it came time to attack, I would care. I would kill them all with my bare hands or my claws, whichever I had at the time to save Mikayla. Secondly, I wanted him to think I was calm enough to believe I was going to get out of this situation. "Alpha Justin. Do you honestly think this is going to accomplish anything? My pack will never accept you as their leader. My beta would take over as Alpha way before my pack allows you to take over."

"Then I will have to ensure his murder as well. You hide behind your mate's shield. Pathetic! Your pack deserves a better leader than you. You cannot even protect your Luna. She protects you."

"You should take your men and leave now Justin while you still can. You have already lost two in this pitiful excuse of an attack."

"I have plenty more men willing to lay their lives down for me. How many will do so willingly for you?"

"My pack is faithful to me. How many of yours are willing or did you command them to do it, leaving their mates and families behind for your power-hungry quest?"

"Jason, you and I both know Mikayla cannot hold this bubble forever. Your men are not going to make it to you in time to save you. I may not be able to kill you both, but I will have one of you for sure before they get here."

"You underestimate my mate's power and my strength. You will not be victorious today."

"I am giving you one chance to relinquish your pack to me. Give up your Alpha status and I promise to kill only you and let Mikayla live as part of my pack. She will be revered once she comes into her full potential."

I mind-linked Matt, "Alpha Justin is here. He wants me to give him the pack. It's clear he wants Mikayla alive. He wants me dead. I need howls to come from different directions, the louder the better to make his pack feel you are closer than you are."

"Let me be clear Justin. You will never lead or have command over the Eclipse Moon Pack. I had no intention of warring with you; however, this act condemns your pack to war. When I kill you, you should remember this was the moment your fate was sealed."

Justin laughed almost hysterically, "you are up against a wall and dare say these words to me. You are a little pup playing in his dad's office. I have taken down far better than you. It doesn't matter if it happens today or 10 years from now. I have patience."

Howls were heard in the distance from multiple directions. I knew Chris and Scott were coming from the direction we had been run off the road.

I smiled at Justin, "you are running out of time."

"Your mate isn't looking too good there Jason. You and I both know this bubble is coming down before your pack gets here."

"Then why do you and your pack seem nervous, and I am sitting here confident?"

Mikayla's POV

I could hear ramblings of Jason and someone else. It must've been Justin, but I wasn't sure. I was focusing all my energy on holding up this bubble for as long as possible. Mia also supplied her energy to give me a boost. I was draining her quickly and she would need a while to rest. Mia was able to tell me and Titus, she was almost done and sorry she couldn't help more. Knowing she could hear my thoughts, I thought to myself, "you helped enough. You bought us more time."

As I concentrated my energy, I tried to pull power from anywhere I could find it. I had grounded myself by sitting on the ground. I don't know how much time had passed but I was starting to feel my body parts going numb one at a time. It started with my limbs and moved towards my body from the top of my head, my fingers, and my toes, down my neck and arms and up my legs. I knew once the numbness reached my heart, I would be unconscious again and completely tapped out of power. I didn't know how long it would take me to recover from using the magic this time, but I hoped I could wait it out with Mia in her space again. It was serene. I felt relaxed and enjoyed spending time with her frolicking about under the willow tree by the lake.

There were many wolves surrounding us. Jason sat beside me. I could've absorbed power from him as well, but I didn't want to leave us completely defenseless if I could not hold on a little longer. His calmness was washing over me in droves. How was he remaining calm and having a casual conversation like he was out to dinner? I regret not being able to mind-link him. Had I accepted him earlier, we wouldn't be in this situation, or we might have mated and marked each other by now so we would have the upper hand and at least be able to mind-link. I had to focus on the matter at hand. The ground and cliffs and trees nearby all have energy and I tried my best to pull from all of it, but I wasn't strong enough. I should have practiced the magic and not listened to the warnings of my parents in the letters. Was this going to be the end for us? We were only starting our life together. Every time I think life is in a good place some disaster happens. What is this dark cloud following me everywhere waiting for me to be happy to rain down on me? It's infuriating. As my anger rose inside me, I felt the numbness moving up my body slow down a little. I kept fueling myself. Who does Justin think he is trying to kill us and take our pack? It belongs to us, and he cannot have it. I am its Luna.

I gained a few more minutes, but I was fading fast. The bubble was coming down. I hope our pack is close. The bubble started to flicker. The numbness was almost to my heart. I turned to Jason, "It is time." He reached out to me and helped me lay down on the ground gently as he whispered, "I love you, Mikayla." My eyes closed and I succumbed to the numbness and darkness that crept over me.

Chapter 30: Alpha Justin

Jason's POV

Mikayla's body went limp in my arms, as the bubble started to fade. I laid her body down gently.

"Titus, are you ready? If we can take out Alpha Justin, everything will be over. He needs to be the target after ensuring Mikayla's safety," I thought.

"I'm ready. They should have brought more wolves." I could feel his excitement at being able to unleash his wrath finally. He was enraged a move such as this was even considered against our pack, and he was out for blood. I wasn't going to hold him back from teaching them a lesson, since they risked my mate. As I turned away from Mikayla, I shifted immediately and lunged out of the fading bubble. I caught the onlookers surprised. They would not have known I could exit the bubble while it was still in place. Titus easily ripped through the throat of the largest wolf in front of us to assert his dominance and scare the others into leaving or making a mistake.

Alpha Justin turned around abruptly starting to leave as he instructed his pack, "kill the Alpha, bring the witch to the pack house alive."

He doesn't want Mikayla killed. This information was all Titus needed to go after him. Killing him would remove all his commands on his men. Those willing would be slaughtered when my pack got here and those who were not, would be given the opportunity to live. Titus sprinted in the direction of Justin, when he was tackled from the side by another wolf. We rolled a few times fighting for control. Titus was victorious as he bit down on to his throat and ripped it out. Another wolf came at us but was stopped.

"Alpha, I thought you were going to wait for us," Chris chimed in through mind-link as he sunk his canines into the wolf. A loud howl escaping his mouth as they plunged deeper into his skin.

"We have some pay back to exact for our brother," Scott added.

I couldn't be happier to see these two in action. They took out two wolves without breaking a sweat and were already on to the next. The three of us were a force to be reckoned with. I mind-linked them back, "I need to go after Alpha Justin, you two keep fighting, the rest are not far, but make sure they do not take Mikayla. She is on the ground at the bottom of the cliff unconscious." I turned to follow in Justin's path. He had a considerable distance on me as he retreated and left his pack to their demise. I knew they were no match for my warriors. The three of us had already taken out a total of 7 of them and I had a small scratch on me which was already almost healed. I took off after Justin when I saw Matt and Luke coming through the clearing.

"Jason, what's the status?" Matt mind-linked with both Luke and me.

"Alpha Justin has taken off, the coward that he is, I am headed after him to see if we can end this sooner rather than later. Scott and Chris are protecting Mikayla at the base of the cliff," I answered.

"I am coming with you," Luke replied, "Matt, you help Chris and Luke get our Luna to safety."

Apollo, Luke's wolf, ran after me. I was slowed as another wolf attempted to halt my progress. Titus disabled him almost as soon as he came into view. Apollo was now side by side with me chasing down Justin. "There he is," I exclaimed. Justin slowed almost to a halt and turned around to face us. We snarled at him, Apollo flanking his left side as I moved to his right ready to attack.

Luke's POV

Jason was an incredible fighter, but I wasn't sure he had it in him to kill Alpha Justin. He always believed the best in people and would rather have someone locked in a dungeon for eternity than to end everyone's misery. I had to ensure Justin was put down once and for good. As Titus and Apollo approached him, he slowed. A cowardice like him wouldn't slow down to fight two alphas, knowing one of us was stronger than him alone. He had to have a plan. Before I could mind-link Jason telling him something was amiss, I saw a light reflect from the trees nearby. It was an ambush, and we ran right into it. Apollo lunged towards Titus, tackling him out of the way as a dart whizzed by our heads. I held on to him so we would continue to roll off to the side, as we could hear more traveling through the air.

"Highly concentrated wolfsbane and silver. We need to get out of here. Run! I am right behind you," I mind-linked yelled as Apollo pushed him back in the direction we had come from. Titus took off back as I instructed, turning around when he couldn't hear me beside him.

I felt the burning sensation spread from my back where I had been hit through my body. It was quick and removed the connection with my wolf. I couldn't talk to my wolf; he was beyond injured from the concoction. It forced me to shift back into my human form where I laid on the ground, weakened and defenseless.

Alpha Justin stood over my convulsing body, as he leaned down, extending his claws towards my throat.

Titus' POV

I turned to see Luke laying on the ground in his human form with Justin standing over top of him. "Not the Alpha I was gunning for, but I will take what I can get," he said as he ripped Luke's throat from his body. Jason and I felt Luke's tether to the pack break and I could sense Jason was falling apart. His thoughts rang through me like a bulldozer. "Alpha Justin killed him. Luke was gone. How could I have been so naïve to think Justin didn't have a plan and walk right into it? Apollo saved my life and gave his own for me, for our Luna, for our pack." His grief washed over me, crippling me as I released my frustration and hurt into a howl. Jason was devasted and unable to maintain control. His thoughts were everywhere, and we were in the middle of a battle. Luke's death couldn't be in vain, I tried to pump him up. His response was to relinquish complete control to me.

Jason had never given me full reign before today. He always kept me in check, but not anymore. I sprang back to the cliffs taking my pain out on any unfortunate wolf who got in my way. I didn't care if they were commanded to attack or willing. They all had to die for Luke's and Apollo's death. This was going to be a reckoning they had coming. They dared attack us. Our wrath would be the last thing they felt. I whipped through wolves like they were paper. Hoping each death would make me feel the slightest bit better, but it didn't. The more I killed, the more I wanted to kill. More had arrived since the initial 20 and I noticed quite a few of our pack wolves halt their attacks watching me tear through the crowd of interlopers.

Our pack was completely in charge of this battle now. Our own pack members continued stepping aside to let me through as the bodies piled up. Alpha Justin must've felt each tether break how Jason and I had felt Luke's. Did he care? Probably not, he was selfish and power hungry and he was going to regret his actions of today. His death was no longer a matter of if, but when, I would sink my canines into his throat and rip it out slowly so he could see it in my hands as his eyes glazed over one last time. The thought of his demise sent a thrill through me, and I gained a second wind fighting wolf after wolf until no member of his pack remained alive. None of them were permitted to live after the atrocity they had pulled. Jason probably would be angry with me for my rampage. I wasn't going to wait for him to take control back. I was a wolf, and it was kill or be killed. I wanted blood and nothing was going to stop me from avenging Luke's death. The combined deaths of them didn't amount to the loss of our brother in life and arms.

After they were all gone, I could hear Matt trying to mind-link with Jason. Jason was unresponsive. He had hidden himself away deep into our minds. I would get us back to the pack and then force a shift to his human form where he would have to regain his composure but for now, he needed to be away. I strayed over to where Mikayla lay on the ground trying to reach out to Mia. She was also unresponsive. I laid down next to Mikayla. I was covered in blood and gore, but I needed to feel her. Her body was warm next to mine, and I laid my head across her stomach.

Matt came over to us and shifted back to human. He was instructing others to help our wounded and secure the bodies of the fallen. We would be holding a ceremony for them as per normal. He sent four wolves, including Chris and Scott to retrieve Luke's body if they could find it.

Telling them to stay on the alert. The wounded, along with Mikayla, were carried back to the overpass, we originally were thrown over, where transport waited to take us back to the pack hospital. I stayed close to Mikayla. Being near her was the only thing keeping me calm. I wanted to run after Justin whether I died or not, I wanted to challenge him. Unfortunately, he was always hiding behind some rouse or plan. He never actually fought himself. Did he even know how to fight? He paralyzed Luke then went in for the kill. I was letting out growls as my thoughts flitted through my head. Then, I heard Matt, "Titus, you need to calm down. You are scaring...well...everyone."

I looked at him, then placed my head back on Mikayla who was now lying on the bed of a pickup truck heading towards our territory. If only he knew, this was me being calm. The truck pulled up in front of the pack hospital. I watched as they took Mikayla out of the truck. A car came speeding down the road, tires screeching, coming to a halt across from where the truck was being offloaded with the injured. It was Mom and Dad. How could we face them and tell them their son was dead? They ran over to us, and Allison fell to her knees and hugged me. She then whispered in my ear, "please return Jason to me. I know he is hurting. I can feel it. I need to hold him." I forced Jason to shift back to human. As he laid on the ground, his mother wrapped her arms around his neck telling him repeatedly, "it was not your fault. Alpha Justin will pay for this." Matt covered his body with a blanket and handed   clothes   to   Jonathan   for   him.

Chapter 31: Aftermath

Jason's POV

Four days had passed since Luke's assassination. Luckily, we were able to recover his body and include him in the ceremony for the fallen. The mood was somber. Everyone seemed on the same page, vengeance would be ours. Luke touched so many lives being the head trainer and traveling to packs all over the country to gather improved fighting methods for our pack. Our victory the other day was in large part to him. We would continue his training methodology and it will become his legacy, never to be forgotten.

Elliott was locked in his room when everything went down, and no one had thought to release him. He was furious when he was finally let out and updated on the events of the evening. It was clear Luke's passing impacted him also. Even though it was a short amount of time, they had some invisible bond. Elliott had always wanted to be a warrior and asked if he could be trained as such. He spent almost every hour he was out of his room in the training area. Mostly working with Luke, but the others took part also. If he wasn't training, he was strategizing with Matt, Kirk and I or he was sitting in the room with Mikayla.

I don't know if I would ever be the same without my little brother. In some areas, he far exceeded my expertise and together we were unstoppable. His death is a great loss to our pack. My mother and father have been quiet. Their grief overwhelms them, and they find solace in spending time together in their quarters. They are okay but asked for privacy while they grieve. Other than the cleaning staff and those bringing food, I am the only person they have let into their area.

Mikayla hasn't awakened yet. I have strategizing and planning to do as we move from the defensive to the offensive in a war against Alpha Justin. She didn't sustain any injuries and from all the tests seems to be sleeping peacefully. Titus has reached out to Mia every time we are with Mikayla, but she has yet to respond also. We know they both severely drained themselves. They are needed here. The pack needs their Luna and Titus and I need our mates. Mikayla has been moved into a bedroom adjacent mine and literally every night I end up crawling into the bed with her to feel her beside me. Titus is a mess in my head screaming for his mates to return. Touching her is the only way he calms down and allows me to sleep. I crawl into the bed with her and rest my head on her shoulder draping my arm across her waist. Titus has receded to the back of my mind when he suddenly jolts up.

"It's Mia. She is awake. She is asking what happened," Titus excitedly told me.

"Is she okay? What does she remember?" I ask.

Titus begins to growl in my head. I can tell he is frustrated, angry, and scared. "Mikayla isn't with her," he informs me.

"What do you mean Mikayla isn't with her?" I ask perplexed.

"Last time Mikayla went into Mia's space, and they were able to talk together and spend time until Mikayla recovered, but she isn't anywhere, and Mia cannot talk to her. She has been trying for a few hours now. Until we touched her, and she woke up from the sparks, she thought she had died and was alone" he explains.

"How can she not be there? They are the same person. Where the hell is she then?" I can feel my heartbeat escalating.

"She doesn't know either. She is asking me what happened after she passed out. Let me update her on everything and then we can see if we can figure anything out. Mikayla is alive or her body wouldn't be here with Mia still intact and communicating. She has gone somewhere other than Mia's space though, we will have to find out where."

Titus is the voice of reason in this situation. Now I know the world has gone into complete chaos.

Epilogue

It has been almost two years since I lost my brother and Mikayla to Alpha Justin's unprovoked attack. We have been at war and both packs have suffered greatly at each other's hands. Wolves have been lost, finances drained, buildings destroyed, famine and fatigue. I fear I am losing some of my pack members who can barely remember why we are fighting this war now. If only they knew how merciless and ruthless Alpha Justin could be. I am worn and haggard, barely taking care of myself each day. I am the Alpha, so I make my rounds of our territory and am often on the frontlines of defense when we receive an attack or force an attack. We seem to be at a deadlock. Alpha Justin may be cowardice, but he is intelligent enough to have foresight into our battle. Our lands were vibrant and green, growing crops to sustain us and now it is burnt and smoldering. Barely anything growing around the outskirts of the territory. The packhouse garden is still intact.

Titus is on edge every day. I can't control him most days. His anger and frustration at Mia being trapped within Mikayla's body and Mikayla has yet to return to us. We have investigated her situation and found there are others like her. The first has been unconscious for over 20 years. Dylan's friend, Aurora, came from the Light Magic Coven and gave us all the information she had as she wept over Mikayla's circumstance. It was clear she had been a part of her early years and her parents sending Mikayla away was a futile effort given her current predicament. I feel like I am going crazy these past two months. Mikayla seems she is near me. I have even turned my head a couple of times to look for her, thinking she will be standing there looking back at me. It is such an eerie feeling. I asked Titus if he noticed anything and of course he makes me feel completely insane. Maybe I am.

It has been a long night and after 40 hours of fighting and taking down the latest attack, I am sitting in the room with Mikayla. Matt and Jacqui are here with me. The three of us have a late dinner together pretending life isn't as bad as it is at this very moment. After polishing off, Goddess only knows how much food, I sit back in my chair and grab Mikayla's hand in mine from the bed where she is resting peacefully. It was then I heard her voice, "Mark me," she said. I looked at her, then at Matt and Jacqui. "Did you hear something?" I asked.

They both looked at each other then, at me, and simultaneously shook their heads. "What did you hear?" Matt questioned looking quite concerned.

"Mark me," almost a whisper like it was words traveling in the air from a far-off place. I know I heard it now.

"There it was again. Did you hear it that time?" I asked.

Quizzical looks all around. Then Titus spoke up, "I didn't hear anything and neither did Mia. However, Mia said she feels something different in Mikayla's body. She cannot hear or feel her, but something is off. She doesn't know what."

"Mark me now!" It was louder this time, and I knew it was only me who could make it out. Deep down I knew it was Mikayla. She was reaching out to me and had been for some time. I couldn't recognize it, but now here, holding her hand and three times couldn't be my imagination. Was it really her? Asking me to mark her. Typically, a Luna would be marked in a ceremony in front of the entire pack showing the bond and strength the Luna and Alpha gained in their union with witnesses. I had to listen to the voice. It was nagging at me and every fiber in my body told me I had to listen. I mind-linked my parents, Kirk, and Elliott to come immediately to Mikayla's room. I needed to have more witnesses to the marking, other than Matt and Jacqui. People who were equally invested in Mikayla's recovery.

While we waited for the others to arrive, I lifted Mikayla's top half of her body off the bed and slid in behind her with my legs on either side of her, and let her body lean up against me for support. Her back was now to my chest and her head was draped over my shoulder. I knew I was going to do it but no one else did. They would probably try to stop me. First because of the whole marking ceremony tradition and secondly because being marked by an Alpha and becoming a Luna required verbal acceptance from the incumbent Luna. She would be unable to do this, but I know it was her reaching out to me, telling me what had to be done. I would face the consequences afterward.

The others all arrived and came into the room. Kirk asks, "what is happening, Jason? Is everything okay? It's the middle of the night."

"I needed you all to be here as witnesses," I responded. Before anyone could say another word, I grabbed Mikayla's head turned it to the side and sunk my canines into her neck marking her. I felt her blood flow into my mouth as my canines went deeper and deeper into her. The power I felt was incredible and nothing I had felt before. Images flashed before my eyes of a dark place, and I could see her. She was in the middle of a circle surrounded by six individuals who were chanting something. Blue light encircled them all. The blue light swirled around and then congregated where Mikayla stood in the center of the circle, then it blasted out from

249

her in all directions flinging the six others back onto the ground. They stopped chanting and I saw them slowly rising and looking at each other. Mikayla was gone. Where did she go?

I heard gasps from those in the room and Titus was doing somersaults in my head. "You did it. She is awake." I opened my eyes and retracted my canines, licking her wounds to close them. I helped to turn her head towards me where her eyes looked into mine and a smile graced her lips.

"Hello there, stranger," she said in a raspy, barely audible voice. The most beautiful words I had ever heard. Tears soaked my eyes, and I grabbed her promising to never let her go. The others stared in awe and disbelief.